A TALE OF OAK AND MISTLETOE

A Tale of Oak and Mistletoe

TIME WALKERS BOOK 4

E.B. Brown

KIRKBRIDE

Contents

PART THREE 187

Prologue

James County, Virginia

October 2012

Winn

He ran his hand over his head, his fingers brushing down through the prickly short hairs on his fresh shorn scalp. It felt strange without the weight of his braid down his back, and he could feel the autumn breeze at his nape as he crouched down. The journey through time had been very much as Maggie described; pulling his body down, the unseen force urging him to submit, until finally, when he pressed his face to the earth the sky exploded into darkness.

He woke lying flat on his back, staring up at grey storm clouds overhead. Scattered raindrops dotted his skin as he sat up. As he looked around to gain some sense of reality, he saw an English-style house with the soft glow of lights inside through the glass windows. To his other side was a large red barn with the door slightly ajar. The future had some fragrance of the past, but most of the scents assaulting his senses were dank. As he crept up to the house and kneeled down next to the window, he could hear the sound of a man speaking. Without being able to see who was in the house, he could only assume the man was daft by the way he carried on a conversation alone. He peered through the window and saw one of the things Maggie had described to him. It was a picture box, one where people acted out stories on a flat screen. Although his wife had told him it was called a television, his heart still raced at the sight of it and he recalled a fight they once had.

"You have no idea what my life was like!" she shouted.

Yes, she was right.

No matter how much she described the future, he still had no idea. The truth of her words felt heavy in his belly as he sat there in her future time, so far away from all those he loved. *What if he was unable to return to them?*

Winn swallowed hard and took a deep breath. There was no time for hesitation. He needed to find Marcus and get what he came for. As he stood up, suddenly the door flew open and slammed against the shingles of the house and a woman stalked outside past him. She clutched a red coat around herself, muttering under her breath as she bent her head against the wind.

His heart hammered in his chest as she turned his way. Her auburn hair whipped over her shoulder and her soft green eyes lay beneath red-rimmed eyelids. Her face was round and she carried more weight on her frame as she had on the day they met, and as he took in the rest of her attire he could hear his own pulse throbbing in his head.

Maggie stood in front of him.

The denim trousers, the heavy buckskin colored boots. The strap of a pink undergarment peeking out at one shoulder where her thin cotton shirt exposed her skin. She shoved her hands in the front pockets of her trousers and raised her eyebrows at him. Defiant and unamused, the woman who would someday be his wife stared at him with restrained indifference.

"Well?" Maggie said, as if he had failed to answer a question. His words caught between his dry lips as he stumbled over what to say to her. She made no effort to hide her eyes as she surveyed him head to foot, her brows squinting down and her lips pursed. If he had ever thought her behavior bold before, the way she confronted him now leant some indication of how she was accustomed to speaking to men.

"Wh – what?" he stammered.

"Were you gonna knock, or just stand there? If you're looking for Marcus, he's in the kitchen," she replied, as if impatient with him. Winn knew his face must have looked addled, so he made an attempt to slow down his breathing and make his words more confident. It confused him that she would not ask who he was or what he wanted, but instead she merely offered him entrance to her home.

"Yes. Yes, I am here to see Marcus," he said slowly.

"Whatever. Later," she said as she shrugged. She turned away to leave, but before he could stop himself he reached out and snatched her hand. He wanted to pull her into his arms, to feel her heart pound against his. But this was not his wife yet, he was no more than a stranger to her, and he could not endanger the success of his journey by falling prey to his aching soul.

"Wait," he whispered hoarsely. "I think you dropped this."

Winn pulled her watch from the pocket of his tunic and placed it in her hand. She stared down at it but did not pull away. Her fingers felt warm against his despite the brisk air, and she slowly looked up at him.

"Thank you. I've been looking for that," she said softly. Her green eyes softened as they met his, creases forming as her lips twitched and dropped slightly open. "Who did you say you are?"

He continued to hold her hand, fighting the urge to draw her close.

"An old friend," he replied.

"Oh, okay. Well, thanks. See you later," she said, and this time her words were stammered out as her cheeks filled with color. She uttered a nervous laugh and pulled her hand back before she walked away. As he watched her go into the barn, he had no doubt about what day he had arrived in the future. Any moment she would be taken to his time by her Bloodstone, and he could recall every detail of their meeting as if it had happened only yesterday.

Part One

1

Norse Village, 1634

Maggie

Curled on her side, her limbs still felt heavy from the dreams of a rested sleep when she felt the touch on her ribs. Inquisitive, testing, his fingers traced up across her belly, then paused before his warm palm came to rest. His hand squeezed lightly, a question more than anything, and she answered him with a slight, but definite nudge of her elbow into his ribs.

"I'm awake," Maggie said. A smile crossed her lips as she felt him slide one leg over hers. Winn was a furnace, his skin aflame against her even when she needed layers of furs to keep warm. She snuggled deeper into him.

"I'm sorry. I did not mean to wake you," he whispered. His breath was hot on her neck as he spoke, and by the sound of his voice she knew he was anything but sorry. It seemed he certainly had no intention of sleeping.

"Sure you didn't," she replied. "I thought you'd be with the men longer."

"I should be," he admitted, his fingers sliding up to cup her heavy breasts. She closed her eyes with a little moan at the contact. "But I've heard nothing of what they speak of for the last two hours. All I could see was you, across the hall, with my son at your breast..."

He squeezed her gently to demonstrate, and she let out a tiny shriek.

"Winn!" she laughed.

"...then you left, and I've been standing at attention ever since," he whispered. She could feel him stirring against her.

"Well, that doesn't sound very comfortable," she admitted. She inched backward, inviting, eager to relieve his burden, but he shifted so than he could look down on her. Leaning on one elbow, his eyes glazed wide with desire, he bent to trace his lips over her skin. Down her neck, then to her full breasts.

"No, it was not," he agreed. "Then I realized there is a solution to my, uhm, problem."

"Oh?"

"Well, I am Chief. If I wish to ravish my wife, I will do so," he muttered with a grin. He settled his body over hers and parted her legs with his knee, and in that single motion slowly joined their bodies. "Ah, that is better now."

"So it's good to be the Chief," she murmured. A brief echo of her past surfaced at her clumsy attempt at humor, but when he stared down at her she was glad he did not understand it. Silent now, his gaze slicing through her soul, he remained motionless inside her, his breath coming slow and controlled.

"I am only your husband now," he said softly. "And this is where my duty lies." He retreated, then bore her back down with his next thrust. She let him clutch her head in his hands as he moved, knowing that he needed that connection for a fleeting moment. Winn spoke with his touch rather than his words, the shadow of flesh upon flesh drawing him deeper than anything spoken. His gleaming eyes never left hers.

"Then do your duty, husband," she whispered, and he did.

***

Winn left early the next morning as was his usual routine, taking eight year-old Dagr with him to meet with the men. She wondered what her son might learn with his father today. Would it be to hunt? To learn the ways of being a Chief, as his father was? Or might it be a lesson in killing?

The possibilities unnerved her at times. Despite her best efforts, Maggie still had difficulty going along with life in the seventeenth century. Sometimes she thought of how her life might be if Winn had journeyed to the future, instead of the magic of the Bloodstone sending her to the past. She had no doubt and no regret that her life was joined with his, but she could not help but wonder how things might have been different.

As she made her way to the Northern Hall, what the Norse speaking members of the village called the *Noroanveror Skali,* she spotted Winn grappling with Dagr in the courtyard. She adjusted two-year old Malcolm on her hip to watch them as her daughter Kyra ran ahead.

No, she thought with a secret grin as her husband taught her son a lesson. *Winn was meant for the time he was born to, and she was meant to find him.*

Winn's arms stood out in welcome beneath his simple fur-lined vest as he taunted his son, and Maggie let out a groan when Dagr rushed his father haphazardly. The boy was promptly upended onto his backside, eliciting an uncharacteristic swear word in Norse from the youngster. Maggie tried not to smirk when Winn reached down and ruffled Dagr's mane of thick black hair, which did nothing to stem the tide of obscenities coming from his mouth.

"That cannot possibly be my son talking like that," she commented as she joined them. A crooked grin graced Winn's face. With one hand holding the squirming Dagr flat on the ground, he glanced down briefly at his son before he greeted her.

"Do not blame me. He's your son," Winn chuckled. When Malcolm reached out two hands toward his father, Winn released Dagr and took his younger son from Maggie.

"Da! Down! *Nior!*" Malcolm cried, his demand relayed in both Norse and English.

"It is not time for you to fight yet, Mal. Soon, I promise," Winn said to the child. Malcolm pouted but stilled in Winn's arms, sticking a thumb in his mouth as his dark eyes turned to his father.

Maggie caught her fingers in the edge of Dagr's braies before he ran off.

"You!" she admonished him. Dagr had the good sense to know when he was in trouble. He stood bravely beside her, his narrow chest rising and falling rapidly as he struggled to contain his ire. "I'll wash your mouth out with sand, don't think I won't!"

Dagr scowled when she kissed his cheek.

"Aww, Ma!" the boy hissed. He twisted away from her kiss and raced off to join the older boys who were gathered by the well. Dagr was built like his father – lean but solid, thick through his shoulders, with a strength from his core that gave him an undeniable aura. With his dark skin and long hair, he could easily blend in with any of the Indian tribes just as his father had. Yet in the village, he was the young son of the Chief, unique in his own special way among the Norse.

Ahi Kekeleksu grabbed Dagr around the neck as the boy ran straight into a mob of young men. Keke, son of Winn's brother Chetan, had turned into quite a stout young man over the winter. Gone was the boyish shyness and the uncertainty when speaking with others. Keke seemed the leader of the pack of youths in the village, those who were new to manhood and testing the limits. Iain was his closest friend, the half-Indian son of Roanoke survivor Ellie, and Tyr was a Norse youth that kept company with them.

When Keke let young Dagr pummel him before he shoved him toward the meal table she smiled. Although quite a bit younger than his cousin, Dagr still assumed a spot of honor amongst the boys. After all, Dagr was Chief Winn's eldest son.

Across the expanse of the Northern Hall, Maggie spotted Rebecca. With her long blond curls hanging loose over her shoulders and her skin flushed with radiance only happiness could give, she sat quietly beside her husband Makedewa as he spoke with the men. Although she was close to term with her pregnancy, she carried small, her bump only scarcely visible under her long gown. Rebecca gave a quick wave to Maggie when they spotted each other across the room, but the younger woman quickly returned her attention to her Indian husband.

Maggie smiled. Perhaps she could corner her friend later to ask how she was feeling, without Makedewa near. Rebecca would never admit any discomfort with her husband within earshot.

As Maggie and Winn joined the group, Winn swung Malcolm onto his shoulders, a place of prominence that the child loved. Winn held the youngster's kicking feet in place with his hands and Malcolm pointed and laughed at his kin.

"Winn is here now, let him decide," Cormaic called out. Maggie's cousin was a bear of a man, standing taller than her husband with a set of arms to rival any body builder from her future time. His physique was earned from a lifetime of labor, hewn from endless hours spent hunting and fighting. Maggie was surprised to see him agitated, being that gentle Cormaic usually kept his stronger emotions under wraps. Standing next to the Indian Makedewa, however, Cormaic appeared anything but happy. Cormaic handed Winn a tankard of mead.

"On what shall I decide?" Winn answered.

"There's more woodland being burned, and now it's close to the Nansemond village. We should send some of our men to protect them," Cormaic replied.

Winn took the proffered mug and drank half of it before answering, his eyes scanning the men before him. He kept one hand on his son's heels, and Malcolm rested his hand on Winn's head.

"So they want more fields for their tobacco," Winn said. Cormaic nodded, casting a look at Makedewa.

"The English are never happy. They keep taking the land, destroying it with their crops. They burn too much and leave nothing for the tribes," Winn's brother replied tersely.

"Has Pepamhu sent for help?" Winn asked. Maggie was not aware of any emissaries from the Nansemond village, nor of a visit from Makedewa's father. It was a sore subject for both Winn and Makedewa, since the Nansemond sheltered the last of the Paspahegh people. Among them was Winn and Makedewa's mother, now first wife to Pepamhu, the Nansemond leader of that particular tribe.

"No," Makedewa answered.

Winn handed Malcolm back to her when the boy grabbed for his mead cup. Maggie took the child without a word, intent on listening to what the men discussed.

"Send a rider to the village. I need word from Pepamhu before we act," Winn said.

"I will go."

Winn nodded to Makedewa at his offer. Maggie knew it made sense for the younger man to carry out the duty, yet she wondered how Rebecca would feel over her husband's departure.

Hoisting the toddler higher up on her hip, she made her way over to Rebecca as the men continued to discuss their plans. Things had been quiet in the village for some time, with no interference from the English or threats from any native tribes. They kept close ties with the Nansemond, a tie that gave them some standing with the Indian community and kept them relatively safe. With the English, however, relations were strained, and it seemed only a matter of time before the English curiosity grew into something more. Over the last few months, Winn had restricted the men from journeying into town for trade; they went only in groups of heavily armed men, and they only ventured out when there was the utmost need.

Despite all their efforts, it seemed they would soon be right in the path of the English expansion. If they were burning fields near the Nansemond, it would not be long before they reached the Norse village as well.

"How are you?" Maggie asked as she reached her friend. Rebecca brushed the back of her palm over her brow, wiping away the bead of fine sweat at her hairline. Her blond curls lay matted at her nape, her cheeks plump and flushed. If anything bothered her she hid it well, striking a wide smile as Maggie joined her.

"Fine," Rebecca answered. "But I will admit I am ready to meet this wee one. I canna hardly see my toes this morning, and I feel so clumsy."

"Soon, I think. Gwen seems to think so as well," Maggie replied. Malcolm squirmed away and hid his head in her shoulder when Rebecca tried to give him a kiss.

"I should hope so," the younger woman smiled. Rebecca perked up when Makedewa lifted his chin to her across the room. He split away from the group of men and moved to join them.

"I'll leave you to your husband," Maggie whispered, giving her friend's arm a squeeze. She nodded to Makedewa. "Morning," she said. He scowled and grunted a greeting under his breath, causing Maggie to roll her eyes with a sigh. Always coarse and unmanageable, Makedewa's stony demeanor was a constant they could all rely on. Except when it came to his wife, there was little that would crack his facade, and even the impending birth of his first child had not softened him. If anything, his tension seemed to swell with each day that passed. She wondered if Rebecca was truly ready for the birth, or if she only wished to end her husband's distress. It was anyone's guess.

Maggie made her way across the Northern Hall. On the long table was the remnants of the morning meal. She let Malcolm chew on a piece of hard bread as she gathered food into her small pouch, taking enough to fill her belly and soothe the child. The rest of her family managed on their own; Winn ate with the men, and Dagr sat with his friends. Maggie spotted eleven year-old Kyra with her aunt Gwen near the hearth fire, and she knew all those she loved were fed. There was little she had control of in her world, but it was one thing she took comfort in seeing to.

Malcolm toddled ahead, happy to explore on his own as they left the hall and walked through the courtyard. Winn's eyes met hers as she passed by the men. She ducked her chin down and kept going, knowing he was busy and she should leave him to it. Tending the village was a full-time occupation, and as Chief, Winn took it upon himself to see everyone's needs were met. It was a duty that kept him long hours into the night, sometimes only returning to her bed in time to see the morning sunrise in the sky. As such, it was her responsibility to support him, and she tried her best to be the sort of wife he needed.

She was surprised, but entirely pleased when she felt Winn come up beside her, his stride matching hers. He took her elbow and pulled her to a stop. Although his eyes were still on the men, he dipped his head to her ear and his hand slipped down onto her hip. He rested it there for a moment, his fingers kneading her gently as his breath tickled her cheek.

"Did I say you could leave?" he asked, his voice low and teasing. She bit back a giggle and gave him a demure half-bow.

"No, *my lord*," she shot back. Her surly response sent the corner of his lip up into a grin.

"You should mind your tongue, wife," he said. He touched her neck with his fingertips, sending a shiver straight through to her toes. "You know I hate when you call me that. I would rather hear my name on your lips."

"Oh, would you, *my lord*?" she laughed. His grip tightened on her and he pulled her close, despite the fact that they were in the middle of the busy courtyard and that people milled around them. She felt a rush of heat fill her cheeks.

"Yes, I would. Perhaps you have forgotten it. I could put off my duties if you require a lesson in how to address me properly," he whispered. She swallowed as his blue eyes flashed with mock ire, his gaze drifting from her eyes to her lips.

"I'm not sure you can teach me anything," she stammered. His brows narrowed.

"Oh, you will regret that," he murmured. He took her hand and placed it flat against his chest, flush to his skin beneath the edge of his vest. His pulse beat madly under her fingers, showing her exactly how serious he was.

"I hope so," she said softly as she caught her breath. She gathered her flailing wits and planted a playful kiss on his cheek as she whispered, "Have fun with the men, *my lord*. I'm very busy today, I have no time for talking."

With his lips pressed lightly to her ear, he uttered his hoarse reply.

"When I see you next, you will have no need for *talking*. That, my wife, I promise you."

She kept the rest of her retorts to herself when he left her standing there. He shook his head as he turned and left, and Maggie sighed with a grin spreading across her face. As she caught up ahead with Malcolm and swept him up in her arms, she glanced back at the men.

Winn was surrounded by the others, yet his eyes met hers through the crowd. She could see the promise in his gaze as clear as the sun blazing above them.

Oh, yes, she thought. Next time she saw him, there would be very little talking.

2

Kyra

"Oh, I cannot *stand* it! Make it stop!" Kyra muttered. She squeezed her eyes shut and clenched her palms over each ear to muffle the screams of childbirth, yet the clamor continued despite her efforts. There was no escape from Rebecca's shrieks, which she thought had been going on an awfully long time in spite of there being plenty of help. Why didn't Aunt Gwen do something to ease her pain, or have Gramma Finola utter a spell? Surely, there was some way to make it better!

"Are ye all right?"

She cracked open one eye, just a slit, but enough to cast a glare at sixteen-year-old Morgan. He kneeled beside her in the grass, looking idly toward the village and the sounds of Rebecca's pain. The chaos seemed not to bother him so much.

"No. I think it's killing her. The blasted wean is killing her, I'm sure of it!" she whispered. Unwilling to say much more, she shook her head in defiance and clamped her hands tight when another squeal pierced the air.

"Nay, it will be fine," he assured her.

Morgan patted her arm, the motion hesitant but still comforting. In her panic to stop the screams from reaching her ears, Kyra ducked her head into Morgan's shoulder. She heard the older boy let out a sigh as she burrowed into him, but he relented and made a clumsy attempt to comfort her by gently hugging her. Although she was only eleven, he still looked out for her, and she did not know what she would do if she did not have his friendship. They sat on the ground next to the moss-covered log as Morgan stammered words of consolation.

"Kyra!"

Uncle Chetan stood above them, his eyes wary, his hands planted on his hips. Chetan was not a man easily angered, so when Kyra saw the dark glare in his eyes she was instantly worried. He grabbed her by the elbow and yanked her up off the ground, out of Morgan's arms, his face contorted as he surveyed them.

"What the–never mind! Be glad I found you instead of your father!" Chetan growled. Then he turned to Morgan, who was sprawled beside the log. "And you! Go back to town. I think you are too old for my niece to follow you any longer. Go. Now!"

Morgan slowly rose to his feet, his skin burning with crimson color from his neck to his ears. Although Chetan's grip on her arm was unbreakable, his eyes were still fastened on Morgan. Kyra stomped her foot and tried to wrench her arm away from her uncle, but he held fast.

"Why must he leave? Uncle–"

"Not another word, *Kwetii*," Chetan snapped. Her heart seemed squeezed by a fist as she watched Morgan mount his pony with a flying leap and take off away from the village.

Chetan escorted her to the Northern Hall, where her father was sitting at the long table with the other men. Uncle Makedewa sat beside him, not drinking like the rest, merely staring into the tankard he gripped it in both hands. It was clear the other men tried to console him as his wife labored to birth their child. As Chetan brought her into the hall, her father rose from his seat and met them near the door.

"Where have you been? Your mother was worried," Chief Winn chastised her. She grimaced under his narrowed gaze and ducked her head. She knew she had been ordered to stay near the Longhouse, but when she saw Morgan had come to visit she could not help but escape with him to avoid hearing the wails. Everyone was so caught up in the birth of Rebecca's child that they did not even notice when she slipped away. She didn't understand why her uncle seemed so angry. After all, she had not been far away, and nothing bad had happened.

"I found her with Morgan White near the woods," Chetan said. Kyra scowled at her uncle but quickly hid her scrunched face when her father turned his attention to her.

"Is that true, *Kwetii*? Did you disobey your mother?" Father asked. She nodded sourly, keeping her eyes down at her feet. Great. She would be in trouble again. She hoped they would not make her sit in the corner. That was her mother's favorite punishment, and Kyra found it entirely boring.

"I think Morgan is growing too old to play with Kyra any longer," Chetan added. Kyra's head snapped up at that.

"He's not that old! I'll be older soon, too!" she interrupted. Winn grunted a warning at her, and she put her head back down.

"Too old, hmm?" Winn asked. From the corner of her eye, she saw Chetan nod, and the two men exchanged a peculiar glance. Kyra did not like it, not one bit.

Chief Winn bent down, placing one hand on her shoulder. His gaze was still fierce, but his eyes held a twinkle of softness that she needed to see from her father.

"I know you grow older with each sunrise, but he is the age of your cousin and needs friends his own age. I think you should play with the girls from now on, daughter," he said. She tried to stop the swell of tears that surfaced, wiping angrily at her eyes with one dusty fist.

"He's my friend," she said softly. Father squeezed her shoulder.

"I know. But he is no longer a child. Would you want the other boys to think him weak?"

"Morgan doesn't care what the others think."

"Maybe not, little one. But I do. You are my daughter, and I must look out for you. No more playing with Morgan in the woods. Play with the other girls. Make new friends."

"Yes, Da," she muttered. She said it, but she did not mean it, and she was certain her father could see through her shallow promise quite easily.

"Good. Go to your mother, she worries after you."

Kyra shot one more seething glare at her uncle, then picked up her skirts and ran from the hall.

Well, her father might be Chief, but she still had two legs. There was no way he could command her to stop being friends with Morgan.

She stalked across the yard to their home, pausing outside the open door. The sounds of Rebecca's screams reached a pealing squeal, yet still there was no sound of a babe. Kyra bypassed the door, went to her tied pony, and mounted up.

***

It had been a long time since she had been allowed into town with her father, but the path was worn into a thin sandy line through the woods by the many times Morgan had traveled back and forth. Her pony followed the path without much prodding, which was fortunate since she was lost in her own thoughts as she approached Elizabeth City. She knew Morgan had moved there with his guardian, John Jackson, who was an acquaintance of her father's. John Jackson was a gunsmith, and Kyra had heard Morgan speak once or twice about working at the local ordinary. It was not much to go on, but she was determined to find him. She needed to tell him that they would always be friends, no matter what her father or uncle had to say.

The town was much different from what she was accustomed to. People milled about, so many people that no one seemed to notice her at all. It was a comforting thought, since she was utterly exhausted of people butting into her business at every turn. Her mother could tell people to "mind your business!" but Kyra, unfortunately, was not allowed to speak to her elders that way.

She followed the sounds of music and bawdy laughter into the center of town. There, a brightly lit tavern stood, cramped full of bodies as daylight left the sky and settled into nightfall. She imagined someone there could help her find Morgan. After all, how many boys could there be named Morgan White in one town?

After tying her pony to a hitching post, she slid in through the open door. Lacking in manners in such a situation, it was all she could do to stare at the passel of English as she pushed through them. Some wore frilly finery, dressed in bright fanciful colors and covered with jeweled baubles. Others wore the clothes of laborers, with muted shades of homespun on breeches and tunics, pointed wool hats and work-stained hands. It fascinated her to see them all in one place, such a hodgepodge of different likes and tastes. So caught up in taking it all in, Kyra was startled when a hand suddenly closed on her upper arm.

Her first reaction was to look down at the hand. It was large, quite large, in fact, and it was latched securely over hers as if the stranger held some authority over her. Who dared handle her in such a way? Well, obviously he did not know who she was, and her father would surely have words with him over his attempt to manhandle her.

"I beg yer pardon, ye ignorant old fool!" she hissed, trying to jerk her arm away.

The man bent down, and she clamped her mouth shut at the sight of him. He was bigger than her uncle Cormaic, even larger than her own father. A swatch of unruly black hair fell over his brow as he bent down to her level. His eyes were a deep, blazing blue, seeming alight with what she could neither discern as annoyance or amusement.

"Quiet yer tongue, lass! What on God's earth are ye doing here?" he replied, shaking her a bit as he spoke. She peered up at him. Even kneeling, he was still a monster, and for the first time since her hasty escape from the village a sliver of fear infused her.

"I–I'm looking for my friend. It's none of yer concern, sir!" she sniped. She figured at least if she sounded brave, he might think she was.

He glanced over his shoulder toward the long wooden bar, then turned back to her as he uttered a sigh. His face softened, only a bit, but enough to ease her mind that he meant her harm. Truth be told, the man seemed perplexed.

"Not quite eleven years old, and here in a tavern. Well, I suppose there's a first for everything. Where's yer father? Does he know ye've run away from him?"

"No," she admitted. She saw a woman approach, and Kyra knew the strange man noticed her as well. The woman rubbed a glass in her hand with a cotton cloth as she approached, her eyebrows upraised in question. The man stood up straight as the woman joined them.

"What have ye got here, Benjamin?" the woman asked. She was pretty, Kyra thought, for an Englishwoman. More of the height of Kyra's mother, the woman's head barely reached the man's shoulder. She did not seem intimidated by Benjamin in the least, tossing her loose brown hair back as she crossed her arms over her chest.

"Nothing fer ye to worry on. Just a stray from town, I'll see her back to her folks," Benjamin said. Kyra started to open her mouth, but clamped it shut instead. Something unspoken was going on between the two adults, and somehow she was plunked right smack in the middle of it.

Before Kyra could protest, she was shoved unceremoniously out the door, her arm still firm in the man named Benjamin's hand. It suddenly occurred to her that she was in a heap of trouble. Lost in town, with no idea how to find Morgan, no one would know where to find her when she ended up dead. As much as the fear ignited her anger, she felt tears spring onto her cheeks as Benjamin dragged her out into the street. Despite her tears, he did not stop dragging her until they were alone in the shadows behind the tavern, out of sight of anyone she might call out to for help.

"So tell me where yer father is, so I might return ye to him," Benjamin said softly, finally letting his grip on her arm loosen. He was no fool, however, and he did not let go entirely as he bent down again to her level.

"He–he's not here," she admitted as she started to cry. "And he's gonna tan me good if I ever see him again!" Despite meaning not to, she burst into tears.

"Och, there, mite, don't cry, I'll take ye back to yer father. Ran away, did ye?" he asked gently, patting her back as she cried. She nodded. "Oh, I see. Like that, hmm? Sick of his uppity orders and such?"

She choked back a sob as she nodded and glanced up at him through her tear-soaked lashes.

"He said I couldna play with Morgan anymore. He said Morgan's too old. But I'm almost grown! I'll be older, soon, I will!" she explained.

Benjamin smiled. He took a clean cloth from his pocket and wiped the tears from her dirt-stained cheeks as she tried to control herself. Somehow, the stranger did not seem so threatening any longer. In fact, she felt quite comfortable with him.

"Well, if yer speakin' of Morgan White, then I must agree with yer Da. Morgan's a young man now, and he shouldna be playing with bitty girls like ye," Benjamin said.

"Do ye know Morgan?" she said, her tears instantly squelched at the prospect. Benjamin nodded.

"Aye, I know the lad well. As I do yer Da."

Benjamin looked a little sad at that confession, and Kyra wondered how they knew each other. If they had met before, she was certain she would have remembered him.

"I need to find Morgan."

"Ye need to go home. C'mon. I'll see ye back the way ye came."

He kept hold of her hand as if she might run. As they rounded the corner to where her pony should have been standing, she let out a groan when she saw Blaze was not there. Oh, sweet Odin! Not only had she run away, but she'd lost her horse. If she made it home, she was going to be walking bow-legged from a busted arse for a solid week.

"My pony's gone. Da's gonna tan my arse," she whispered. Benjamin's eyes burst wide open and he uttered a deep laugh despite her dismay.

"He might, *Kwetii*, he might just that," he agreed. A rush of unease surfaced at his use of her Indian name. How did he know it–and how did he know *her*?

"Here, we'll make a stop, and then we'll get going."

She walked obediently with him down the street, for lack of options or lack of wits about her, she did not know. He had to be friends with her father if he knew her Paspahegh name. They stopped at a small cottage, and it was not long before she realized where they were. With the smoke stack above and the smell of gunpowder, it could only be the gunsmith's house where Morgan lived.

When Benjamin knocked on the door it parted open only a notch, but he spoke swift and softly to the occupant. The door closed and a moment later Morgan came outside, rubbing his eyes with his closed fists with his hair sticking out in blond tangles around his face. He was dressed in a long shirt over a pair of breeches, hastily pushing them down into his tall boots as he joined them.

Thrilled to see him, Kyra moved toward him, but Benjamin held her firm. She was glad at that moment, because Morgan glared at her in a way he had never looked upon her before, and it tore what was left of her childlike heart into tiny pieces.

"I'm sorry, sir. I'll help ye return her," Morgan muttered and turned sharply to her. "Yer father will have yer hide, ye little fool. Why would ye defy him? He'll kill ye when he finds out, be sure of that!" Morgan brushed past Kyra without another glance and readied his horse. Benjamin lifted her easily onto a second ready horse and then mounted behind her, and they took off in a brisk lope toward the outskirts of town. They did not slow until they reached the seclusion of the wood line and the lights of the town were just dim glimmers through the trees when she looked back.

They looked longingly back at Morgan as they rode, but he refused to meet her gaze. She didn't understand why he was so angry at her, and how her plan had spiraled so horribly out of control. She had only wanted to assure him they would always be friends, that there was no other who could replace him in her heart of hearts. Even when separated, that is what it meant to be friends, and she would stand by that vow until she grew old enough for him.

"I meant no harm," she said. She saw Morgan stiffen upright in his saddle.

"Ye never do. Yer a spoilt child," Morgan replied.

"I'm not that much younger than ye, Morgan White!"

"Yes, ye are! And I doona want to see ye anymore. I'll never turn a lady's eye with ye following me about. It's best ye listen to yer Da."

Kyra felt the warmth of tears as they slid down her cheeks, and she turned her face away so Morgan could not see. She choked back a sob, and she felt Benjamin's arms tighten around her.

"That's enough, lad. She knows she's done wrong. No need to be so harsh," Benjamin admonished the youth. Morgan uttered something low she could not decipher, and then pushed his horse forward to ride ahead of them.

"Yer broken heart will mend, lass. I promise ye that," Benjamin commented. Kyra sighed.

"Why is he mad at me?" she asked.

"Because he's a young man and yer only a girl, and he doesn't need ye following him about. He doesn't want to hurt ye."

"How do ye know so much? And how do ye know my parents?"

"Well," he replied. "Ye look like a ghost of yer mother at the same age, there's no mistaking who yer ma is. And I happen to be well acquainted with yer Da, ye wee hellion."

"He never speaks of ye," she replied. At that she felt his arms stiffen, and she bounced with the stilted gait of the horse.

"No, he wouldna. Nor would yer ma."

Benjamin fell silent after that, and she relaxed enough to close her eyes a bit. It was well past her bedtime, and the excitement of the day wore heavy on her.

Finally they arrived in a meadow near the Norse town, which she knew was only up over the next ridge. They dismounted, and Benjamin spoke quietly to Morgan.

"Take her into the village, and see her back to her Da. Make sure she goes in, make no doubt of it," he ordered Morgan. Kyra had scarce time to wonder why Morgan took Benjamin's instruction without issue, as if he knew Benjamin as well and had cause to respect the man. "And you. Don't let me find ye in town again, or it willna be yer father tanning yer hide. Bide my word, *Kwetii*. Yer place is here, with yer kin."

She didn't know how to answer his demand other than to nod in agreement. Benjamin put his hands on her waist to lift her onto Morgan's horse, when suddenly the air grew still. Only the sound of a snort from the horse punctured the silence, and Kyra felt the tiny hairs on her arms stand at attention. Benjamin froze, his hands tight on her waist, then pushed her behind him as if to shield her. An arrow whizzed by her, clearing her by a good foot to impale in the grass at her feet, and Kyra knew with certainty that the archer had meant to miss.

The tall grass at the edge of the meadow rustled, and every Norseman she knew then stood up from the cover. Chetan had his bow poised for another shot; Erich held a flink-lock musket perched in aim on his shoulder.

And then her father parted from the men and strode toward them, his face an echo of a legion of hell unleashed as he raised his *bryntroll.*

Chief Winn stopped a few paces away, his eyes darting back and forth between Benjamin and Kyra. Kyra kept behind her new protector, putting off the inevitable of facing her father as long as she could. Benjamin stood up straighter and met Winn's gaze. For two men who were friends, surely they were acting right barmy, Kyra thought.

"My daughter. Was she harmed?" Winn said evenly. Kyra had never heard her father utter such strangled words before, and it sickened her. She instantly regretted her rash actions.

"I found her in the tavern. She's fine," Benjamin replied tersely.

The two men were silent for a moment, and then Benjamin broke the pause by pulling her forward. He bent down on one knee and gently wiped the remnants of tears from her face.

"Go on, lass. Go to yer Da," he said softly. She was utterly confused but she did as he bid her, walking dutifully to her father's side. Once she reached Winn and he had a hand on her shoulder, she saw her father lift his *bryntroll* and then gently lower it. The Norsemen behind him lining the meadow lowered their drawn weapons.

"Her pony returned without her. I feared–I feared she was hurt...or worse," Winn said quietly. Benjamin broke the standoff by taking a few paces toward them, and Kyra heard the rustle of the Norsemen in the trees behind them.

"She came to no harm, and no one followed us here," Benjamin replied.

She saw some unspoken message between the two men, and she suddenly knew there was much more to this encounter than the issue of her return. Who was Benjamin, and why did he speak to her father so boldly, as if the Englishman had no fear of him? Other than her uncles, she had never seen a man confront her father without fear, yet Benjamin stood straight and sure in front of them as if he had some secret assurance Winn meant him no harm.

Benjamin was either a fool or the bravest Englishman she had ever known. She was not sure which.

"My thanks for her safe return," Winn said, his fingers tightening on her shoulder. "I give you safe passage to leave. None of my men will harm you."

Benjamin's gaze did not waver from Winn's at that moment, but Kyra saw the way the Englishman's fists tightened at his sides. She looked up at her father, and then to Benjamin, confused at the threat lying beneath her father's words.

"Da, he helped me, he's done no wrong!" Kyra interrupted. At her protest, her father snapped. He grabbed her by her chin and turned her face upwards, his face awash with a mixture of fear and fury she had never witnessed before.

"This man is our enemy. Be glad your heart still beats, and that he took pity on a foolish child!" her father growled. She squirmed to break the hold he had on her chin, but he was relentless, his blue eyes boring through her until tears coursed down her cheeks. Finally, he released her chin and she looked up at Benjamin through her misty eyes.

Her savior's face held no shelter. Fixed as if carved from stone, there was no more trace of the kindness she had seen in him.

"Your father speaks true. Do not return to town. Ever. And be glad I am the only enemy who knows who ye are," Benjamin said, staring down at her. His voice slanted to a coarse octave when he raised his eyes back to Winn's. "Your secret is safe. For now."

Winn nodded, and Benjamin returned the gesture. Before Kyra could utter another word, Winn turned abruptly and hauled her back to the village. As they reached the safety of the trees, she turned her head.

The pounding of hooves thudded like thunder across the damp earth, and she could only see the haunches of two horses as Benjamin and Morgan galloped out of sight.

3

Maggie

"You have to push now! Push!" Gwen demanded. Maggie's aunt took a firm hold of Rebecca's knees, urging on the younger woman in the midst of labor. Sweat dappled Rebecca's forehead and the mop of blond curls on her head lay limp and plastered to the skin around her face. As Gwen shook her Rebecca let out a long sigh, more of a sob than anything. The desperate sound caused Maggie's toes to curl in her boots.

Something was wrong. Rebecca's pains had started before the sun graced the sky that day, yet still there was no baby as the moon rose above them. Gwen, always the stalwart one, suddenly appeared unsettled and her directions to Rebecca seemed more frantic than direct. Maggie swallowed hard at the sight of Gwen's hands covered in bright red blood.

As Rebecca collapsed back against the pillows, Maggie grabbed Gwen's wrist. When Gwen's sad green eyes met her own, Maggie knew her suspicion was correct. Rebecca had been bleeding for the last hour, and the trickling flow showed no sign of stopping.

"She needs to push. The babe must come out, it's right there!" Gwen said to Maggie's unasked question. "You sit behind her, make her sit up. Hold her legs, it'll help the wean come down."

Maggie pushed herself behind Rebecca and did as Gwen commanded. She put her hands on Rebecca's knees and drew them back, despite the moan of resistance Rebecca offered. Rebecca's head lolled back onto Maggie's shoulder, her eyes staring blankly up at her friend.

"Only a few more pushes, the baby's almost here," Maggie murmured. She felt Rebecca's body shudder with the onset of another contraction.

"Again! Oh, I see the head, one more push, girl!" Gwen shouted.

Rebecca leaned forward suddenly as if she regained her strength, screaming long and hard with the last push she could tolerate. Tears coursed down Gwen's face as the babe slid into her arms, and when they heard the throaty cry of healthy newborn they all broke into sobs.

"I did it," Rebecca whispered, a smile creasing her lips. Maggie kissed her cheek, hugging her tightly as she helped her friend lay back in the bed. Gwen cleaned and wrapped the squealing babe then placed the infant gently in Rebecca's arms.

"A boy. A fine son fer yer man," Gwen announced.

"He's perfect," Maggie added. She tucked the blanket down at the babe's chin so they could look properly at his face. He had large round eyes, staring up calmly at them as if he wondered what all the fuss was about. When he opened his mouth to yawn, tears streaked down Rebecca's face.

"Do ye know how much I wanted ye?" Rebecca said softly as she stared at her son. Maggie helped her put the boy to her breast, and Rebecca smiled when he latched on with a hearty suck. The babe made soft snoring sounds as he fed, taking his fill for some time before Rebecca laid her head back on her pillow. "You look just like your father," she whispered.

She was right. With a swatch of thick black hair and a set of the darkest eyes Maggie had ever seen on a newborn, the boy was the image of his father. The infant stared solemnly up at his mother, eyes wide and soulful beyond what a newborn should possess.

Maggie drew back away from the bed, giving her friend some space with her child. She knew better than anyone how little time a woman actually could keep her son beside her. Now that Malcolm was weaned, it would not be long before he joined the men in their duties and learned the ways of the village. If Makedewa was anything like his brother, Maggie knew Rebecca would be seeing her son grow up faster than she could blink.

Gwen remained at the end of the bed, delivering the afterbirth and massaging the new mother's belly. Maggie assumed her aunt was just cleaning up, but when Gwen's face tightened and her lips pursed into a line a surge of unease shivered over her skin. Gwen should be happy now that the babe had arrived healthy, shouldn't she?

"What is it?" Maggie asked. Gwen shook her head, as if to herself, then pushed a bundle of bloody furs onto the floor. Blood pooled on the bed beneath Rebecca, so much that it dripped off the side onto the soiled pile at Gwen's feet.

"Sister, would ye take him for a bit? I think I shake too much, I might drop him," Rebecca asked with a tiny laugh. "I doona see myself having as many weans as ye, if this is what one wee mite does to me," she added. Her head fell back onto the pillows and her lids closed over her weary eyes as Maggie took the babe from her.

"Of course I'll hold him. Just until you're steady again," Maggie replied. Rebecca smiled at that, and Maggie could not help but notice her lips had taken on a bluish tinge. In fact, her once rosy skin seemed flat and much too pale, as if the life was draining from her with each moment.

And it was.

When Gwen met her gaze again over Rebecca's still body, the reality of what was about to happen numbed her.

"It willna stop. There's too much blood," Gwen said softly. Rebecca squeezed her eyes shut at Gwen's declaration, and a tear streaked down her cheek.

"I know," Rebecca whispered in return. Gwen continued to massage Rebecca's belly with long strokes, pushing her fists into the new mother's soft skin. It did little to stem the bleeding.

"It will stop, it will," Maggie said, clutching the newborn in her arms. Gwen shook her head, tears staining her cheeks.

"We must send fer her husband. Stay here, I'll find him," Gwen muttered. She clutched her arms around her full waist as she rose as if comforting herself to the task. The older woman wiped her bloodied hands on her apron and left without another glance at Rebecca.

"Shh now, sister. Bring him to me. I should like to see him again," Rebecca said. Her face seemed caught in a grimace, her teeth biting down into her lower lip as tears continued to fall from her shining eyes. She tried to lift her hand, but it fell weakly to her side. "Please...wipe my face. I canna let my husband see me so."

Maggie dutifully sat down next to her friend, blotting at her pale skin to dry the dampness. Even as her fingers were tinged blue, and her neck looked mottled with splotches along the collar of her shift. Rebecca knew she was fading, and it tore at Maggie's heart to see her friend so calm as she faced the other side.

"Put him next to me, so I might warm him," Rebecca asked. Maggie placed the swaddled babe gently beside her, tucking the child in next to his mother.

"Here, he's right here," Maggie replied.

"Make sure he's warm. Ye'll see to it, won't ye? That he's always warm?" she asked. Maggie pressed her face into Rebecca's hair and clutched her tight. Did Rebecca truly understand she was bleeding too much? Did she accept there was nothing they could do to stop it?

"Of course. Of course I will," she promised. Maggie wondered what was keeping Gwen from finding Makedewa as her resolve to be strong broke into tiny fragments. When Rebecca let out a long sigh and grew quiet Maggie bit her own lip to muffle her sob, yet Rebecca's chest continued to rise and fall with her shallow breaths.

How could this be happening? Women didn't have to *die* in childbirth! Why did they have to sit back and watch it happen, without interference? What was the good of having magical blood if she could do nothing with it?

Malcolm's blood was too old to help Rebecca.

There was nothing in her power to do to help her friend.

Maggie looked up when Winn pushed open the door. He glanced down briefly at the tangle of bloodied furs at her feet and then shifted his blue eyes to hers. His throat was tight, his face carefully composed as Makedewa came into the room with Chetan.

Makedewa shrugged off the hand that Winn placed on his shoulder and sank down onto his knees beside Rebecca. He stared silently at her for a long moment until her eyes fluttered open and he kissed her gently on her clasped hands.

Maggie felt Winn's hand at her waist and she let him lead her from the room. Chetan nodded as they passed by, crouched down on his haunches by the doorway as he watched Makedewa. The sound of Rebecca's voice was too faint to hear, only a whisper left between the two lovers as they held each other.

4

<hr>

Makedewa

HE PLACED HIS HANDS over hers. Although there was sweat on her brow, her skin was not warm, but she smiled at him despite any discomfort she felt. He felt her attempt to squeeze his hand, so he gathered her fingers between his palms and shook his head.

"Rest, *chulentet*," he said. "Close your eyes, I will stay here with you."

Her body relaxed, her head falling back onto the pillow as she uttered a sigh. Strands of her golden hair stuck to her face, so he gently brushed the tendrils away. He needed to see her clearly, every bit of her sweet heart-shaped face. If ever he had known another's soul, it was hers, and if by looking into her eyes he might find some truth, then he must look.

Gwen said Rebecca was too far gone.

Gwen must be wrong.

"Our son is perfect," she said softly.

Makedewa did not look at the babe. There would be time for that later, when her strength returned and they could tend to the child together. Until then he could not bear to consider the boy in her arms, lest he linger on the anger at that small spirit for draining the life from the woman he loved.

"Let Gwen take him," Makedewa said, his voice more gruff that he intended. "Gwen –"

"No, leave him. Please," Rebecca insisted. She tried to sit up, causing his heart to clench as she faltered and fell back down. He took her in his arms, ignoring the little beast swaddled at her side.

"Let him stay, but you must rest. I need my wife at my side again."

"Husband," she whispered. "I must tell ye –"

"Tell me nothing –"

"The life we have, this life we have made – it is so precious to me. When I was broken, ye made me whole. I have lived a beautiful life," she whispered, "Because of ye."

When she grimaced, he realized he clutched her too hard, so he slid down onto the bed beside her. Her body surrendered, molding against his, tucked into his chest where she belonged. Slick with sweat, her forehead rested in the crook of his arm, her flesh clammy despite his efforts to warm her. *She hated being cold. He must make her warm, and then she would feel better.*

"You will live your life at my side," he insisted, his voice hoarse.

For a long moment, she did not answer, her eyes closed as her mouth fell slightly open. Finally, with a sudden burst of strength she stirred, clutching his tunic with her blue-tinged fists.

"Please, stay with me," she said.

"Always," he replied.

He meant it.

Makedewa held her long after the breath left her body. If he did not let her go, she could not leave him.

5

Maggie

The men stayed away from Gwen's dwelling while the women tended to cleaning up. They were all accustomed to their duties and expected to carry on, each member of the community pulling together to finish the task. The sounds of muffled sobs littered the air inside the longhouse as they worked, scattered among the scent of childbirth and blood.

Maggie patted Gwen's hand and tilted her head, giving her aunt notice that she needed a moment. Gwen nodded, and Maggie wiped her hands on her apron and left. Away from Rebecca's shrouded body. Away from the sweet woman who had called Maggie sister.

Away from the squalling babe in the cradle who would never know his mother.

Although the Northern Hall was quiet, Maggie imagined the men must be gathered there with Makedewa. Wishing to feel the crisp night air across her face, she pushed her wool hood off her head and took a deep breath.

Oh, Rebecca, she thought. *It was so unfair, so wrong.*

The courtyard was empty save for a lone man who sat by the well. He was not difficult to make out, sitting on the edge of the well with his face in his hands. The fur mantle shrouded his slumped shoulders, and while his face was difficult to see in the moonlight, she noted the glimmer of dampness on his cheeks.

In his own way, Cormaic had cared for Rebecca. Despite his brawn, there was a gentle side to him, one he let loose around those he cared for. When Rebecca married Makedewa, it was Cormaic at her side pledging to remain her friend. It was Cormaic who honored her by making Makedewa fight for her hand. Whatever feelings he had for her he kept silent, supporting her choice and giving every outward appearance of acceptance.

Maggie gently touched his mane of copper hair. He uttered a deep sigh but did not look up, keeping his face buried in his massive hands. For want of knowing how to comfort him, she remained silent, merely sitting down beside her cousin. She looped her arm through his elbow and laid her head against his shoulder, feeling tears slide down her cheeks as he shuddered.

Finally he placed his hand over hers. A slight squeeze, enough to acknowledge the pain they shared. He raised his head and stared off into the sky, wiping the back of his hand over his face.

"She was not mine to mourn, but still...still it pains me," he said quietly.

"I know," she whispered.

His jaw tightened and he sat up straighter.

"Is that Makedewa?" he asked.

Maggie turned to see who he referred to, and sure enough, it was Makedewa stalking across the yard toward them.

"I thought he was with his brothers," she replied. As he drew near, the look on his face sent a current of despair down deep in her bones. Whether it was grief that drove him or anger she did not know, but from him she knew to expect anything.

She stood up and walked to meet him, concern winning out over fear. Although he had not yet held his son, she hoped he might remedy that and find some comfort in the child Rebecca had wanted so desperately.

"I – I'm going back to help Gwen. Your son –"

"Heal her," he interrupted, grabbing her wrist. "Use your magic, use the Bloodstone. Heal her as you healed me once."

His grip was on the edge of painful, but she tried to ignore the sting as she looked into his desperate face. His mouth was set firm, his breath coming in short bursts. Black eyes reflected his darkness, and with a sickly feeling of recognition, she saw the beast within him surge to the surface.

"I – I can't," she stammered. He knew as well as she did that only the newborns of her line held that power. The power to heal was a sacred gift, one that was too potent to carry as one aged. It was Dagr's blood that had saved Makedewa's life once, and now all the Blooded MacMhaolians were past that time. The only way she could heal death would be to give all of her blood, and as such, her life.

"You cannot? Or you will not?" he asked.

"Let her go," Cormaic growled, his voice surfacing at her side.

"Makedewa," she said softly. He was her husband's brother, her family. He would not hurt her. Or would the grief drive him to place he could not return from?

"You saved my life once," he hissed. "Why? So I should live without her?" She felt the sting of his fingers as he clenched her wrist, but it was the desperate depths of his black eyes that kept her attention. She tried not to move, afraid her efforts would send him further over the edge.

"We all love you," she said, at loss to give him any sensible answer.

"I have nothing."

"You have a son," she whispered. His eyes narrowed.

"I only wanted her," he replied.

Cormaic placed his hand over Makedewa's, and chaos broke loose as she was jerked free. She hit the ground bottom first, scraping her palms on the stony earth as she was shoved away from the melee.

She winced as Makedewa threw a punch, landing it squarely in Cormaic's ribs. Cormaic bent over at the blow and rammed his shoulder into Makedewa's gut, sending both men crashing to the ground. They rolled together, entwined in a knot of flailing arms and kicking legs, each striving for the upper hand in a battle no one was meant to win.

"Stop it!" she shouted to no response. They were too lost in the fight, too embroiled in pummeling each other. She heard shouts from the Northern Hall as the two men continued wrestling, and her breath caught in her chest when Makedewa rose above Cormaic with his knife drawn.

"No!" she cried.

"I'll kill you," Makedewa growled, his brow dripping with sweat and blood. Cormaic was bested for the moment but he was not a man to underestimate; both men were bloodied and bruised.

Moonlight glanced off the blade in Makedewa's hand. When Makedewa pressed the knife beneath his chin, Cormaic slowly let his head fall back.

"Kill me then," Cormaic said, the words ground out between gritted teeth. "Do it! Release yer burden. It willna bring her back."

At that, Makedewa pulled away, falling onto his haunches next to Cormaic. He hovered for a moment then scrambled to his feet, staring first at Cormaic and then at Maggie. He took a step backward and stumbled a pace, righting himself as he looked at the blade in his hand. His eyes widened and he swallowed, as if seeing the weapon for the first time.

His haunted eyes met hers. The knife slipped from his hand, impaled in the dirt at his feet. His lips parted as if he meant to speak, but his voice failed to surface.

She watched silently as he turned and left.

"Here. Yer bleeding," Cormaic said. The sound of fabric tearing was dull, muted by the ache in her chest. Cormaic pressed the makeshift bandage to her scraped hand. She had not noticed she bled until the sting of the cloth hit her palms. When she looked up at Cormaic, she was relieved to see he was bruised but otherwise intact.

"What happened here?" Winn asked as he arrived with the other men. She watched as Makedewa disappeared into the woods and she knew Winn saw him as well. When he moved to follow, she grabbed his hand.

"Let him go," she said softly.

He turned back to her as if to protest, but then his eyes fell on the bloodied cloth she pressed to her hand. As he inspected the wound, she closed her eyes briefly and leaned into him.

"Was it him? Did he do this?" Winn demanded. Her voice faltered in her dry throat, the urge to deny it strong. As much as Makedewa had frightened her, it was clear he suffered. When she shook her head in denial, Winn clenched his hands on her shoulders.

"Cormaic?"

Winn's voice did not waver. Erich joined them, and she spotted Chetan standing by the wood line.

"Aye. It was him." Cormaic paused, his green eyes meeting hers before he answered. "He was not himself," he added.

Winn sent a silent message to Chetan with a slight nod of his head, and Chetan disappeared into the woods.

"I'm going back to the longhouse," Maggie murmured.

Winn dropped his hands away from her.

"Have Gwen tend your wound," he said. "And I will join you soon."

"All right," she agreed.

Maggie left while the men stayed behind. It was up to Winn to decide what to do for his brother, and for once, she was glad to follow her husband's orders.

***

She found Gwen alone in her longhouse, rocking the baby as she sat by the fire. Maggie's uncle was a skilled craftsman, constructing the rocking chairs she described from the future with only her description to work from. A rocker sat by nearly every hearth in the village, and each time she spotted one she was reminded of where she came from.

"How is he?" she asked quietly. Gwen gazed down at his face, smiling as she answered.

"Fine fer now. But he willna live if we cannot feed him. He canna survive on water and mash, not now. Maybe if he was a mite older, but…" her voice trailed off. Maggie swallowed hard at her aunt's blatant assessment of the situation. Gwen knew the infant would not survive without milk, and she made no bones about it. To her, it was simply a fact of life.

"We can send to the Nansemond for help. They must have someone who can nurse him," Maggie answered. Gwen shook her head sadly.

"It will be two days before they could return with a woman, if one agrees to it. It's too long. Perhaps we should just send the babe to them, and let his father come for him if he pleases."

The child opened his mouth into a yawn, and then released a tiny cry. Patting his bottom, Gwen soothed him back to slumber.

"Gwen?" Maggie said. Lost in her own heartache, she finally felt strong enough to ask the questions she kept buried. She needed to know more about the magic in her blood – how it worked, how she could wield it. How could she be useful to anyone without the knowledge to control her own power?

"Hmm?" Gwen replied.

"I need answers. I know you think you're protecting us by never speaking of the how to use the magic, but you're not. I need to know how it works. I need to know how to control it, how to use it," Maggie said. "Please. Please tell me."

Gwen did not stop rocking, nor did she raise her head. Her cheeks, however, betrayed her discomfort with Maggie's demand, and a flush blazed across her skin. She shook her head, as if to herself, and then let out a short sigh.

"Yer own mother died using that bloody magic. Is it worth that much to ye?" Gwen asked.

Maggie swallowed hard but nodded. If she could bring Rebecca back, yes, it was worth it.

"Yes. It is. Tell me what you know, and let me decide for myself."

"She was barely grown when she met yer father," Gwen said. Her voice lowered a bit and she cleared her throat. "Yer father dinna tell her who he really was, and when she found out it broke her heart. I think she never did forget him, even when Dagr took her away to your time."

"I can't remember her at all," Maggie whispered.

"Ye have her look about ye. It's quite clear," she added, raising an eyebrow to glare at Maggie. "She was young – and foolish. Ye have that part of her as well."

Maggie bit her lower lip but said nothing.

"Dagr told me Esa tried to return here from yer place, but she went to the wrong time. She met herself here, and that is why she died. One cannot return to a time once lived. It's just not natural."

"But why did she die?" Maggie asked.

Gwen stopped rocking and leaned forward in her chair.

"A soul cannot beat in two hearts at once. If ye go back to a time and find ye face yerself, then yer own heart will stop. She made a mistake, and she paid for it with her life."

"Wait. A mistake?"

"Some of us still know the runes. If ye paint the runes on yer skin, ye can make it take ye where ye need. 'Tis the only way to truly control that bloody stone. Else it takes ye where it *wants* ye to be, and then yer truly and rightfully fooked," Gwen said. "Yer ma had not yet learned the runes. Old Malcolm knew Esa was not ready."

"So my raven didn't bring me here?" Maggie sputtered, still grasping to understand. If the magic could be controlled, directed, then there was some use to it she could wield. Could she change what had happened to Rebecca?

"Of course it did. All those trinkets are marked with a rune. They link them together. That's why Benjamin dinna travel far when he tried. Ye gave him his eagle, and it was tied here, to the others."

"My raven. And the other ones Erich made."

Gwen nodded. "It helps when one gets lost. 'Tis easy to find yerself trapped and alone when ye mettle with time."

Maggie glanced at the figurines on the hearth. She noticed a few new ones in the bunch, all made in the image of an animal. A deer, a turtle, and a fox graced the ledge, each a tiny replica made with great care.

"So my mother was a fool. And what of my father, Gwen? Why is he never spoken of?" Maggie asked quietly, keeping her gaze steady on the figurines. Afraid to look at what she knew would be condemnation from Gwen, she tried to keep her voice steady with her demands.

Instead of Gwen's response, the gravelly voice of her uncle cut in.

"Because he was a Sturlsson and our enemy," Erich said. Maggie turned to face him, swallowing hard as she noted her husband beside her uncle.

"It's my right to know," she said, trying to keep her voice from wavering. She raised her chin a notch, her hands falling to her sides where she clutched her gown.

"Aye, it is. But what do ye mean to do with this knowledge, niece, if it not something foolish? I will tell ye what ye wish to know, if I have yer promise not to act on it. There's a reason we fall under command of the Neilsson Chief, a good reason," Erich said. His shoulder sagged as he removed his weapons, laying them across the table before he sat down. He motioned to the bench at his side and she took his invitation, sliding stiffly down beside him. Winn moved closer to the fire but remained standing, watching them in silence.

"I won't do anything foolish," Maggie muttered. She was incensed when everyone in the room laughed, even Winn, who coughed and tried to pretend he had not joined in. Erich, however, chuckled and sputtered in his amusement, finally taking up a mug of ale to clear his throat.

"Oh, no, ye'd never leap with yer heart first. Not my niece," he muttered. Winn looked at the floor, hiding his grin.

"Yer like yer mother, through and through," Erich added, his voice leveling off to a more thoughtful tone. He wiped a trickle of mead from his greying beard and leaned back. "Her heart was kind, as I know is yers. I loved my sister, but for the Gods, she was a stubborn one! She met the Sturlsson boy and hid it from us, and we dinna find out until it was too late."

"Too late?" Maggie asked. Erich nodded, and Gwen looked away.

"When yer father revealed his plan to my sister, the deed was done. She was with child, and it broke her heart to know he only meant to use her blood for his own gain."

Maggie glanced at Winn. Quiet throughout the conversation, Winn's jaw seemed tight and he would not meet her gaze. With a sickly feeling, Maggie realized that this was not news to her husband. She wondered how long he had known, how long he had chosen to keep the details to himself. True, she rarely spoke of her parents, but only because they did not seem real to her. She was not a woman who had grown up longing for the care of her missing parents; rather, she had learned early on to harden her heart to those who had abandoned her and take comfort in the love she was given by her grandfather and Marcus. For her entire life, it had been enough, but now, standing before her uncle, she was taken over by the desire to know them.

To know her mother. To know her father. Perhaps it was because she was a mother to her own children, or because she was a wife to her husband. Her lifeline was entwined with that of her kin, and even though she could not miss a mother she had never known, she felt some kinship with the image of her. It irritated her to hear her uncle thought her foolish like her mother, but on some level, it warmed her. At least she shared something of the woman.

"What did he plan to do?" she asked quietly. Winn looked up at her question and glanced at Erich. Erich stood up from the bench before he answered, facing the fire with his back to them.

"He wanted yer mother's blood to take him back in time," Erich took a swallow from his mug, then spit into the fire. "He planned to take her back, see ye born, then use yer blood to change his father's death. Then he would have control of her, and all the Clans would bow to him. In that place in time, the Chief that held a Blooded One had all the power."

So her father had used her mother, in one of the most heartbreaking ways a man could use a woman. Her fist tightened as she stared at her uncle, and she tasted a stab of that betrayal her mother must have felt. To know she was only a means to an end must have been devastating, and then to be left carrying his child? Well, Maggie could not condemn her mother. Even knowing that truth, the fact that own father was a bloody scheming scoundrel was difficult to process.

Erich and Gwen told her often she was like her mother. Yet the burning question in her mind was how much she was like her *father*.

"Why not just have my mother take him back to prevent his father's death? Then he wouldn't need the blood of a newborn," Maggie muttered. It was more of an observation than anything, but Erich made a low snorting sound at her question.

"Have ye heard nothing? One canna go back to a time once lived. Yer father couldna go back to his kin, fer he was there with his da when he died. Yer father is a brazen swine, but he's a smart one. He would never risk his own life if he could serve up yers instead." Erich ran a thick hand over his head with a sigh. "If ye meet yerself in another time, girl, best ye run the o'er way," he said.

"You've said that before to me, but why?" she demanded. "If you teach me to use the runes, I can control it. I can go back exactly where I need to, I can change things – I can make it better. Why do we just – just *sit* here, doing nothing? Why can't I try?"

Erich turned back to face her, but it was her husband's voice that broke the silence.

"Because I will not allow it," Winn said quietly. "The desire of one man – or woman – is not enough reason."

"It's not just me," Maggie whispered, struggling to control her tone. She felt a flush rise in her neck and she straightened her back. "Are there any of us who do not want Rebecca back?"

"All of us do. Yet the decision is mine, and it is made," Winn replied. "And you will not interfere in the matters of men."

Gwen's eyes widened and Erich sat back down beside Maggie. Feeling the beast of frustration rise in her belly, she stared long at her husband. The fact that Winn seemed to know much more about her blood than she was privy to was a topic they would discuss later – alone. Yet his unyielding command was something else entirely and it took all of her self-control to steady herself without a harsh retort.

"Ye see, niece, I fear ye knowing how to bend this magic. It's a dangerous thing. If ye let yer heart lead ye, ye might use it when ye should not. And if that happens, then it shall be my fault." Erich turned and reached for her, taking her hand. He urged her fist open, tracing his thumb over her scar. "I can show ye how to use the runes, but to what end? If ye make a mistake and I lose ye...well, I have enough death to bear o'er my back. I'd not take on anymore, and if ye could oblige me on that, I'd be a grateful man."

She closed her eyes, squeezing his hand. Words would not come, her throat dry and her lips creased in a tight line.

"I can't help thinking about it. Is it so wrong to want to do something, to make it all better? Rebecca was my – my friend. And Makedewa...I'm afraid for him," she said softly.

"Even if you went back, what could you change?" Winn asked. "You could not stop the bleeding, even if you knew it would happen. Maybe you could keep her from marrying him, and then change destiny for all of us. Where would it end? And where would you begin?"

She stared at her husband, unable to make a reply. He was right, of course. She could not have changed the outcome, no matter how much she knew of what was to come. Saving Makedewa's life with blood from Dagr's heel was one thing; going back in time to change an entire sequence of events was another entirely.

The sharp cry of the newborn pierced the silence, reminding them all that there was yet another future to consider. Gwen patted and rocked him, but the boy would not be consoled, the demands of his empty belly much stronger than his need to sleep. Although it had been a few days since she weaned her own son, Maggie felt the tingle of answer in her body at the cry. There was something clear about a child's hungry wail, one that stirred a mother to her core.

In the absence of his own mother, there was a void to fill. If she could not use her power to change things, if there was truly nothing she could do to bring her friend back, well, then at least there was the life before them to watch over.

As Maggie took the newborn from Gwen's arms, she looked down on him and smiled. *Yes*, she thought. *This* was something she could do. She could care for him. She could feed him.

And in some small way, perhaps, she might change his future.

6

Winn

Winn settled back into his chair in the Northern Hall, listening to the murmur of Erich's voice as he reported on the status of the village supplies. His thoughts were distracted over his brother's absence, and it was with a heavy heart that he carried on with his duties. Although Makedewa had only been gone for a week, Winn feared he might never see his youngest brother again. The warrior had been careful to cover evidence of his path, disguising his trail so well that even Chetan could not track him.

When Makedewa wished to return, he would. Until that time, there was nothing Winn could do to help him. Life in the village continued on and the demands of the people who lived there did not diminish. There were mouths to be fed, a home to protect, and a new young life that depended on them. Winn found his duties a reprieve from the worry over his brother.

"…hunt for perhaps two days. That should suffice, I think. My lord?"

Winn squinted at Erich, aware he had not heard most of the older man's words. Shaking his head a bit, Winn cleared his throat and nodded.

"Yes. Hunt for two days? If you think it needs be, then we shall make it so. I trust you will gather the men?" Winn answered.

"I shall. And on the matter of the wean? Ye shall take him as yer own?"

"The child?" Winn asked, aware that he appeared addled. It occurred to him that he had missed more of the conversation than he previously thought.

"Yer brother's child, my lord. Yer wife is here to request yer blessing."

Winn stood up when Maggie was ushered into the Great Hall. In her arms she held Makedewa's son, swaddled so tightly in his bundling he remained soundless and still. When his wife kneeled before him and he saw her red-rimmed eyes, his first reflex was to drop to his knees beside her and comfort her. Yet with a glance around the hall he could see the men were watching him; this was some sort of test, and Winn felt helpless at distinguishing what was required of him.

To comfort his wife would show weakness. To ask others to make a decision would make him powerless. If only he had any idea what they wanted from him, he could try to make a ruling.

"Speak, wife," he said, in the most even tone he could manage.

"I ask you to look on this child with no mother...and no father to claim him," she said softly, her voice barely audible to his ear. "I ask you to wash him, dress him, and give him a name."

Winn grimaced as he looked down on his wife. He did not like the fear spread across her face, nor the way her hands were clenched so tightly around the child. To see his brave woman in such a state riled him to the core, and be it his lack of Norse upbringing or his flaws as a leader, he thrust away his pride and went down to one knee in front of her. He thought his heart might crack when he reached for the babe and Maggie pulled away, but suddenly what was being asked of him became clear.

"Please," she whispered. "Claim him. Give him a name. I cannot turn him out. I'm begging you. Please."

Through dry lips he murmured a word of consolation to her in his native Paspahegh and she nodded, relief flooding her face. When he reached toward her again, Maggie placed the child in his arms. Winn looked down upon his nephew, a child he would now call son, and he looked at the woman he loved more than his own life.

"Wife," he murmured. "You beg of no man."

He rose to his feet with the newborn in his arms, letting the swaddling cloth fall to the floor. The child squealed at the intrusion but Winn still held him up for all to see, raising the squirming mite above his head.

"I claim this child, son of my brother, now son of my heart. His name –"

He paused and glanced down at Maggie, who whispered, "Daniel."

"– his name is Daniel. Let him live a long life!"

It never occurred to him he would need to claim his own nephew, but Winn knew he had made the right choice when he finished to cries of *"Daniel, Daniel!"* Maggie held a copper basin as he bathed the crying child, and then together they wrapped Daniel in fresh swaddling clothes. Winn made the sign of the hammer over the wean's head and the ceremony was complete; Winn claimed the boy, and as thus, the child was one of them.

"Thank you," Maggie said softly. Winn placed his hand on her waist and she leaned slightly into him, the child wedged between them.

"Have no doubt," he replied. "What you ask of me, I give it gladly. Your fear wounds me, *ntehem.*"

"I'm so sorry. Finola told me I must present him to you, or he could be cast out with no one to claim him. And it had to be you – a man – I mean, I'm not allowed to claim him. I would have, but it's not in the rules, and –"

"Ah, enough," Winn said. A smile turned up the corners of her lips, and as difficult as it was for his wife to show deference, he grinned when she bowed to him. "Go now," he added. "Take the boy to join our children. I shall be finished here soon."

Maggie nodded. She gathered the child snug to her breast and turned to go, but not before glancing up at her uncle. Erich responded with a slight dip of his head toward her, the edge of his mouth tight in what might have been a grin. Winn briefly wondered what his MacMillan kin had been plotting behind his back, but dismissed the thought as fast as it surfaced. Let Maggie and Erich have their victories; Winn was glad to oblige them.

The scream of steel suddenly pierced the air and every man in the Northern Hall responded in kind. It was Cormaic who drew first as he stood guarding the entrance, his broadsword unsheathed and held in readiness. Maggie, who was near the door, was thrust behind her cousin where she had the good sense to remain as newcomers approached. Winn stood up and was immediately flanked by the Norse and Indian men of the village, with Erich barking a terse command to *be ready* in his foreign tongue.

"Goor viroar!" Erich grunted.

Winn stayed on the dais only so that he could see over the heads of his men as visitors entered the hall. When he noted the leader of the group he realized why his men were so unsettled.

It had been years since a Powhatan emissary had stood before the Norse. And if Winn recalled his father's family history correctly, he suspected the last time the two groups collided it had ended in the near extermination of the Norsemen from the lands of *Tsenacommacah* before Winn was even born.

One warrior stepped forward from the group of five. Dressed in the simple breechcloth and leggings most warriors wore, the man's attire held few clues to his identity. His skin, however, was littered with a swirl of dark tattoos that decorated a path from his neck to his waist, giving Winn the impression it was only a common man who stood before him. Those who accompanied the leader held the same look about them, and it was with some relief that Winn noticed it. He decided to greet them with a simple *welcome friends* and let them proceed from there.

"Sesegan, wìdjìkiwe," Winn called out. Erich muttered an oath in Norse at the use of the friendly Powhatan greeting, but Winn ignored him. Winn switched to English so that most in the Northern Hall could understand the exchange. "Who are you, and what brings you here?"

"I am *Pimiskodjìsì*, sent by Weroance Opechancanough," the leader replied in a stilted tone. "We come to speak with *Winkeohkwet*, nephew of our Great Leader."

"Then you have found him," Winn said. He met Cormaic's eye across the room and gave the younger man a nod. Cormaic obeyed the command and lowered his weapon, the other men following his lead. Winn waited to speak until Erich relaxed his sword hand and then he sat back down in his chair. "What need does my uncle have for his nephew? It has been many years since he sought my counsel."

"He sends these gifts to show his favor," *Pimiskodjìsì* said. Two of his companions came forth, placing bundles of hide-wrapped gifts before Winn. "For you and for your Red Woman."

Winn nodded his acceptance, but his entire body tensed at the mention of Maggie. The warriors obviously had been instructed to deliver the gifts, yet the mention of his wife as the Red Woman was no doubt purposeful. It was very much like his uncle to remind Winn there were thousands of Powhatans ready to strike down a Blooded One upon a single command.

Winn did not need a reminder, nor did he take kindly to threats.

"Tell my uncle I thank him for his gifts. Tell him he need not thank my wife again for saving his life."

Pimiskodjìsì met Winn's gaze. One of the Powhatan placed a hand on the knife sheathed at his waist, and *Pimiskodjìsì* grunted a command at the man. The man dropped his fist.

"Your uncle will be pleased to hear his gifts were favored," *Pimiskodjìsì* said. "He sends us on another matter as well. The English are as rodents, spreading in number. They drive our tribes west and claim the lands for their king."

"I know this," Will replied tersely. His patience was ending after the veiled threat at his wife, and he was in no mood to hear what he already knew. "What does my uncle ask of me?"

"Our Weroance asks that you send five of your strongest men to join us. He has need of more warriors for the journey we must make."

So it was war Opechancanough planned, the true intent behind the gifts and threats. For years Winn had kept his people away from the skirmishes, away from the disputes. Although he would gladly kill any English that warranted it, Winn knew the best way for his family to survive was to stay out of the fray. In the Great Assault of 1622, hundreds of English had been slaughtered, yet even that did not stop their expansion for long. Shiploads of English arrived from across the Great Sea, replenishing the numbers and bringing more weapons. Retaliation from both sides left more Powhatan dead than English; for what purpose, Winn did not know.

What did it mean to fight, if it meant your family lay dead before you? What good was land stained with the blood of the ancestors?

Opechancanough viewed Winn's neutrality as weakness; Winn saw it as the only way to survive.

He leaned forward in his chair as he spoke so that there was no confusion as to the intent of his message.

"Tell my uncle I have no warriors to spare. Tell him I thank him for his gifts, and I wish him the blessings of the Creator."

Winn's men shifted stance, closing in their ranks around him. The Powhatan warriors bowed their heads in deference and turned toward the door. As *Pimiskodjisi* crossed the threshold, the decorated warrior paused. The dark tattoo on his jaw stretched tight as the man shot Winn a sly grin.

"Your brother told us you would not fight. He told us you have abandoned your people. Opechancanough will not be pleased Makedewa spoke true. Many blessings, *Winkeokwhet.* Be proud your brother is there to slay the English for you."

The last of the pronouncement slammed through Winn, but he would not show the Powhatan his weakness. He nodded stiffly to the warriors and motioned to his men to let them pass. As they left, Winn leaned back in his chair.

So Makedewa had proclaimed an alliance.

Winn glanced at his wife who still stood behind Cormaic. She clutched the swaddled child to her chest, her green eyes shadowed in confusion as she met his gaze.

Makedewa made his choice, and there was nothing more they could do but carry on. Winn's life and that of those he loved hinged on the decisions he made as a leader. He had no luxury of chasing after his wayward brother, of asking him to return to his family. Winn wondered if the killing would dampen the hate inside of Makedewa, or if it might consume what remained of his soul.

It was a question Winn feared would be answered soon enough.

Winn unclenched his fingers and gave a slight flick of his wrist. Erich took note and gave Winn his attention.

"Speak on the next matter," Winn said.

He settled back on the chair and placed his hands on the armrests. The sting of splintered wood cut into his palm, reminding him that he was yet still only a man, powerless to stop what tale history had already written.

7

Maggie

The babe latched onto her breast, but all she felt was the tug of his hunger and the failure of her body to respond. She closed her eyes to the sensation, begging her body to let the milk flow. Yet no matter what she envisioned, or where she sent her scattered thoughts, it was Rebecca's face that haunted her thoughts, a ghost that would not be chased away. The boy let out a weak squeal, and she swallowed hard against the lump in her throat. She could feel his frustration, as thick as the despair that rolled through her bones, leaving them both helpless in the face of shared disappointment. She could not give the infant what he needed. The harder she tried, the more she failed, and as his tiny weak hand gripped furtively at her breast she felt the tears slide down her cheeks.

For now, they called him Daniel, but he had no Paspahegh name. There was no one to claim him, with Makedewa still missing in the shadow of Rebecca's death. If the Norse followed their tradition, the babe would have been set out exposed, left to the fate of the wild to decide if he should live or die. At the time, Maggie had been relieved Winn supported her objection to the old ways, granting her claim to the child. Now as she looked down at his pale face and sunken brown eyes, she wondered if it would not have been kinder to leave him to his fate. After all, a swift death would be preferable to slow starvation. Despite her best intention, she knew he pulled no sustenance from her body. The milk simply would not flow.

As she dipped her head to the rush of tears, she felt a pair of hands take the babe from her arms. It was Winn. He tucked the babe into the crook of his elbow. Too weak to object, little Daniel snuggled close to Winn's bared chest.

"You're crying," he said.

"I can't give him milk. It just – it just won't flow. Maybe it's been too long since Malcolm weaned," she whispered. Winn's brows scrunched down and he took her hand in his free one.

"Gwen told me," he replied.

She nodded, wiped the back of her hand over her damp eyes.

"But there's no one else. None of the other women have nursed a baby in months. If I can't do this, he …. he won't live," she said.

Winn pulled her to her feet.

"Come with me," he said simply. She followed, more of duty than desire. Numb with the truth of her failure, knowing the child was suffering for it, it was too much to bear.

Winn led her through the village to the edge of the woods where the bathhouse lay nestled in the mountainside. After he guided her inside he closed the door behind them, and she let him pull her into the warm water as he continued to hold the tiny babe in against his chest.

If her mind had not been so cluttered with grief, she would have questioned his intention. As much as she enjoyed his attention, she hardly felt up to bathing with him. After all, she had insisted on taking care of the child, and spending time with him as if he might live just seemed a cruel reminder of the inevitable.

The babe let out a muffled squeak as they slipped down into the shallow pool. Winn placed the baby in her arms, and then settled behind her. He wrapped his arms around her waist, pulling her snug against his chest as the hot steam moistened their skin. She could feel his lips near her ear and the way his muscles yielded to surround her, shielding her tenderly within his embrace. The water was a warm clasp, sheltering them, pulling them down to the damp depths where she could feel a trickle of hope. The remnant seemed so close, but her painfully full breasts sat unyielding to her demand.

"I promised Rebecca I would take care of him," she whispered. The babe stared quietly up at them, his almond-shaped eyes so unnaturally dark for an infant. His gaze was steady, almost knowing, as if he could see through to her heart and know her true intent.

"You will keep that promise," Winn said softly. From his place behind her, Winn's legs wrapped around hers and one of his hands slid up. "Close your eyes," he murmured. "When Makedewa was born, my mother could not feed him. The village women bathed her with warm water until the milk returned. I remember watching them, hoping the Gods would help her and my brother would live."

She leaned back against him with a sigh as his fingers caressed her torso. Across her belly, up over her ribs, then beneath the crease where her breasts lay heavy on her chest. At first she was confused, thinking his touch meant something different, but as he continued to stroke her skin lightly with his fingertips, she realized his pure intent.

"The women told my mother to think of her other children, the ones she made strong. They said if she could picture it, the milk would return," he said softly. "Think of Kwetii, the first time you held her to your breast. And of Dagr. You said once he was greedy, like a little piglet, taking more than he needed."

"Winn, I can't –"

"Yes," he insisted. "You can. You will."

He lifted one breast, and when his thumb brushed over the tight nipple she let out an involuntary sigh. She felt the rush, the downward pull, the warmth as the milk swelled forth. He raised the babe to her breast, and she closed her eyes as the seeking mouth latched on. Winn's legs entwined through hers as he continued to caress her, his fingers slippery as he moved in an easy rhythm from her ribs to her breasts, urging the flow to continue. Her limbs felt boneless, relaxed beneath his gentle touch.

She pictured Kwetii as a newborn, and that precious time where her only tie to survival was what could be found in Maggie's arms. Then it was Dagr, a robust babe who took greedy satisfaction and never went hungry. Finally, it was Malcolm she saw, the tiny son she feared might not live. *Daniel was like her youngest son,* she thought. So tiny, so needful. His fist clenched and unclenched as he sucked, and as the warmth of the letdown filled her, she could hear his satisfied suckle.

Winn's cheek lay pressed to hers, his chin on her shoulder as he watched. There was little she had master of in her life, but this, this giving, it was something she could wield. As the babe finally quieted, her body relaxed back against Winn.

"See?" Winn whispered. "You will feed him, and he will grow strong. Only you can give him this gift, the gift of living. The Gods smile on you now, *ntehem*," he said.

Soon the babe stirred, arching his back and pulling away from her. His mouth dropped off from his feeding, staying draped open with a trickle of milk on his chin as he succumbed to slumber. As Winn washed the babe's face, she realized it was the first time she had heard the child snore.

***

The babe slept well that night, tucked in next to her between the furs. Maggie woke to Winn's arms surrounding them both, his large hand keeping them secure in his embrace. She uttered a groan of dismay when Winn stirred and left the warmth of their bed, but smiled at his promise to see her later in the day at the Northern Hall. As he woke Dagr to take with him on a hunt she dozed, and they stumbled about the Longhouse in a sleepy haze as they tried to ready themselves without waking the women. Winn kissed her on the cheek before he left, his fingers brushing gently over Daniel's head in acknowledgement.

The matter of a Paspahegh name for the boy was something they would need to discuss soon. With Makedewa gone the entire subject seemed in limbo, with neither she nor Winn wanting to take that task from the child's father. Yet the longer Makedewa stayed away, the less hopeful she felt he would ever return, and the simple fact was that they needed to carry on.

After rising for the day, Maggie took Kyra and the boys to the Northern Hall to join the other women for the morning meal. Malcolm followed his sister, seeming happy to go wherever she might lead him.

Gwen was eager to get her hands on the newborn so Maggie handed him over after teasing her aunt a bit. With the hearth fire warming the Longhouse and the women bustling about preparing food, it was a morning like any other.

"Mama, I'll eat later. I'm gonna go hunt rabbits like Da showed me," Kyra said. Busy peeling carrots, Maggie glanced at her oldest child. The eleven-year old had been subdued since her adventure into town. Shortly after her dramatic return to the village Rebecca had died, and Maggie felt like Kyra had retreated inside herself somewhat. Normally outspoken and bold, the girl hung back in the shadows more often than not. She stopped playing with the older boys as her father had demanded, but she did not try to socialize with the girls, either. Instead, Kyra stayed close to home and her brothers and moped about as much as a girl her age could muster. The only thing that had caused her to perk up in the last few weeks was Winn talking about taking the boys on a hunting day, but of course, Kyra was crushed when Winn left her behind.

"Why not help me with the cooking, *Kwetii?*" Maggie called. She wiped her hand on her apron and watched her daughter shrug. Her tangled mane of dark hair fell like a cloak around her face, hiding her eyes, but Maggie could still see her heart shaped lips pursed into a frown.

"Nay. I can hunt as good as Dagr can. He's only eight," Kyra muttered.

"Of course you can. I'm sure your Da will take you next time. I'm sure he just thought you might want to spend some time with us women," Maggie offered.

"Why? So I can act like a lady? I'll never be a *lady*, Mama. *Never.*"

Maggie bit back her smile.

"There's nothing wrong with being a lady, sweetheart. And it's something you can't help, if you're asking. You'll grow up whether you want to or not."

Maggie instantly regretted her carefree response when Kyra's fists clenched into knots at her sides and her round blue eyes filled with tears. Placing her working knife aside, Maggie wiped her hands and took Kyra into her arms.

"Sweetie, what on earth is going on?" she murmured, kissing her daughter's forehead. A muffled cry escaped Kyra, and Maggie felt her body shudder.

"I don't ever wanna grow up. I never want babies, I never want a husband. Not even Morgan!" Krya sobbed. Maggie sighed and held her tighter, rocking her gently as she had when she was a babe.

Gwen and Ellie looked up at them over the steam of the house kettle but did not approach.

"Shh, shh," Maggie whispered. "Someday you might change your mind on that, but for now you needn't worry on it."

"Rebecca *died*, Mama! She's dead, all because of–because of that *baby!*" Kyra insisted.

"It's not his fault. It's not anyone's fault," Maggie replied, at loss to console her daughter. She wanted to tell her that these things rarely happened. She wanted to tell her it was not *normal* to die in childbirth. Yet the stark reality of it was that her explanation would be a lie.

Perhaps in the future, women did not routinely die in childbirth. In the seventeenth century, however, it was more likely to happen than not.

"Then why did Uncle Makedewa leave? Why won't he come home?" Kyra demanded.

"I don't know, sweetie. I don't know," Maggie replied. She wished she knew the answer to that question as well.

"Promise me you'll never make me get married, Mama. Please." Kyra fussed like a hummingbird in her arms, her dirt-stained fingers clutching Maggie's shift.

"Kyra...someday you might feel different."

The child twisted suddenly away.

"I won't, Mama. And if ye make me do it, I'll hate ye. I will. And Da, too!" Kyra shouted. Maggie closed her eye with a sigh as Kyra darted out of the Longhouse, her ermine cape flapping behind her.

When Maggie looked back at the women, Gwen made a shooing motion as she rocked the baby.

"Go on, I'll see to this wee one," Gwen said. Elli shook her head and resumed her chores as Maggie left to catch Kyra.

She scooped Malcolm up into her arms and kicked at the dirt with a swipe and a sigh as she walked. It was a juvenile gesture, one more in line with what Kyra would do, but heck if she had any experience with angry adolescent girls. Bereft of a mother and raised by two men, she did not have much insight into how a mother would console a child. She could only do what felt right, try to answer Kyra's questions, and let the girl know how much she loved her. It seemed the only thing left to do.

As she searched the courtyard for Kyra, her eyes fell on a figure by the corral. Tall and dark haired, his broad shoulders sheltered by a thick wool cape, Maggie did not recognize him right off. She knew the men were hunting, she was sure none had stayed behind except maybe crooked Old Olaf, and he spent most days rocking in a chair next to Finola. Since the tall man tied his mount to a post by the corral with the other horses she did not feel alarmed, but when she saw Kyra approach him, her panic sensors sparked into overdrive. She plunked Malcolm down firmly on the ground next to the well.

"Don't you move until I come back," she said, giving him her stern look. Mal grinned in return and she set off to see what business the stranger had in her village.

His back was to her as she approached. Still too far away, she watched him bend down to speak with Kyra. To her dismay, a tentative smile creased Kyra's face.

When the stranger lifted Kyra onto his horse, Maggie pulled her knife from her pocket and broke into a run.

8

Benjamin

"There should be no trouble, my lord," Reinn assured Agnarr.

Benjamin continued working his ledger book, keeping his eyes cast downward as he listened to the conversation. Neither Agnarr nor Reinn made any care to conceal their discussion, yet another plan to drive the Indian tribes further west. Every parcel of land that Agnarr helped clear was another workable piece of property – one that tobacco would grow on, and another means to line his pockets. There was a reason Agnarr was one of the wealthiest citizens in the colony. His willingness to eradicate the natives was matched by none.

"Good. Ye say it is a small village? Send only a few men, then, and leave the rest." Agnarr leaned back in his thick tufted chair as he answered, taking a long drag from a carved ivory pipe. It was one of the many unique trinkets he confiscated from new arrivals to his port, including his last search of a ship carrying trade goods from the Far East.

"Aye, a small one, but the leader is a fearsome sort. Our Indian tracker says they call him *Winkeohkwet* – The Raven."

Benjamin's hand tightened into a fist beneath the table. He had watched the English destroy village after village, forcing the Indians to move or be moved. Although he knew someday Winn's village would be in danger, the reality of it hit him like a blow in the gut.

It was time. His debt must be paid, his duty satisfied.

He would not allow Agnarr to harm his kin.

"Oh, fearsome, ye say? Well, shall we make a day of it? I will accompany ye, and we will take a few soldiers as well. What harm can a few arrows be when we have so many muskets to make our persuasion?" Agnarr answered.

"As you wish, my lord," Reinn agreed. "I will prepare the men."

Benjamin did not look up as Reinn left the room. Even when Agnarr cleared his throat in that definitive manner that meant he was preparing to speak, Benjamin continued to focus on the ledger numbers on the desk. Never one to be ignored, however, Agnarr was quick to engage Benjamin in a dialogue.

"So it seems I shall be engaged for most of the day. I expect you will keep matters in order here?" Agnarr commented casually, as if his words were mere requests instead of commands. Benjamin nodded, scribbling figures into the ledger book.

"As always," he answered. He felt his skin prickle at the nape of his neck and the telltale dampness of sweat on his brow. He had to do something, warn the villagers – but how, without arousing Agnarr's suspicions? Hurriedly he added, "I must retrieve the ledgers from the tavern, but that shall not keep me away for long. Profits were good this quarter, ye shall be pleased with the return."

"Fair enough," said Agnarr, standing up from his chair. He glanced at himself in a wall mirror as he turned toward the door, unable to resist smoothing back his elegantly coiffed hair. With a wry grin at his own reflection, he uttered a low chuckle. "And Jora will join us for the evening meal? I do so miss her. It seems you hide her away from me."

Agnarr's declaration was grumbled as he admired his own countenance.

"Of course not. I am sure she will be pleased to join us tonight."

"Good. See that she does." Agnarr finally abandoned admiring himself and pushed open the door. "Oh, and Benjamin?"

A bead of sweat slid down his face, tickling his ear as it went on its path. He swallowed slowly, trying to ignore the nagging sensation.

"Yes, my lord?" he answered evenly.

"Has my ward been absent for some reason? Perhaps her condition warrants rest?"

Struggling to contain his composure, Benjamin met Agnarr's gaze across the room.

"My wife was feeling poorly, but she is recovered. It was no matter to worry over, and it is passed now. Ease your mind. Ye need not dwell on it," he replied. He chose his words with care, giving Agnarr enough information to provide the older man assurance without leading to more questions. Every moment they spent making small talk was keeping him away from helping his brother; Winn needed to be warned of Agnarr's arrival – and Benjamin was the only one who could do it.

Agnarr nodded, his hint of a grin leveling out into a thin line.

"Until tonight then, my friend."

When the door closed behind his partner, Benjamin let out a deep breath. He wiped the sweat from his brow and rested his chin on his clasped fists for a moment, knowing he had precious little time to dwell on his worries. He must act and he must do it immediately, lest the life of those he was swore to protect would be in danger.

He shoved away the part of him that said to wait, to gauge his options, to come up with a sensible plan. Instead, he embraced the loyalty that still bound him, the loyalty that would not leave him no matter how many times he stood by and watched Agnarr's devious deeds.

Jora was dressing when he entered their room and he quickly stepped up behind her to help tighten the stays she struggled with. Her long dark hair brushed his wrists as he tied her, her breath expelling in a squeak when he pulled too harshly.

"I thank ye," she said, her words strained. He noticed when she placed her hand on her waist, closing his eyes for a moment when her palm slipped down briefly over her lower belly.

"How do ye feel this morn?" he asked.

"I shall abide," she sniped. He sighed. She did not move away when he placed his hands on her shoulders, and for a moment he thought he felt her lean back into his arms. Yet Jora was stronger than that, and as quick as he had felt her soften to him, she moved away even faster. "'Tis better now that the courses have stopped," she said softly.

He gripped her shoulders at her words, swallowing back his own grief. It had been more than a week since the loss of the babe. Despite the imminent danger of what the child could mean to Agnarr, Jora had been happy when she told Benjamin the news. She said she saw their future, and despite Benjamin's fears she knew that someday a dark-eyed little boy would be at Benjamin's side. Her sight had always led to the truth in the past, something they could rely on to point the way when the path was unclear. This time, however, he wondered if her heart had not led her gift astray.

"I am glad to see ye well," he replied. At loss to form words that might ease her pain, he stumbled over how to console her. The valley between them was wider than the strain of their recent loss. It was a marriage mottled with mistrust and fear, neither of which he had any notion of how to dispel.

And when Benjamin told her he must leave, he knew it might be the last nail in the coffin of what tenuous bond they still shared.

"Stay here for the day, away from the men. I must leave ye now, but I shall return soon."

Her shoulders stiffened beneath his fingers as she turned to face him. She did not pull away from his touch, but her chin dipped down and she shook her head a bit, as if to herself.

"How can ye leave now? I know I mean verra little to ye, but ye would let me face him myself –"

Not entirely meaning to, he shook her as he bent to meet her lowered gaze, producing a swell of tears let loose from her round eyes.

"Ye are my wife. I willna let Agnarr harm ye, that is why I ask ye to stay here. He is off with Reinn today on business, but even so, I will rest easy knowing ye are safe in our room."

"As long as ye rest easy, then I shall do as ye say," she said. He words were compliant, but her tone was anything but submissive.

"I would not leave ye now if there were another way," he replied.

"Then I wish ye a speedy return, husband," she whispered.

He wanted to argue, wanted to hold her, but there was no time for such things and she would not permit his attention in any case. He knew there was something broken inside her and he knew he was responsible for it. Someday he hoped they could mend it – someday when he did not have a duty he must place above all others.

Letting his hands fall away from her, he stepped back and opened the door. He could feel her gaze bore into his spine as much as he had felt her flesh beneath his fingers only moments before.

"I know ye think ye must go. But ye have reason to stay here, as well," she said.

He bowed his head, closing his eyes for a moment before he stepped through the door.

"I will return to ye," he said quietly.

He did not wait for her response before he left.

***

It was not long before Reinn and Agnarr departed with a group of hired men and a handful of English soldiers. Benjamin followed shortly after, leaving the safety of the common trails and instead making his own path through Indian lands. Agnarr was a man who would not sacrifice his own comfort for a day of dalliance harassing the natives, and Benjamin was counting on them sticking to the much less troublesome main routes.

Smoke escaped from the top of the Northern Hall as he rode into the village, but other than that telltale sign from the smoke hole, there seemed to be very little activity. He could hear the murmur of voices and the squeal of a child, typical sounds of a busy village.

Everything appeared normal – except that he saw or heard no men.

His horse stomped at a fly as he looped the rein over the corral fence. There was little time to waste before the English arrived, and if Benjamin were found aiding the villagers, he could be hanged. He needed to act without haste.

"Why are ye here?"

Benjamin turned to find Kyra staring up at him, hands perched on her hips as if she meant to scold him. If the situation was not so dire he might have laughed, but being she was one of those he meant to protect he stifled his amusement.

"Well, to see ye, of course," he replied, bending down so that he might look her in the eye. She seemed to appreciate the gesture, flashing a wide smile at him.

"Have ye seen Morgan, sir?" she asked, her cheeks flushing with color. "I mean, he's not visited of late."

"Nay, I havna seen him. Tell me, where is yer father?" Benjamin replied. She pushed her hair behind her ear and shrugged, her sunny smile fading into a scowl.

"Hunting. All the men are hunting. They'll no return 'til dark."

It might be good fortune that the men were away, but the cold feeling in his gut surged in spite of it. There was no reason for bloodshed when Agnarr's men arrived; it should be a simple notification of the Crown's intent to make use of the land. With no men in the village to argue, the transaction might occur without incident. It was only when the natives resisted that there was trouble.

"Where is yer mother? With the women?" he asked.

"Yes. They're *cooking*." Kyra pointed to the Northern Hall with a shrug. She let out a squeak when he picked her up and tossed her onto his horse. "I canna leave, Momma willna let me!"

"Quiet now, keep yer seat. I'll fetch yer brother and Ma, and then ye need to ride downstream. Doona kick that beast yet, he's a flighty sort."

He was pulling the girth tight when he heard footsteps behind him, and before he could utter a word in defense, he was grabbed by his arm and fingernails bit into his flesh. His reaction was one of self-preservation when he saw the flash of a knife.

With his two large hands he subdued her, closing one hand over her mouth and the other around her waist. She twisted around in his arms, but he easily blocked her blows until she sank her teeth into the flesh of his hand. At that, he turned her to face him, shaking her like a rag with one hand as he plucked the knife from her fingers.

"Just what do you think you're doing with my daughter?" Maggie demanded. "You won't be taking her anywhere –"

"Jesus, Maggie! There's no time for this!" Benjamin hollered.

"Benjamin? What the hell? What are you *doing*?"

Stunned for a moment, she tried to draw away from him but he held her without fail.

"Where are the boys?" he asked. "*Where are the boys, Maggie?*"

His frantic voice lowered an octave as he shook her and she stared back at him as if she had lost her sense. For a moment, he thought she had.

"Mal is by the well. What is going on –" she stammered, but he cut her off.

"There's no time. They're coming here to the village. Where are all the men? Why are there none here to protect ye women? Tell me!" he snapped. She went rigid as he shook her again, her eyes glazed with confusion.

"They're with Winn," she whispered. "The men are all hunting. They're not here."

"Jesus. They leave ye unprotected? Alone?" Benjamin cursed.

"They're not far – and we need the food!" she shot back, obviously incensed with any criticism of Winn. Benjamin stifled the rest of the rant that bubbled to the surface. It was none of his concern how his brother tended his village.

The peril of their situation suddenly burned deep. They were about to be raided by the English, and they needed to come up with a plan.

"The English, ye say?" Gwen interrupted. Benjamin loosened his hold on Maggie, who promptly stepped back. Gwen eyed him up, a scathing glare from head to foot, as if his very presence offended her senses. With a grubby hand clutching her skirt, Malcolm toddled behind her.

"The English are coming to serve ye notice. If ye do as yer bidden they'll serve ye and leave, but best Maggie and the children stay out of sight. Agnarr travels with them."

He noted Gwen's eyes widened, but there was no additional sign of recognition from Maggie, whose face remained pensive. He did not have time nor was he willing to discuss why Agnarr was a danger, so he was relieved to see Gwen understood.

"I thought that wee bastard was dead," she said.

"Not hardly. He keeps to his own, except when he has cause." Benjamin looked Gwen in the eye, willing her to understand. "Best we send Winn's family away for a spell."

Gwen nodded, her throat visibly tightening. She darted a glance at Maggie, who cocked a brow at the both of them.

"So we'll take the women and hide. We can go downstream to the Nansemond until Winn and the others return," Maggie said.

"No, that willna work. If the English come upon this place and find it abandoned, they will burn it to the ground. It would save 'em the trouble of making a peaceable request," Benjamin replied.

Gwen cleared her throat.

"Then you must get the children and Maggie away. Take them now, and let us face the English when they arrive."

"Gwen, no, you can't stay here! None of you can –"

Gwen reached for Maggie, who quieted when the older woman took her hand. Gwen smiled, a gesture that served to muffle Maggie's protests for a fraction of a moment.

"Of course I can. It's my duty as yer kin and yer duty as our Chief's wife to see yer children safe. Now is the time to lead, *my lady*. We shall be waiting here fer ye once the English have crawled back to their snake holes."

When Gwen's sad eyes met his he swallowed hard. He nodded at the unspoken request in her voice.

"Ye'll see them safe, will ye not?" Gwen said softly. "Maybe ye are yer father's son."

Yes, he thought. *He would keep them safe. For that was his duty, and he would not abandon it.*

"Mama?" Kyra called out, her voice pitched high in question. Benjamin looked back toward the horse where he had deposited Kyra with strict instructions to stay put. The horse lifted his head straight up, ears pricked and eyes focused on the wood line.

The rustle of movement through the brush and the disjointed shouts of strangers reached them, making the idea of a threat into instant reality. Maggie plucked Malcolm up off the ground.

"Ride, sweetheart," she whispered, kissing his head as she placed him behind his sister. With shaking hands, she hugged Kyra as Benjamin spoke softly to his niece. Kyra promised to follow the river path downstream to the Nansemond village, where she would wait. In turn, he promised that her mother would not be far behind.

Kyra ground her heels into the horse's flanks and the beast took off into the woods. He grimaced as Malcolm jerked backwards, but the boy recovered without issue and remained astride behind his sister. Benjamin took Maggie's hand.

"Go!" Gwen insisted.

Maggie followed him mutely into the woods, gripping his hand with the strength born of panic. He had known her very well once, and he knew fair well when she was afraid. That unguarded part she struggled to contain flared like a beacon with every emotion on display, as if she dared anyone to tell her she should not act on what she felt.

It was clear she did not want to leave the village. He had no doubt she was bold enough to face the English on her own – and he had witnessed her capable behavior on more than one occasion – but there was much more at stake than that. Apparently, she did not recognize the name of her own father, and for the life of him, Benjamin did not know why. Had Winn not told her that her father lived? Nor Erich? Did they think it best she not know of the man? Whatever the reasons, it was clear Maggie was in the dark. The true danger to her and the children was not the English – it was the Norse Time Walker with a vengeful streak who would stop at nothing to claim her if he knew she existed.

"Come on," Benjamin growled. He could see the English through the trees as they rode into the village and he knew their time to flee had run out. He pulled Maggie into the woods toward a small alcove surrounded by slate boulders, a place he recalled the children often played. Sitting well above the Northern Hall, those in the niche could see the village below, but were unlikely to be seen in return.

"But the children –"

"They're far gone by now. Ease yer self. We'll stay down until they leave," he whispered.

Benjamin tried to control his breathing as he drew her close and they kneeled down in the dirt.

"They willna hurt anyone. He's here to give them the King's decree, then he'll go," Benjamin said softly, more to convince himself than to placate Maggie. He knew she could see Agnarr down below for the man stood out amongst the English as a gemstone gleamed in the sun. It was not only the expensive clothes he wore and healthy horse he rode, but the way he carried himself lent no argument as to who was in charge.

"Who is he?" she asked.

"An enemy, if ye must know," he snapped. She twisted around at his harsh reply and shoved him in the chest, which surprised him but did not budge him an inch. It had been years since he had spent time with her, and truth be told, he was no longer that same man. Despite the danger before them, having her in his arms stirred something down deep in his gut. Memories assaulted him, causing a scowl to form on his face.

"Yes, I *must* know!" she shot back.

"Ye need know he's dangerous. He'll recognize ye as a blooded *MacMhaolian*, and he'll stop at nothing to take ye," Benjamin replied. "And yer weans," he added.

Maggie stopped arguing. More than a dozen men on horseback poured into the courtyard below amidst a cloud of dust, shouting amongst each other as if they feared no retribution. When he saw the band of English soldiers flank the group he realized why. Every man among them held a musket, even the plain dressed Englishmen who were in Agnarr's employ. Benjamin wondered why they seemed armed for trouble rather than for a simple notification, yet he knew in his bones the answer.

Agnarr did the King's bidding – when it suited him. Sturlsson always had another motive in his dealings, however, and being vigilant in the search for other Time Walkers was his ever-present task. Holding fast to the notion that not all the Norse colonists had been exterminated by the Indians, Agnarr lived for the moment he might stumble upon one.

And Benjamin, as such, lived to prevent him from doing so.

Agnarr dismounted slower than the others. Shorter than Benjamin but still marked with considerable brawn, the man straightened up in a refined manner and surveyed the others. His bright blond hair was coiffed fashionably back with a ribbon, his velvet and brocade attire more reflective of a gentleman than a rogue.

"What is his name?" Maggie whispered.

Benjamin sighed. He saw no reason to keep it from her.

"Agnarr. My employer," he answered. Let her chew on that morsel if it would quiet her. With a touch of inappropriate amusement, he noted that Maggie still had no control of her emotion. Always defiant, forever willing to give a challenge instead of acquiescence, he supposed that was one of the things that drew him to her. He adjusted his hand at her waist, aware suddenly that he was gripping her entirely too close as they watched the scene below.

"So you've gone back to the English, and this is what you do? Why not join them now? How many villages have you raided? You traitorous bastard –"

"Damn ye, woman, quiet yer tongue. I've done no such thing. Did ye ever know me at all?" he snapped.

He could see her pulse throbbing madly along her tight jaw as she glared up at him.

"I thought I did," she whispered.

His voice was hoarse when he answered.

"You did know me," he said. "You knew me like no other ever had."

Her eyes glistened with the swell of tears and he looked away before she could shed them. His belly was a heavy knot, the warmth of her in his arms sending him back in time to that place where she belonged to him. He shook off the memory as quickly as it surfaced.

The past was over. Now was time to pay for his sins.

Two of the soldiers dragged Gwen from the Northern Hall. Maggie jumped up and Benjamin immediately jerked her back down.

"Doona move!" he ordered.

"They're hurting Gwen!" Maggie cried. He held her tight, but she refused to turn away from the scene below.

"They willna kill her," Benjamin whispered.

The tone of his utterance did not console her. She tried to twist away from him once more.

"Let me go, we can talk to them–" she pleaded. Gwen wasted no time displaying her opinion of the intruders, spitting in Agnarr's face when he approached her.

Benjamin was surprised to see Agnarr turn away from the woman, but his stomach clenched when Agnarr plucked at his glove. Finger by finger he removed it, folding the glove neatly in half before he nodded to his companions. One of Agnarr's men grabbed Gwen and pulled her out into the middle of the courtyard.

They tied Gwen to a tall post by the well in the yard. Maggie gripped his forearm.

"We have to do something!" she said.

"There is nothing to be done!" he replied, his voice strangled with fear. Agnarr had no cause to harm the villagers. His only duty was to inform them they should move further west, away from the English as they cleared more land for tobacco farming. Benjamin had visited many villages with Agnarr where they had done the same, ending the visit peacefully with no harm to any person. Yet those villages had been filled with Indians, and none of those people held interest to Agnarr. Not like the tiny settlement Winn's family lived in, a mix of whites, Indians, and random stragglers that kept to themselves.

Benjamin did not expect Maggie to relent, but he was still startled when she renewed her struggle. She struck out at Benjamin and connected with his cheek, her nails scraping his skin. He grabbed her wrists then and crushed her to his chest, holding her head down as Gwen began to scream.

"I promised to keep ye safe. I promised her – and my father. If ye go down there now, I will go after ye, and it will be for naught because they will kill me where I stand." He felt her jump at the crack of the lash. "I willna let them harm ye. *Never*," he whispered fiercely into her hair.

He had made that vow, and he planned to keep it. Maggie let out a muffled moan against his chest when Gwen screamed again.

They could hear each snap of the strap and the resultant cry from Gwen until finally the lashing ended. They were too far away to hear what the English were saying, so he could not determine what the man said to Gwen as he bent his head to hers. He only knew that there were too many men to count, all armed with gun power, and he was helpless to do anything except stay hidden until it was over.

He felt like a coward, but he knew he had no choice.

"Is that Ellie? What is she doing?" he whispered. When Maggie looked up at him, her face had taken on a pale tint. She followed his gaze back down to the courtyard, where Elli approached the intruders.

"She has Daniel with her," Maggie whispered.

"Whose wean is that?" he asked.

"Mine. I mean, Rebecca's. She–she died giving birth. Makedewa left. I'm watching over him until his father returns."

He bowed head and closed his eyes. Makedewa had been his friend, his companion. To know his friend had lost a wife and now wandered alone was a sickening thought. Benjamin knew what isolation was like, to feel as if your home was no longer a place you could stay. It was a loneliness they had held common, one they had worked to vanquish as they traveled together. He wondered where Makedewa was, and how he fared.

He wished to convey his sadness, but he had no right to behave as if he were still part of the community. Keeping his thoughts to himself, he simply said, "I am sorry." Maggie gave a slight nod at his words, but her eyes were focused on what was unfolding in the courtyard.

In Ellie's arms was baby Daniel, bundled securely as she spoke with the English. Elli stood straight as she confronted the intruders, but they were too far away for him to hear what was said. Benjamin's breathing stilled and he loosened his grip around her.

"What's happening?" Maggie asked.

"I doona know. I think they're leaving," Benjamin replied.

He was right. After speaking with Ellie, the English mounted their horses. Agnarr spoke once more at Gwen and Ellie, and then he turned and slowly surveyed the village.

He raised his chin as if the villagers sullied the very earth he walked on, glancing down his chiseled nose at something on his jacket. With a flick of his gloved hand he brushed at the shimmering brocade, then swiftly mounted the horse one of the other men held for him.

Maggie leaned forward in Benjamin's embrace. Bored, disgruntled, Agnarr's countenance bespoke a smoldering anger undisclosed. Once securely astride, Agnarr's horse turned in a tight circle and the man looked into the woods. Maggie stiffened when Agnarr seemed to stare straight at them, but it was only a momentary glance before he turned and galloped off.

"I will never forget his face," she whispered as the men rode away. "How does he know me, Benjamin? Tell me."

"'Tis not my tale to tell. Do not ask it," he said quietly.

"I deserve an explanation," she replied.

His throat contracted when he swallowed and his hands tightened on her arms.

"Then ask yer husband and yer uncle. I'm sure they know more about this feud than I do. Tell Winn I will be at the tavern in town if he should care to speak."

He knew his brother and Erich enough to know that they would not let Gwen's beating go unpunished. For whatever reason Agnarr had ordered it, the consequence would be more bloodshed. Benjamin feared this was just the beginning.

Ellie untied Gwen and the older woman fell to her knees. Maggie opened her mouth as if to question him again, but closed it and instead.

"Wait here until I see it's safe. Stay down," Benjamin replied. More women assembled in the courtyard to help Gwen, but Benjamin would not be satisfied until he was certain the English were gone.

Maggie made to move away, but Benjamin held her for a long spell, feeling as if he were lost somewhere that he could not return from. He stood up and pulled her to her feet with him, forgetting for a moment where he was as he spoke softly to her.

"Do ye see the ridge, over on the far side of the meadow?" he asked. She nodded. "Look there. When I see they're gone, I'll wave to ye. Stay here until ye see my hand."

"I – I want to see Gwen – but the children –" she stammered.

"I'm sure they're safe. I will see them returned to ye," he said softly. She nodded.

He released her. Maggie's cheeks were streaked with tears, but her demeanor was controlled as she gathered her composure. His mouth twisted with the hint of a grin as he thought he would rather fight the English than stand between Maggie and her family – the family he had once meant to call his own.

He stole one last glance at her before he turned away.

God strike me down, he thought *if I should still love her. For how can I feel anything else, when I would give my life for hers?*

Marcus had given up everything for the sake of his vow. His father had protected the blooded MacMhaolian with his last breath, using his final moments to elicit a pledge from his sons for her safety. In the time Benjamin knew him, Marcus had never spoken of loving a woman, not even Benjamin's own mother.

Was that the future for one who protected the blooded MacMhaolian? To love her from afar and pledge his life to her protection? It had been easy at that moment, when his father asked it of him.

To realize that he could let her return to Winn without an ounce of regret was another matter entirely. That ache was gone, that tiny part of himself that demanded he keep her was buried, not even an ember of it burning as he walked away. It was a different sort of love, one he could use when needed and look on with fondness. One he could live with without regret or shame.

Relief settled heavy in his chest. His brother would return soon, and Winn's family was safe for now. He heard the whisper of her voice as he left her, carried to him over the gentle roar of his heart.

"Thank you," she said.

He nodded and kept walking.

9

Winn

The men returned from hunting not long after the sun dipped behind the mountains, but the moment they reached the village Winn knew something was amiss. Be it the stillness in the air or the lack of welcoming cries from their women, it was a silence that sent his heart to racing.

His motions were blunted in a blurred haze as he left his horse ground tied and gave his son an order to stay in the courtyard. Chetan and Erich called out to him, but he could not decipher the words if he had wanted to. All he could manage to focus on was the path to his longhouse, and until he held the sight of his family safe before his eyes, he would not rest.

It was Chetan who reached him as Winn opened the door to his empty dwelling. If not for his brother's hand on his arm, he might have exploded at the sight of the cold hearth. *Where were his wife and children?*

"They are with Gwen," Chetan said, the question clear on Winn's face. "Men were here."

"Powhatan?" Perhaps Winn had brought retaliation down on his people by refusing to help Opechacanough.

"English."

Torn by his anger and overwhelmed with relief, he followed his brother to Gwen and Erich's longhouse. There he found Maggie sitting beside Gwen, silently watching her aunt sleep. Kyra and Malcolm curled up beside each other in a pile of furs next to the fire, and Makedewa's son slept peacefully in a cradle beside the fire. All those Winn loved were safe, the guilt of relief washing over him as he looked down upon them.

"Will she wake?" Erich asked, placing his hand on Gwen's shoulder. Her body tensed but she did not stir, and Maggie shook her head.

"I gave her a drink for the pain. The poppy made her sleep," Maggie said softly.

Winn heard his wife gasp when Erich parted Gwen's dressing. Erich looked down on Gwen's flayed skin, his body unnaturally rigid as everyone fell silent. When Erich gently replaced the bandages and turned away from the bed, Winn thought his wife's uncle was in control. Yet striking quick as a serpent, Erich whirled away from the bed and buried his fist into a thick wooden beam, leaving his hand bloodied and ragged as he turned to the fire. The older man was surprisingly quick in his temper, uttering a hoarse oath as blood dripped from his torn skin. He ignored the wound and placed both hands on the mantle, leaning over the fire as he struggled to speak. His ragged voice emerged, low but steady as he stared into the flames.

"I willna let this go. Give me two men, Winn, that is all I ask of ye," Erich growled.

Winn paused before he answered, knowing his words would only serve to incite Erich further. Winn feared Erich's willingness to retaliate against the English could not be stayed, but he had to try somehow to make his friend hear sense.

"Stay with your wife until dawn," Winn answered, placing his hand on Erich's shoulder. Erich grimaced, his fists clenched tight upon the mantle. "Then I will go with you."

Erich remained still for a moment, and then his shoulders and head dipped down. He nodded, his gaze still focused on the fire, and Winn knew the man was at his breaking point. Winn could not fault Erich for the desire for vengeance; it was a desire that Winn was most familiar with. Yet it was the strength of a Chief that Erich needed then, and giving in to primitive desire without a plan would serve no one.

Winn turned to the bed and gathered up his sleeping children. Kyra stirred in her sleep with a tiny sob, her cheeks stained with the remnants of dusty tears as she burrowed into his chest. Malcolm, thankfully, stayed asleep, merely tucking his face into his father's neck. Maggie followed mutely behind him with the babe in her arms. Winn called to Dagr to join them, and soon his children were all accounted for.

His two sons slept in the back of the longhouse, and Maggie tucked Kyra into her bed in the loft above. Though the infant was not his son, he was still of Winn's blood, and he counted as one of those Winn meant to keep safe. Five beating hearts entrusted to his care, five people he would give his own life to see protected.

Yet it was greater than that, a greater duty than even the ties of love he felt for his family. He had promised to lead the villagers, the blending of Norsemen and Indians that looked to him for guidance. Winn had taken his father's place, pledged to honor his ancestors by seeing their bloodlines go on.

It was with a coldness stealing over his skin that he knew they could not go back. If being Chief meant he would hide his people and allow the English to abuse them without retaliation, then Winn was no Chief.

He would find them, and make them suffer. The man who harmed Gwen would die, and all those who aided him would bleed. It did not matter that it was the way of the Paspahegh, or the way of the Norse. In the end, it would be a husband's vengeance, and Winn would stand beside Erich when he struck that final blow.

As he lay next to his wife he stared into the darkness, letting the echoes of old battles with the English clutter his thoughts. Although Maggie curled up against him with her hand resting lightly on his chest, the images haunted him. The screams of men, the feel of bloodied flesh beneath his hands, it stayed with him even when he meant to forget.

Perhaps the taking of life would always plague him. After all, could any man truly hold the soul of another in his grasp? To send another to the afterlife left some trace. It was a stain that could never be washed away.

"What will you do?" Maggie whispered. He knew she did not sleep, and he was not surprised at her question. It was the same question he asked himself.

"What I must," he replied quietly.

Her fingers tightened into a fist on his skin. When he placed his hand over hers, she relaxed her hand flat against his chest.

"Winn?" she asked, a tentative question in her voice.

"Hmm?"

"Teach me to how to use the musket. It was sitting here, I could have used it –"

"No," he replied. He repeated his command, so there would be no question that she would obey. "*No.* You did your duty today, and that is all you must do."

"I ran away like a coward, and Gwen suffered for it," she said, her voice unsteady.

"Would it console you if you killed one Englishman? The musket cannot kill them all. Gwen would still be beaten. And you would be dead as well."

From where her cheek rested against his skin, a trickle of tears dampened his skin. She did not raise her head, hiding the frustration he knew simmered in her heart.

"You will not worry on the matters of men," he said. "Give me your word, *ntehem.*"

She did not answer him for a long time. Finally, her head moved where she lay against his chest. It was a slight nod, but it was enough. He had her promise, and that was all that mattered to him in that moment.

It was not long before her breathing slowed, and he listened to her rhythmic slumber long into the night. His sons uttered muffled snores, and he could hear the rustle of the bedding as his daughter shifted in her sleep.

Although his family was safe, the truth of it was enough to strike fear into his bones. Tomorrow they would set out on a new path, and the life they led would exist no more.

"I will do what I must," he said, his voice only a whisper in the darkness.

Those he loved slept on.

***

Winn joined Erich before the light of dawn graced the sky. He was relieved to find his wife's uncle at Gwen's bedside, and although it appeared Erich had not slept, at least he had not left the village on a one-man vengeance spree. It was all Winn could ask for.

"She woke fer a time. She said his hair was black and his speech was queer, like he'd a mouth full of honey. The others called him Hayes," Erich said quietly before Winn even announced himself.

"An Englishman?" Winn asked. Erich nodded. The older man rubbed a thick hand across his eyes, rubbing away the remnants of sleep not taken. He bowed his head to his wife, his thatch of reddish gold hair nearly touching hers as she slept.

"I dinna understand most of what she said before the poppy silenced her, but aye, it was an Englishman who did it."

Winn took a cup from the hearth and poured some warm ale, handing it to Erich, then took a cup for himself. Erich shrugged with a long sigh yet downed it in a single swallow as he eyed Winn over the rim.

"Go ahead. I see yer mind twistin'. Say yer piece. I'll hear it now," Erich muttered.

"You will hear it, yet will you listen?" Winn replied, more to himself than to Erich. His uncle-by-marriage stood up away from the bed.

"If ye mean to tell me we willna avenge this deed –"

"We will find the one who did this," Winn cut him off. "And the ones who helped him. My horse stands ready; I wait only for your word."

"*No.*"

Gwen's cracked voice emerged from the bed. The men turned to see her sitting upright against a bundle of furs, her eyes glazed from the strong herbs but her face set with a stubborn edge. Her hair stuck to the wounds on her back, thick pieces entwined in the poultice and blood. Winn noted her grimace as she took a deep breath.

"Ye canna go after them. Agnarr didn't know me, but if ye go thrashing his men, he'll surely think to come back here. What then, ye brazen louts?" she berated them.

Erich's face turned a peculiar shade of crimson as Gwen railed at them. She continued citing numerous reasons why they were idiots peppered with a slew of colorful insults until Erich exploded.

"Ye'll not tell me how to take care of ye, ye bletherin' harpy!" he shouted. "If I wish to dispatch an Englishman it's my right as yer husband, and ye'll stay here and wait fer me!"

"Oh, will I? Aye, I'll stay 'ere! And I'll shove a stick up yer –"

"Enough!" Winn hollered, slamming his empty cup down on the table. "Agnarr was here? And he did not know you?"

Gwen scowled. "No. I feared he might remember me, but he dinna seem to. Even when I spit in the lout's face."

"Ah, *bruor*, why did ye do it?" Erich said quietly. His voice shook with the uttered endearment, and clearly, the ferocious spat was over. The older man sat down next to his wife on the bedding platform and took her hands in his. "Ye risk too much."

"I know. I regret my temper, but the *things* he said!" she whispered. "I'm so sorry. I should've held my tongue. The risk to our niece and the weans –"

"He might have killed ye," Erich interrupted. "And then where would I be, my love, without ye to rile me?"

Gwen placed her hand on Erich's cheek, tears welling up in her round eyes. Winn stepped outside, closing the plank door quietly behind him.

Seeing the way Erich looked at his wife made Winn's duty seem all the more just. Vengeance still called, but it would wait for a touch of affection to bless them. Erich and Gwen needed a moment, and Winn needed to decide what to do about Agnarr Sturlsson.

***

With a touch of restlessness, Winn dismounted from his horse. Elizabethtown was much busier than he recalled from his last visit, a veritable mess of commerce and excess crowding the marketplace.

Chetan stayed behind to oversee the village, and although Winn had ordered it, he was uneasy with his brother's absence from his side. Cormaic was more than capable of meeting any threat to their party and the Norseman seemed to enjoy giving orders to young Iain and Tyr. Chetan's son, Keke, however, stayed close to Winn's side, soundless as he listened to the prattle of English clamor around them.

Paspahegh to the bones, Keke remained silent as the others made noise, and he studied the townsfolk as his companions gathered their wits. *Onamen.*

Watch. See your enemy before you strike. Every warrior knew that simple truth.

The young men were excited to ride into town despite the risk and Winn could not fault them for their enthusiasm, but his reason for bringing them was more of a selfish one. Erich was not himself, and Winn hoped the presence of the impressionable youths would keep the older man in check.

Winn knotted the end of his rawhide rein around a post, adjacent to the rest of his men's mounts outside the tavern. Since they had arrived in town he felt increasingly unsettled, knowing the risk they were taking by searching for the men who came to the village.

"I trust thy desire is to settle this matter peaceably."

Winn looked over at John Basse, a stout young Englishman with a round face. His cheeks were sunburned in spite of his wide-brimmed hat, a trickle of sweat running down his neck. A devout Christian landowner and one who was adamant about his desire to spread his views to the Indians, Basse was a man Winn held some trust for that he believed would be useful. Satisfying Erich's vengeance would serve no one if they all ended up dead, so Winn decided the best way to deflect attention from their activity would be to engage the Christians. When Winn asked for his assistance, the Englishman was more than happy to comply.

"That is my desire," Winn agreed. He heard Erich make a gruff snorting sound behind him.

"Verily, thy friends should feel the same?" John asked, casting a nervous glance at Keke, who was wiping his knife on his tan leggings.

"They do," Winn replied. His answer seemed to satisfy John.

One might think he would be accustomed to the stench of the English by now, but the rancid odor of too many people in a small space hung heavy in the air, broken by the occasional waft of roasted meat from inside the tavern. He did not wish to follow the scent, but it came from where he meant to go and there was no other way. Winn motioned to John Basse to follow, and nodded to Erich and Cormaic to remain outside.

They had discussed the plan on the ride into town, which involved Winn taking John Basse to speak with Benjamin and Erich and the others standing watch. John Basse was a convenient diplomat in a time of need, but he was no soldier, and as such, the man was little assistance in locating the Englishmen they searched for.

Benjamin was a different matter entirely. Winn was certain his brother would know exactly what men they were looking for and where to find them. The only question remaining was if Benjamin would help them or not.

"Is that thy friend, perchance?" John asked as they moved through the tavern. Benjamin stood behind the bar, but his eyes narrowed on Winn as soon as he entered the room.

"It is," Winn agreed.

Benjamin met them where they stood. From the way his eyes shifted about the room, Winn could see his brother was uneasy, which only served to cause Winn more caution.

Could he be trusted? Years before, Benjamin had abandoned his family and declared his allegiance to the English after the death of their father. Winn knew the reasons Benjamin left, but to see his brother in league with their enemies left one little choice but to question his loyalty. Although Benjamin claimed staying away was the best way he could protect his kin, for all outward appearances Benjamin was just as much a threat as his employer.

Benjamin made a motion towards a table in the corner and they sat down. John Basse stammered a declaration about watching for trouble and left them to stand by the door. Slightly away from the bustle, the shadowed corner gave Winn and Benjamin some privacy. Winn sat upright against the back of the chair, considering his brother's nervous demeanor with suspicion.

"I give you my thanks for your aid to my family," Winn said evenly, "yet I must ask where to find the men who raided my village."

Benjamin ran a hand through his hair, then opened his mouth to speak and reconsidered. With a groan he slammed his fist down on the table and glared back at Winn.

"I dinna do it fer ye! And – and ye need to tell me what ye know! Why does yer wife know nothing of Agnarr?"

Winn leaned forward, gripping the edge of the plank table with his hands.

"She need not know of him," Winn replied.

"Why? D'ye truly think yer safe here? Why not take them away? Why stay here when ye run the risk of being found?"

"So you think I must run from one man? Leave the place I was born, the place my children were born? I think not," Winn shot back, feeling the heat rise to his throat as he bit back his anger.

"D'ye know what they did to the Blooded Ones, in the land our father came from?" Benjamin asked. "How the women were fought over by the Chiefs – at least the ones that might bear children? The barren ones had only one use, and that was –"

"I know the tales," Winn growled. Yes, he knew what had been done to those like Maggie in the past. History was the very reason why the Blooded McMillan needed protection, why the Neilsson Chiefs had sworn an oath to protect them.

"Then why must ye stay? Ye've always been a stubborn lout, but I canna see why –" Benjamin's mouth fell open as he sat back in his chair. "Oh, aye, I see. It's like that? Yer wife really knows nothing, 'tis plain. Who are ye serving by keeping her senseless? Maybe yer Indian uncle?"

Winn rose slowly to his feet. His pulse throbbed in his ears, his muscles taut with desire to throttle his brother. Who was Benjamin to question his actions? Benjamin, who had abandoned them to seek refuge with their foe?

"When you return to your kin, brother, you may question my command. Until that time, you have no voice," Winn said quietly. Old wounds surged in the space between them, betrayal and anger spiking his words. "Tell me where to find the men I seek, and I will leave you to your duties serving my enemy."

Benjamin remained seated, meeting Winn's gaze without waver.

"Ye shall find them at the docks. Sturlsson is expecting a shipment forthright."

Winn loosened his fists and turned to go. John Basse stared inquisitively at him from the doorway.

"He is the enemy to me, as well, brother," Benjamin said, standing up and grabbing Winn's arm as he moved away. "I pledged an oath to protect the Blooded Ones, and that is what I do. I know ye do the same."

Through the rank anger that flared, Winn realized the trace of truth in Benjamin's words. It hit him like a hammer, the thought of his actions squeezing him tight.

Did he stay in *Tsenacommacah* for his family, or did he stay to satisfy his own base desire to remain in his birth land? As a Paspahegh-born man, he knew he was tied to the land just as surely as his soul was a gift from the Great Creator. Yet he had made a promise to protect the Blooded Ones at all cost – even if that meant his own desires must stay buried.

"Uncle!"

John Basse stepped back a pace as Keke entered the tavern, giving the lean young brave a wide berth. Keke's dark eyes were wide as he called out to Winn.

"They went to the docks," Keke said.

Winn shrugged his arm away from Benjamin.

Damn his blasted uncle-by-marriage, and damn his traitor brother. As Winn left for the docks, the others followed.

If they did not all end up dead by sundown, it would be only by the grace of the Gods.

***

A seagull screamed as it dived down from flight, settling on the palisades as Winn and John approached the docks. Tyr and Iain stood beneath the low hanging roof of a mud and stud house near the supply post, close to the port where a newly docked ship was being unloaded. Standing a good measure taller than most young men his age, Tyr's flash of auburn hair blazed like a beacon, making it easy to pick him out of the crowd. Winn knew Erich and Cormaic must be nearby if they had left the youths on their own. Iain nudged Tyr with an elbow as Winn approached.

"Where is he?" Winn asked. He kept his tone even, despite his annoyance.

"Inside," Tyr replied. "The smithy knew a man called Hayes. Said he had half a tongue and spoke queer. Erich thought he might have a word with him since the man was 'ere in thee tobacco inspector's warehouse."

"Seems most reasonable," John said. The Englishman removed his hat, wiping his face with a bit of white cloth he pulled from his pocket.

"It is *not*," Winn muttered. He had no doubt what he would find inside, and it would be a scene that was far from reasonable to the Englishman. "John, keep watch. Knock twice should any soldiers come near."

To Keke, Winn gave a curt order in Paspahegh so that John Basse did not understand. *Watch for trouble,* Winn said. Keke nodded.

John eagerly nodded, and Winn could not help but think the man seemed relieved. If their meeting inside went badly, it would be unlikely John Basse would be willing to help them again. Winn had spent months cultivating a friendship with John, knowing the alliance with him would only benefit those in his village.

They needed to maintain ties with the Christian landowner, despite what Erich planned to do to the man inside. Better John Basse remain outside, taking no part in their business.

Iain and Tyr followed Winn inside. To Winn's surprise, there were a handful of Englishmen standing in line behind a long plank table. One man sat before them, his dark head bent low over a ledger book. The man took receipts from those who waited in line, giving an occasional snort or grunt of acknowledgement as he scribbled furiously on the parchment.

Cormaic and Erich stood at the rear of the line. While Cormaic noticed Winn's arrival, Erich did not. The older Norseman was too intent on watching the man seated behind the table.

"Him?" Winn asked as he joined them in line. There was no sense in berating Erich. Winn's only hope was to keep them all alive while Erich satisfied the debt owed to him.

"Perhaps," Erich muttered, his stare unwavering. Cormaic leaned over, speaking quietly to Winn.

"It must be him, but the bugger willna speak. Da needs to hear if his speech is queer before we do it."

"Do *what?*" Winn asked, not really wanting to know the answer. He counted four Englishmen in line and one behind the table. The odds were fair, yet it was still a risk he did not wish to take, especially when they were closed in by the confines of the small dwelling.

"Why, have a wee talk with him, of course," Cormaic said, uttering an undignified grunt.

The current customer at the table raised his voice, slapping an invoice down in front of the clerk. Red-faced and angry, the man threw up his arms in disgust.

"Ye know there are no worms in my hogsheads, ye bloody cuss!" he hollered. "I post my best share – ye have no need to cheat me!"

The dark-haired clerk stood up. Apparently, a simple snort was no longer an adequate response. As the man opened his mouth to speak, Winn felt Cormaic and Erich lean forward.

"Sturlss'n ha no need of yer stank tobacca', now git ye gone – and 'ust who da bloody hell are ye?"

The clerk spoke only the once sentence with a slurred voice before Erich went for him, grabbing the man by the collar and slamming him down on the table face first. The previous customer jumped obligingly out of the way, but several other Englishmen made as if they might be a nuisance.

Cormaic brandished his knife, a particularly long serrated one, pointing it at the other men. One by one he addressed them, looking like a hulking bear about to eat his dinner.

"Ye'll abide for a moment, boys," Cormaic advised them. "We have a bit of business and we'll be on our way." Iain and Tyr flanked Cormaic, standing tall and confident in the older Norseman's shadow.

Winn circled the men and joined Erich, who was grinding the man's face into the wood. The clerk screamed his indignation, slobbering a slew of threats, which only came out as an unintelligible mess as he protested his treatment.

"I'll have yer name!" Erich growled. When the clerk did not answer, Erich picked his head up and slammed it back down, bringing a froth of blood from the man's lips that splattered the ledger book.

"Tell him yer name," Winn said, lowering his face close to the man to look him in the eye. If he was the man who beat Gwen, there was no hope to save him. The Norseman had lived peaceably the village for many years, but there was still the beast of a berserker in Erich that flared darkly in his eyes.

"Hayes, it is! William Hayes!" the clerk cried out. The name came out sounding like *yillium aze*, but it was clear to Erich, nonetheless.

The long table crashed to the floor, overturned by Erich as the clerk tried to scramble away. Although Hayes hit the floor on his knees and then scurried toward the open door, Erich took his time. Calm now, his face bereft of any hint of emotion, Erich unsheathed his knife and followed the crawling man as a lion might stalk his prey.

Erich threaded his fingers into the man's hair and pulled his neck sharply back, placing his newly sharpened blade under his chin.

"Coward," he whispered, his voice as steady as his knife. "Ye lifted yer hand to the wrong woman. A mistake ye shall not make again."

Winn did not look away. It was his duty to bear witness, to tell Gwen she had been avenged, and he must look upon it as if it was done with his own hand. Blood surged as Erich sliced the man's throat, a stream pulsing out onto the wide plank floor. Behind them, one of the Englishmen retched.

"*Far vel,*" Erich muttered, the farewell uttered in his thick Norse tongue. Erich let go and the man slumped to the floor, gurgling and clutching his throat as his skull hit the wood with a sickening crack. They watched him kick in his death throes until he choked and ceased to stir, and only then did Winn glance at the Englishmen who were left. They huddled together by a window, as far away from the dead clerk as they could manage to get in such a small space.

When the one with fresh vomit on his jacket made a move toward the door, Winn met the man's gaze and shook his head.

"Stay and you will live," Winn said. The flighty Englishman stepped quickly back with the others, cowering when Cormaic approached.

"Aye, ye shall live – fer now. Many thanks fer keeping quiet, friends. I should not wish ye to meet *his* fate," Cormaic commented, tipping his head toward the dead clerk. The remaining Englishmen eagerly nodded, wordless in agreement with the beast of a Norseman. There was a collective sigh from the bunch when Winn and the men left.

John Basse had retreated a distance away, choosing to wait near the square. Keke explained John heard the scuffle and was none too eager to walk away when Keke made the suggestion. Winn thanked the young brave. It was better for them all if John Basse did not truly know what had occurred inside.

"Oh, good! Ye all seem hale and hearty. I take it ye honored my counsel and resolved yer business peaceably?" John asked. Cormaic thumped John on the shoulder as he passed by, eliciting a startled *whoop* from the Christian as the breath was forced from his chest.

Winn looked ahead at Erich, who was making his way in a decisive manner toward the tavern with the rest of their party. John grimaced as he rubbed his arm, following Winn as they left.

"Resolved?" Winn replied. "Yes, I suppose it is."

10

Maggie

the bucket splashed her skirts as she walked despite her attempt to keep it from smacking against her knee. Maggie knew she was not the most skilled worker in the village, yet she carried on with her tasks regardless of the snickers and teasing from the other women.

Across the courtyard, Ellie sat beneath a thatched overhang with those who knew how to weave. As Maggie passed by, Ellie smiled and quickly ducked her head back to her weaving. It was just one more task that everyone knew Maggie was completely inept at, and as such she was never invited to sit with the group. Gwen claimed it was out of respect, that the other women would not presume to ask the Chief's wife to do such things. Maggie knew it was just Gwen's way of softening the blow.

Truth was, there was nothing Maggie could do that would earn her their respect. She was painfully aware her only value surged in her blood, and most times, she did not understand why even that fact should make a difference. Yes, she was wife to Winn and mother to his children. Yet the twenty-first century woman inside her struggled with accepting her place.

As she set the bucket down inside the door of her longhouse, the men returned to the village. The playful banter coming from the weaving house immediately ceased and the women paused in their duties. It was not the usual greeting given to the men, but it was no simple day of hunting they had returned from, as every person left in the village was keenly aware.

Winn handed his horse off to one of the young boys. She noticed he did not speak to her uncle, or acknowledge the other men as he left them. Even across the span of the courtyard, she could see the distress etched into his face. Whatever had happened, she was sure he would tell her, but she counted each of the men even so. *Yes, they had all returned.*

He brushed her arm with his fingertips as he passed by, entering their longhouse without a word. She closed the door and followed him inside, unease washing through her.

"Winn?" she said softly. He discarded his weapons into a pile by the fire, taking care to settle his father's knife on the mantle. When he reached to shed his tunic she placed her hands over his, helping him untie the strings and pull it over his head. It was a gesture that often made him smile; his lack of response only served to frighten her further.

"What happened?" she asked.

He raised his eyes to hers.

"Gwen is avenged," he replied. Maggie sighed as he looked away, focusing his gaze on the fire instead of her.

"And you're home safe. All of you," she said. He nodded.

"For now. For now, we are all safe," he murmured. "Sit, wife. I would have your ear for a moment."

She wanted to declare he could have any part of her he wished, but she could see it was not the time for such words. It tore at her to see him so pained, as if what he meant to tell her was something so terrible he could not bear to speak it.

"Your father is a man named Sturlsson," he said. She nodded, not surprised. She knew he was a Sturlsson, but she did not know his first name. It did not matter to her, nor should it matter to Winn, and it was not worth causing her aunt or uncle stress by asking upon it.

"So why should I know this?" she said.

"He is the tobacco inspector for Elizabeth City. Agnarr Sturlsson is a powerful man, one who does the Governor's bidding. He –"

"Wait…what did you say? *Agnarr?*" she interrupted. The events of the day prior rushed back. Sending the children off, hiding in the woods with Benjamin. Watching helplessly as Gwen was beaten.

Watching the way that man's face looked when he stared into the woods where she hid, disgust and triumph seared into his sculpted features as if torturing women was just another day's work.

"Yes."

"You knew he was alive," she whispered. She sat down, as the floor seemed to drop from beneath her feet.

"I did."

"Why tell me now? Why am I suddenly worthy of the truth?" she asked, trying to keep her voice steady. She did not wish to rail at him, yet the sting of betrayal was too harsh.

"Because we must take a new path if we wish to see our children grow old," he said, his voice low. "I cannot protect us here. If Sturlsson discovers you, he will bring the force of the English down upon this place."

Winn turned his back to her, placing his hands upon the mantle. Across his thick back, his muscles surged tight, tense as he lowered his head. "What they did to the Blooded Ones…in the time of my father's father…I will never let that happen to you. To you – or our children."

"Tell me all of it," she said. The sting of her jagged nails bit into her palms as she clutched her hands in her lap, trying her best to beat down the betrayal in her heart.

"Those of your kind," he said quietly, "the *women*…they were fought over. Those of your blood have all the power – power to bend time, control the Bloodstone, to heal the dead…and to bear children who can do the same. As long as you can bear children, men like Sturlsson will hunt you."

"And when I can no longer have children? What use am I then to someone like my father?" she whispered.

"You can bring life to the dead."

"I cannot heal the dead. Only the newborns have that gift," she said.

"It is not only the newborns who hold that power."

She swallowed hard.

He turned to her, his pained blue eyes meeting hers.

"You *can* heal the dead," he replied. "By giving your life."

She knew the way it worked, but until that moment she had not considered the horror of what it meant. A few drops of blood from her infant son's heel had saved Makedewa once; her own blood smeared on a Bloodstone had brought her to the past. Yet the magic was nearly a myth to her, spoken of only in whispers and guarded by the men she loved. The reality of what it truly meant to those who came before her was so much more.

"Sturlsson needs a Blooded One to travel through time, he is not powerful enough alone. He would use you to return to his time, and then he would take your life to save his father."

"Our children..."

"All of our children are Blooded," Winn said quietly. "Do you know how powerful a child would be, born from a Blooded man and woman?"

She shook her head, refusing to acknowledge the horror of what he implied as he kneeled down beside her. He gathered her fingers between his warm hands, lowering his head into her lap.

"It is your right to know this," he said. "Yet, still, I would not tell it to you if there was no need."

"Why keep it from me? I – I trust you with my life. Have you no trust in me?" she asked.

He pulled her into his arms, his lips pressed into her hair.

"I trust you with all I have, *ntehem*. The burden of fear is a heavy one," he said. "It is only that I wished to carry it for you."

***

Later she checked on the babe in his cradle at her bedside, and Winn reluctantly left her. Although she wished him to stay, she understood he had taken time away from his duties and she knew he needed to return to the men. He left her with a few tender kisses and a pledge to return soon, and she settled down to rest on their pallet.

Alone in her thoughts, it was then that she cried. She was not certain what drove the emotion, whether it was the worry over the danger her father presented or the numbing hum of grief that still plagued her over losing Rebecca, but it consumed her. Even when she clenched her eyes tightly shut, it haunted her. Her family would always be in jeopardy, forever hunted. Despite the magic in her blood, she was powerless in the face of the danger before them.

The door creaked, stirring her from her shallow sleep, and she smiled knowing her husband had returned. He knew her weakness, he called it her strength. She needed his arms around her to feel that certainty once more.

Expecting a gentle greeting, she was stunned when a hand gripped her wrist and jerked her painfully up off the pallet.

"What the –" she yelped as Makedewa dragged her to her feet. She stumbled over the loose bedding and struggled to right herself, trying to wrench her hand away from him without success.

"Quiet!" he hissed. Torn between relief at seeing him and confusion at his behavior, she could not hide her rising annoyance. Even knowing what a hothead he was, his behavior was strange even for him, and she tried to stem the suspicion rising in her gut. His face was shielded in the darkness of the longhouse so she could not see if he smiled or sneered, but from the way he twisted her wrist she suspected the latter. Even in the darkness, she could feel the menace in his touch and smell the reek of danger emanating from him.

"What are you doing? You'll wake your son!" she whispered. He stilled at her words, and she stopped struggling against him when he moved closer to the cradle. She could see the outline of his face there as a sliver of moonlight shone down on him through the smoke-hole.

She saw no gentle loving gaze in his countenance, rather what laid there she was at loss to put words to. It was a stranger she stood next to, staring down at the infant as if he would smother the child in his sleep rather than claim him as his son.

"Come with me. Make no sound," he demanded. When she opened her mouth, he shook her hard and then she felt the pierce of a blade against her side. She glanced down at the newborn in the cradle and then at her three sleeping children. None of them stirred, and for that she was grateful. Seeing their beloved uncle behave like a mad man would only frighten them.

He took her from the safety of the longhouse and she did not fight him. Whatever he had in mind, she knew he was as troubled as she was, and to see him so rankled and fearsome caused the sickness in her belly to surge stronger. When he pulled her down the path through the woods, she saw he was leading her toward the hill where Rebecca was buried. Perhaps he only wanted privacy, and the roguish way he was treating her was his way of asking. Makedewa had never been one to share his feelings without strong persuasion.

"Uncle?"

He jerked her around at the sound of Dagr's voice. Dagr stood watching them at the end of the wood line, his eyes wide with confusion.

"Go back to sleep, Dagr. We're just talking," she said, her voice steady. Makedewa's hand tightened on her upper arm.

"But Ma–"

"I said *go!*" she insisted.

Dagr rubbed his sleepy eyes with one curled fist and nodded.

"Aye, Mama. It's good to see yer home, Uncle," he said with a yawn. She let out her breath in a grateful rush as Dagr turned and went back toward the longhouse. Makedewa grunted something coarse and resumed pulling her along without haste.

She stumbled as they neared the grave and he released her wrist. Rubbing her bruised hand, she watched him walk a few paces away, then turn back to her. His eyes, always dark, were like burnt embers in an empty shell. Although things were far from pleasant in their relationship, she cared for him as a brother and it twisted her heart to see him in such pain.

"I'm glad you're back. We were all worried about you," she said. At her words he gave her his back, and she heard him utter a snort as she approached.

"Speak no lies to me, Red Woman. You worry for no one, save yourself."

Despite her desire to comfort him, his accusation hurt her and she lashed out in return.

"Oh, do I? Is that why I have been caring for your son? Is that why I feed him from my own breast, as if he were my own? You're not the only one who lost her! We all miss Rebecca–"

He was on her in the next moment, his fingers wrapped tightly around her throat. Her vision blurred as he squeezed.

"You know *nothing* of what I feel. I will not hear her name from your lips," he growled. His grip loosened and she sputtered into a coughing fit as the air surged back into her lungs.

"I loved her, too," she whispered. She dared to speak the words, knowing it would inflame him even more, but unable to keep the truth from tumbling past her lips. His face shattered then, his eyes glossy with unshed tears as his mouth fell slightly open.

"Then bring her back to me," he said softly.

The moonlight gleamed across his shoulders, his muscles straining as he glared down at her. A bird screamed from a nearby nest. Was it a raven? She did not know.

"I cannot," she whispered. She would not lie to him by saying she would if she could. She had given Winn her promise, and she could not break it. She could not tamper with the laws of the living by changing the past.

"You mean you will not."

She gave him no answer, but he knew it without the words. She flinched as he drew his knife.

"Let go of me!" she cried. He dragged her closer to the edge of the peak, so close she could see the white-capped waves crashing against the rocks below, glowing like silver peaks along the beach.

"If I spill your blood, will it bring her back? Tell me how the magic works. Tell me!" he shouted. The knife dug into her side and she felt the sting of the blade pressed through the layers of her dress. It pierced her skin and a trickle of warmth surged forth, only a flesh wound, but enough to make itself known.

"I don't know–"

"You lie! If I kill you here, will it bring her back? This magic brought you here, surely it can return her to me!"

His fingers slid, slippery with her fresh blood, and suddenly he pulled her into his arms. She clutched him, shaking with fear and despair, even as he continued to hold the knife to her.

"I'm sorry," she whispered. "I'm so sorry."

His throat tightened and he bent his head downward.

"I tried. I tried to go on, as she would want me to do," he said softly. "She was not meant to leave this life before me."

Maggie stroked his head as she would have comforted a child, listening without question as he let his agony spill forth. His fingers twisted among her dress, clenching and unclenching as he shook. She felt the dampness on his cheeks and the shudder of his body as he held onto her, his grip that of a desperate man clinging to the last shred of reality.

"If it were you that died, would my brother feel this way? Would he wish to leave this earth and follow you?" he asked. She stiffened at the thought. It was not something she wished to have answered, nor ever think on. Could she fault Makedewa for his rash acts in the shadow of his grief, and would she or Winn be any better if they lost each other?

She shook her head, as both an answer to him and a denial.

"We should go talk to Winn. Your brother –"

"I am not my brother," he replied. "And my wife...my wife was everything good and pure. She was what kept me tied here. Now there is nothing of worth left inside me."

For a moment, she felt him waver, his embrace softening as if he meant to share his grief. Yet as fast as it happened, it disappeared moments later, and from behind them, she heard the sound of angry voices coming toward them.

It was Winn, and she could hear Chetan's shouts as well. Makedewa held her firm, so she could not turn her head to see them, and she felt him turn the blade away from her.

"Makedewa...let me go. Come back to the village with us. Come see your son," she whispered. Her cheek smeared with tears as he clutched her to his chest with one arm, his lips close to her ear. His fingers were tangled in her hair, his voice hoarse.

"No. It is too late," he said softly. His hand tightened on her back. "I have drawn your blood. There is no return from that. There are things even a brother cannot forgive."

When he released her, she did not move away immediately. She knew what would happen between them, her instinct strong to stand between the two men and the actions they would regret. Yet Makedewa would have none of her peacemaking, and with a steady hand he shoved her toward Winn.

She saw Winn's eyes flicker from her face to her side, where her dress held the spreading bloodstain from the shallow knife wound. A rush of cold panic surged through her as her husband's gaze turned to his brother.

"Come here, wife," Winn said slowly. She darted a glance back at Makedewa before she complied. The younger warrior stood straight before them, his chest rising and falling in a tortured cadence as he returned his brother's stare.

She went to Winn, who did not acknowledge her as she passed, but merely continued to level his gaze at Makedewa.

"Tell me my wife's wound did not come from your hand. Tell me, brother, so that we may welcome your return," Winn said.

Maggie opened her mouth to speak, but closed it when Chetan placed a hand on her shoulder.

"I cannot tell you that in truth," Makedewa replied.

Winn took a step toward him. The scream of metal pierced the thick night air as Winn drew his sword.

"Then tell me it was some other evil, that another guided your blade. Ask for my mercy and I shall give it."

Makedewa slid the *bryntroll* from the harness on his back. The long-handled axe had been a marriage gift from Winn at a time that suddenly seemed so long ago. As the warrior lifted the weapon and pointed it at Winn, Maggie shifted her stance, but Chetan held her tightly when the two brothers began to circle each other.

"Stop them," she whispered. Chetan shook his head.

"They must settle this. There is no other way," Chetan answered.

Makedewa was leaner than Winn, a picture of wiry strength against the raw power of his older brother. Neither seemed ready to strike, as if the consequence of their actions echoed between them. Winn raised his sword with both hands, his thick forearms strained tight as he aimed it at Makedewa.

"Mercy? You have the power to return my wife to me, yet I should ask for your mercy? Why should I not take the life of your Blooded One? Tell me this, brother. Tell me why you decide who lives and dies!" Makedewa barked.

She saw Winn's jaw tighten as he remained otherwise steady.

"I make no such decisions. None of us could have saved her, even by going back –"

"You lie!" Makedewa bellowed, brandishing his *bryntroll*. Winn landed a crushing blow with his sword that ripped the axe from Makedewa's hand, and Makedewa launched himself at Winn. The men crashed to the earth, the sounds of their shouts and grunts exploding through the night. Bodies collided, fists pounded flesh. Winn was bigger, stronger, and it was not long before he held his brother's face into the dirt. Although Winn jammed a knee into Makedewa's back and held him down, the younger man continued to struggle, unwilling to abandon his misery.

"Enough!" Winn shouted.

"You should have killed her from the start. I promise you, brother, I will do what you could not!" Makedewa grunted. Winn closed his eyes for a moment, panting shallow as he shook his head.

"I will kill you first," Winn said, his voice hoarse. He slowly rose to his feet, releasing his hold on Makedewa as he stood. Winn retrieved his sword and sheathed it, then picked up Makedewa's fallen *bryntroll*. "Go," Winn said. "Go now, while you still take breath."

Winn tossed the *bryntroll* into the dirt at Makedewa's feet. The younger man's eyes seemed to burn black as he stood up, ignoring the weapon.

"Our uncle was wise. We should have obeyed him, in this and all things," Makedewa said quietly.

Maggie felt her vision blur and realized she had been holding her breath. As Makedewa turned and walked away, she let it out in a rush. This time when she moved toward Winn, Chetan let her go, but she was stopped by Winn holding up his hand. She could not see his face with the way he held his back to her, and for some reason that scared her more than anything she had witnessed that night.

"Go to the children," he said, his words low.

She watched as her husband's shoulders dipped downward and he raised his hands to grip his head. It was not the time to make him ask twice, so she obeyed his bidding and left them alone. On unsteady limbs she made her way back to her children, the blessed numbness of grief sending her back down the hillside with it.

***

Sleep would not come. The empty bed beside her was all she could think of. Dagr had stirred when she returned, but he surrendered to his dreams with a few words of assurance and a pat on his back. The child had no idea what had happened that night, and truth be told she feared knowing the consequence as well.

Again, their lives had changed. Death and pain and anger, always a constant to balance the task of living. Would it ever change? She had no answer.

She could not stifle the gasp that left her lips when Winn's body slid over hers. He was as stealthy as an assailant, as if he meant to pillage what belonged to another, and when she felt the force of his touch on her body she suspected that assertion was not far off. Should she speak to him? Should she comfort him? What could she possibly say to ease his pain? There was nothing she could summon that made any sense, and if taking her body was what he needed then she would gladly give it to him.

One of his hands slipped over her mouth, holding her head down, his face so close to hers. Sometimes he would warn her that way so as not to rouse the children when he snuck into bed at night, but this time his hand remained. His eyes bored like daggers into her, unseeing, brimming with rage and destruction. Whatever had invaded his soul, he was bent on submission, seeking to plunder. She squirmed beneath him but opened her legs, inviting him in, confused when the motion seemed to drive him further into darkness. His chest was stone against hers, abrading her breasts and pressing her deep into the furs. Without seeking her readiness, he growled an oath and drove into her, causing her to cry out beneath the palm of his hand, and with only a few deep thrusts he emptied himself of his need. She bit him then, hard, and it was that which finally stirred him from his furious haze as he jerked his hand away. He blinked once, twice, then just stared at her for a long moment, and she saw his throat contract as he swallowed. In the dim light of the dying fire, she could see the outline of his face, etched taut to bursting, and a glimpse of dampness on his cheeks.

When she reached for him, he recoiled back as if burned, leaving both her body and her soul empty in one swift motion. Never had she felt such ferocity from him, even in the darkest moments they had taken from each other, but bereft of his weight on her body she was left boneless and broken.

"Don't go," she whispered. When he sat up and turned away she wrapped her arms around his waist, her hands running up his chest and strained shoulders. She pressed her lips to the nape of his neck, breathing in his thick scent, the taste of salt and smoke and the remnants of their joining like a brand on her mouth.

"I cannot stay," he replied. She closed her eyes.

"Of course you can. This is home," she said. She took one of his hands and laced his fingers through hers, reminding him of where his heart should rest.

"I...I cannot make this anger fade," he said, his voice hoarse as he pulled away and bowed his head into his hands.

Fighting the urge to flee took every bit of strength she had left. They had lost so much, she would be damned if they would lose each other. She would not let him push her away. She slid onto his lap, trapping him as she kneeled around him and pressed his head into her breasts. His hands trailed up to hold her as if by their own accord and he let out a guttural groan when she reached between his thighs. Yes, he was still ready, if he had ever been truly spent in his furious burst of need.

"If it is anger you have, then I will take it, and you will give it to me," she whispered, pushing him back onto the furs. "I am yours." When he opened his mouth to object she covered it with her own, thrusting her tongue to his to show him she would give him what he needed. She mimicked his possessive embrace, trying to bend him, until suddenly the thing inside him snapped and he let loose the tide of rage. In an instant he switched their places, flipping her over onto her belly and covering her with his rigid body. He was tight as a bowstring, tensed, his hands splayed over her waist. She moaned when his fingers dug into her skin and he yanked her hips up toward him. His breath was hot on her neck, coming quick as he made no effort to control his ragged gasps.

"I will not stop," he whispered as he parted her thighs with his knee.

"Don't," she replied. She meant it, and so did he.

***

He was not spent until the early hours before dawn. Even then, she did not think it was enough to tame the demon. Something was broken inside him that would not yield, no matter how hard he buried his despair in her body, nor how many times. He heard none of the soothing words she whispered, and by the time he was satiated she felt as hollow as the emptiness in his eyes. Her flesh felt bruised. Her soul was battered.

Early in the morning she felt him reach for her. It was only a questioning touch, a brush of his fingertips across her shoulder, but it was enough to let her fall back into the recesses of uneasy sleep. Yet he was gone when the sun finally rose and she woke. She busied about the morning tasks of tending the children, herding the tiny mob toward the Northern Hall as she placed Daniel in a sling. The child eagerly set about nursing as they walked through the village, content in his chore as the other children whooped and hollered around them. Kwetii grew annoyed with Malcolm stumbling alone, so she picked up her youngest brother and toted him along, finally plunking the child down on a bench once they entered the hall.

"Here, give 'em to me," Gwen called, waving her arms. Maggie handed Daniel over to her aunt, glad for the reprieve and eager to find Winn. The men had not yet split off into work groups so the hall was quite crowded, the benches filled shoulder to shoulder as they grappled amongst each other for the morning meal.

Maggie finally spotted Winn. He was standing apart from the others near the head of the table, speaking with Erich. With the events of the night prior still haunting her, she hoped he would acknowledge her as he usually did. The way he slipped from their bed as she slept troubled her. She knew he was mourning his brother's absence as they all were, and that to Winn it was a deeper pain than others endured. She did not recognize the man he had revealed to her, and that was the most frightening aspect of all. Had Makedewa taken Winn with him on his journey? And if he had, would he ever be able to return to her?

She was not consoled when Winn merely lifted his chin briefly in her direction, barely meeting her eyes across the room. Enough of a gesture to show he saw her, but enough to convey he would not speak with her. As she watched him leave the Northern Hall without another glance, her ire simmered. Yes, he was hurting. But she would not let him leave without a fight.

After checking that Gwen would watch over the children, Maggie followed Winn outside. She was stunned to find he readied his horse as if he prepared for a trip. His mount was packed with enough supplies she guessed for a two-day ride; so he meant to go visit Pepamhu at Mattanock. It made sense that Winn would wish to speak with him. She did not fault him for his journey. What rankled her was that her husband seemed to be leaving without even saying goodbye.

He was tying off a strap when she approached, but she knew he heard her by the way he paused. The muscles tensed across his arms, his shoulders tight beneath the edges of his silver fur vest. His voice was quite low when he spoke, controlled, as if he still fought his demons of the night before.

"No goodbye?" she said quietly. She came up close behind him but did not touch him, and he did not turn to face her. His skin bristled with goose bumps where her breath hit his bare arm, and she saw his fist clench and unclench on the rawhide tie. So he was not too far gone to be unaffected by her. At least she had that.

"You need no words. You know where I go," he said simply.

His response stung. She struggled to stem her rising temper, reminding herself he was damaged, and that he needed something more from her than she had ever given him.

"You're right. I know," she replied. "I suppose you're finished here."

She was sure he did not expect her acquiescence. Perhaps he wanted a fight? He let out a sigh and his shoulders slumped forward, only slightly, but enough that she could see the battle leave him. The hand wrapped around the rawhide tie gripped into a fist, and he bowed his head toward the horse. She ached to touch him but did not, giving him the space to reach out in the way he needed.

"When I saw his pain, I grieved for him. I raged for why the Creator would take his woman. I would have forgiven him if only he asked," he said softly. "Yet now, as I stand here, I tell you this: he will never spill your blood again. I will kill him first. My brother is now only another enemy. He has made his choice."

She clasped her palm over her mouth, shaking her head as he turned toward her. *No,* she thought. *Surely he did not believe his own words.*

He reached for her, holding her at arm's length. He caressed an outline down the edge of her face, then took a length of her hair between his fingers, staring at it for a few moments in silence before he dropped it. Finally his eyes met hers, and it was all she could do to match his gaze. Hollowed, barren blue eyes stared back at her.

"He was right when he said it was too late."

"Winn, no –"

"What does that make me, Red Woman, that I would do such a thing?" he asked. His use of the title unnerved her, sending a shiver over her skin.

"He was wrong. You – you wouldn't have hurt him. He's your brother – I *know* you," she whispered. He pressed his warm lips to her ear, his fingers tightening around her face. His breath sent tremors down her spine.

"You. Don't. *Know,*" he said softly. "You don't know…what I would do…to keep you."

His lips traced across her cheek until his warm mouth settled over hers. He tasted bitter at first, a touch of the morning mead, but as he explored her mouth with his tongue he was hers again. Tender, then firm, giving and taking, until finally he sighed and bent his forehead to hers. His breath hitched as he crushed his lips to her hair and she let out a muffled moan.

"I know that you belong to me. Your body. Your soul. It is *mine.* Yet still, I ache for you. I am never finished with you. We never end," he whispered. He pressed his lips to her ear. "We never will."

When he pulled away she closed her eyes, hugging her arms around herself. She dug her fingers into her palms to stem the flow of tears. He deserved a brave wife, and she would give him one. She watched, wordless as he mounted up.

Though she kept her eyes closed, his voice echoed through the pounding hooves as he rode away.

"Two days," he said.

She nodded. She would wait.

***

Chetan leaned back against the bench, sitting at her feet as the night grew dark. A spray of stars dotted the sky, a sprinkle of twilight springing to life overhead as they sat together. Maggie's backside felt numb on the rough-hewn bench, her arms and legs aching from the work of reaping the harvest all day. With the summer drawing to a close and the scent of autumn nearly upon them, it was still warm sometimes at night and she was happy to enjoy it. As the children slept soundly inside the longhouse and night settled upon them, the only thing missing was Winn.

"It's been two days," she commented, more to herself than to Chetan. Yet he cocked his head up at her in response and made a low snorting sound.

"He will return. Spare no worry on that, sister," he replied.

She felt her heart skip a little beat at his use of the endearment, and she battled the urge to embrace him in a fierce hug. Chetan was a kind-hearted man, but she suspected her unabashed displays of affection often embarrassed him. When he addressed her as sister, however, it melted the icy fingers clawing at her heart. It was the closest he had come to kindness toward her since Makedewa left, and she missed his friendship terribly.

"Thank you," she said softly. He nudged her knee with his elbow, looking up at the sky.

"For what?"

"For being here."

"Ah, where would I go?" he snorted. He continued to stare up at the sky as if her words were only casual conversation instead of the tentative stab at discussing their shared loss.

"I thought you might go to your father..."

"No. This is my place. I will be here when my brothers return."

"Do you think Makedewa will come home?"

Chetan nodded.

"His spirit is so troubled, he must wander now. Yet a part of it is tied here, in the heart of his son, and I know he cannot run from that forever."

"Oh," she said softly. She was not sure exactly what to say to his explanation, but it made sense in some way. The Paspahegh believed the spirit of a man must be shown the way through life, and sometimes part of that lesson was the act of taking a journey. She knew Chetan had performed some sort of ritual near the ground where Rebecca was buried, but it was only natural that he would consider the flight of his brother's spirit until he was at peace once more.

"There? See it? The star you tell stories of, the one that points the way. Perhaps it will point my brothers back to us soon," Chetan said. She raised her chin and looked in the direction he pointed. He was right, it was a star they had spoken of together many times. Chetan enjoyed hearing things from the future, and sometimes she just needed to talk about the life she once lived.

"The Northern Star. I see it. I think you're right," she said.

"Hmpf," he muttered with a grin. "Of course I am."

She smiled. The clear night sky held many stories, a welcome distraction from the things they could not change. It was enough for them for the moment.

11

Winn

PEPAMHU LOOKED thinner than Winn recalled. His mother's husband walked with a stilted gait, his legs bowed with the weight of time. As Winn watched him sit down across the fire, Pepamhu was seized by a fit of coughing, one that appeared to take the strength from the older man. Had it been so long since he last saw them? Surely Pepamhu's hair had not been so white before, nor his hands so unsteady.

Winn listened to the elders speak, keeping his silence as they discussed the business of the village. He knew some of the older men, noting Pimtune with the crooked upper lip and old Kayaro, but he did not recognize many on the council any longer. Those left from the decimated Paspahegh tribe blended in with neighboring villages, and as far as the English were convinced, the Paspahegh had been exterminated.

The Nansemond had many of the same problems as the Norse. With the English expanding into Tsenacommacah, the Powhatan people were forced to leave or fight. Game was scarce, forcing the men to leave the villages for longer periods as they struggled to feed their people. Many of the smaller villages simply disbanded, their numbers decimated by disease or the fury of the English. Those who left their lands merged with other tribes, blending to gain some semblance of strength. The ones who stayed lost not only their homes, but their lives as well. Although Winn and Pepamhu were of like mind in keeping their people neutral, it was clear that time was coming to an end.

Soon there would be no choice. Fight what Winn knew was a losing battle, or abandon his homeland to the English forces. Neither option was one he was ready to accept.

"John Basse seeks an alliance, if our people will accept his Christian God," Pepamhu said. Winn noted the abrupt silence. Powhatan men listened first before they voiced dissent. Although it was considered polite to give the speaker their attention, it was clear by the stony faces they did not care for the topic.

"He is a friend to me. If you choose that path, I think it will be a wise one," Winn answered. He was truthful in his response, knowing what he did of the future. If Winn could encourage even a few of the Powhatans to the way of survival, then he would feel there was something he could do to ensure their blood lived on.

"Will you accept the White Christ, *Winkeohkwet?*" Pimtune asked. The old warrior's twisted mouth turned up in a grin as he placed his palms flat together. He bent his head over his hands with a shrug. "I do not see how they call their God. He does not answer when I do this."

A chorus of laughs broke the silence, bringing a smile even to Pepamhu's lips.

"John Basse will ask us to be Christians, but he will not force it on those who object. He is not like the other English," Winn said.

"He calls his land Basse's Choice. Is that where you would have us live?" Pimtune asked. All faced turned to him at the question, silently awaiting his answer.

"It would be a safe place for our people. One where our women would be safe when we must leave them. One where our children need not fear attack – at least from the English."

"Opechancanough will slaughter them, just as he will any Englishman. If our families are at Basse's Choice, they will die as if we were traitors," Pimtune said.

Pepamhu straightened his back as much as he could, rising up onto his knees as he leaned forward onto his walking stick.

"My son knows more of this than any man here," Pepamhu said. "Speak, *Winkeohkwet.* We will hear your voice."

Amidst the snorts and grumbles, Winn told them what he knew, and with each part of his story to them, his own future became clear.

The path was not one he wished to take, but it was his path, and he could no longer avoid it.

12

Winn

He watched from the edge of the tree line, his presence masked by the shadows of early evening twilight. He arrived home to find his wife missing, and when Gwen gave a mumbled excuse for Maggie's absence, he suspected there was something amiss. It did not take him long to find her in the meadow with her uncle and cousin.

She was stubborn, he knew it well, but this time...well, this time his wife had gone too far. Winn knew she was troubled in the time since the English came to the village. Now, staring at his wife dressed in braies and wielding a sword, it became clear. Although their sword blades were swaddled with rags to blunt the blow, it still made a solid thud on impact. Cormaic landed a graze across her shoulder, and Winn did not know if he was angered or proud that his wife did not flinch.

Once again, Maggie defied him. She disobeyed his orders, and even worse, she cajoled his men into casting aside his command as well. Erich stood with arms crossed, surveying the training with his careful eye. Cormaic looked to be struggling more than Winn though he should as Maggie went at him with a sword. Cormaic was a skilled fighter; Winn could see he taught Maggie well.

Should he turn around and leave, pretend he never stumbled onto her secret? One part of him wished to let her have her glory, let her feel secure in her newfound skill. That was the voice of the one who loved her, the one who was a mere man when they stood next to each other.

It would be easy to give it to her. After all, Maggie's biggest fear was being beholden to others for her own safety.

Yet the command of the Chief within surfaced, and it was that man that could not let his woman carry on. Maggie had given her word she would stay out of the men's business, and she had broken it. The danger of her broken vow had deeper implications than just the act; it was the false sense of security it gave her that was the most pressing problem. Maggie could not continue to think she was capable of standing up to fight. If he allowed her such illusion, he was betraying all he was as her Chief, and as her husband.

The snap of brush under his boots announced his presence as he left the shadows. Erich placed a hand on his knife and turned quickly to the sound, but when Maggie's uncle realized it was Winn he relaxed. Erich's eyes met his for a long moment, during which neither of them spoke. Finally, Erich swallowed hard, as if he prepared himself for some punishment. The older man ran a hand through his silver-streaked copper hair. As much as Erich deserved it for aiding Maggie, Winn would not chastise him. It was Maggie who was in need of a lesson.

"She fights well," Winn said. Erich nodded.

"Aye, she does," Erich agreed. Maggie ducked a blow and delivered a crack to Cormaic's flank in return, and Erich smiled grimly.

"She disobeyed me."

Erich appeared chagrined at that comment. He lowered his head with a sigh.

"She is my niece, Winn. If she must wield a weapon, it should be her kinsmen that teach her."

"Her kin will protect her. There is no need for her to fight."

"She has the heart of a warrior inside, surely ye see it. Ye know she is different than other women," Erich said quietly.

"She is still only a woman."

Erich snorted. "Well, I'll leave ye to tell 'er that. I'd have her put down her sword first, fer sure." Erich whistled low against the tips of his two fingers. Cormaic and Maggie paused and looked toward them.

Cormaic had the good sense look away from Winn's seething stare, but Maggie was full on defiance. After the initial surprise at seeing Winn, she planted her legs and crossed her arms over her chest, her sword cradled between her breasts.

Despite her bluster, Winn could see her breath coming quick and shallow, and a touch of crimson creeping up the pale skin of her neck. The battle was evident in her demeanor, in those green eyes he knew so well. Succumb or fight?

As he walked toward her, her scowl deepened.

Ah, well, fight it would be then.

Cormaic muttered something about leaving them alone, but Winn was too focused on his wife to acknowledge it. She opened her mouth as if to explain, then clamped it shut. Instead of retreat as he stalked toward her, she revealed her weapon and met him halfway, her eyes gleaming with insolence and daring him to challenge.

He could not let this go. She might hate him after this moment. Yet if he must choose between her hate and her life, he would always decide the same. She was his woman, his wife. *His life.* And he could not allow her to continue down this path.

Her eyes shifted to his waist as he unsheathed his sword. Her new weapon was slightly smaller, fitted to her stature, yet just as deadly as his own if used well. He could see her effort to slow her breathing as he reached for her, and he knew she expected him to take it from her. Instead, he removed the padding from her blade and tossed it aside.

The lesson between them would not be blunted. Maggie needed to feel the force of the truth, there was no other way his stubborn wife would yield.

"I don't want to fight you," she said.

He leveled the tip of his sword at her breast.

"Why? Because you cannot fight? Because you are weak?"

"I'm *not* weak. I'm—I'm good at this!" she insisted, her voice rising a pitch.

"Then show me. I am your enemy now."

He struck first, his blade screaming as it crashed down on hers. She went down on one knee with her sword raised over her head, blinking rapidly as she recovered. When she thrust upward to shove him away he stepped back, giving her a moment to recover. Strands of her red hair peeked out beneath the cap she wore, and it took one flick of his wrist to snatch it from her head. She let out a screech as her hair fell loose about her shoulders, the thick mass now a burden that impeded her vision.

He hated the anger in her eyes, the rank despair that swelled in her soul. Perhaps it was not normal to know another so well, but to him, it was akin to taking his next breath. He could feel her thoughts as if she screamed them, and when she raised her sword and charged him, he knew he had no choice but to carry on. It was a lesson she must learn, one he trusted no other to teach her.

"Is that all you have learned?" he taunted.

"I'm just as good as some of your men, and you know it!" she snapped.

With some effort he blocked her blows, met each swing of her sword. Yes, she was strong, with a power born of pure frustration and ire. The future life she had been born to had given her confidence, and it was that fire that drew him to her flame. In the end that would not serve her victory; it was her strength that would take her from him if she did not submit.

His eyes widened when she sliced the edge of his tunic with a glancing swipe.

"Oh, you are good, Fire Heart," he agreed.

When he took a step back she grinned, and that moment of introspection was enough for him to pounce. He struck high, side-to-side, giving her half his might, until finally he put his weight into a crushing blow that flung her sword from her hands and sent her to her knees.

She scrambled away to fetch it, and he knew he could not let her. His vision clouded with a haze, and he told himself it was for her that he did it.

She must know she cannot fight like the men.

She must understand.

He snatched her by the back of her man's tunic and shoved her to the ground, slamming her hand into the dirt when she reached for her weapon. As if she did not know she was beaten, she twisted beneath him and clawed at his face, drawing his blood with her jagged nails. He tried to see himself as a marauder, some enemy that would give her no quarter, yet it still burned him to feel her soft flesh gripped in his hands and see how he would leave bruises on the one he loved most.

He tossed her onto her stomach and pinned her with his body, ending any question that she might escape.

"You are not strong enough," he growled. She bucked up against him.

"Get off me!" she screamed.

"I am your enemy! Is that what you say to your enemy?" he shouted.

"I'll kill you!" she insisted, even as he pressed her face into the dirt. He looped his hand across her shoulders from behind, drawing his knife and pressing it into her neck as he drew her upward onto her knees.

With one hand he groped across her stomach, his heart like a blackened ember as he pushed her braies down around her thighs. She had been sneaky to steal his clothes. She writhed but did not cry, her chest rising and falling in rapid sequence as she struggled to free herself. He bent over her, his fingers digging into her hips as he yanked her body against his.

"You are beaten, woman," he whispered hoarsely against her ear. "I will have my pleasure – and perhaps give you to my friends. And then I will end your life."

He drew the knife slowly across her throat, careful to cover the blade with his fingers, but the intention was clear. When he released her she did not move, remaining bent over on all fours, her hair hanging over her face as she panted.

He stepped away and stumbled, his eyes fastened on his wife. She finally stirred. Pulling her braies up with one hand, she turned on him. She stalked toward him, covering the space in only a few paces, then flung herself at him. Her open palm connected with his cheek and then her closed fist pummeled his chest. He let her have her revenge, letting her blows fall on his flesh until she raised her knee with intent to smash his groin.

"You fucking *bastard!*" she screamed. "You just couldn't let it go? Do you have to prove to me how helpless I am? Well, I fucking *know* it! Every single day I'm reminded of it! I may be weak – I may be a woman – but I can still *fight!*"

When she raised her hand to strike him again he caught her wrist, slipping his hand along the nape of her neck to still her struggles. She refused to let him hold her, and he did not blame her as she slapped his hand away.

"No. When the time comes, you will *not* fight. You are weak. You are small. And you cannot win," he replied. Her throat contracted as she stifled a furious sob, and though her eyes still flamed defiance she met his gaze.

"But I can fight. I won't just sit here and do nothing again," she whispered. He tightened his fingers in her hair, as if holding her close was enough to shield her from the truth.

"You can run. You can hide. When the time comes, that is what you will do."

"So I'm helpless."

"No," he whispered. He clutched her face in his hands, smearing the dirt over her tear-stained cheeks as she clenched her eyes closed. He would not let her succumb to self-pity, forcing her to meet his gaze instead of run from it. "You are brave. You are clever. My woman is the most powerful one I have ever known."

"But you said –"

"I do not doubt the strength in your heart. If it took only that to strike down your enemies, then I stand here, trembling in fear for them," he said. "But it is more than that. If you fight you may take the life of a man, even two men. Will you be glad that you felled one man, while your children lay dead beside you?"

A strangled moan escaped her lips. Tears spilled from her jade eyes as she shook her head.

"No," she said softly. Whether her response was to deny him or the truth, he was not certain.

"Then give me your trust. Do as I ask. If a time ever comes where I am not standing before you with my sword, you will run. If you have a choice, you will go, you will take our children and hide. You will see them safe. Only you can do that. Leave this fighting to me. It is my burden, the vow that I made. Yours is only to…go on."

He sighed when she allowed him to pull her to his chest. She shuddered, with rage or fear he did not know, and as she succumbed to his embrace, he felt the fight leave him. The stark anger at her impudence and foolishness ebbed away, replaced with the heavy mantle of devotion he felt for her.

"I will strike our enemies down. I will wield my sword for you. It is I who will carry that task. It is I who will bear that promise. In this life and all others, I swear this to you."

He felt her lips move against his skin.

"Because I am a *MacMhaolian*?" she whispered.

He clutched her harder.

"Because you are my beating heart."

***

Winn joined the men in the Northern Hall after Maggie returned to their longhouse. As much as he wished he could simply stay with her, it was for her and his children that he must make plans. The sooner he could discuss the future with his men, the better off they all would be.

"That went well for ye, I see," Erich chuckled, his eye on the tear in Winn's tunic as Winn took a tankard of ale from him. It was not as sweet as the mead, but supplies had been scarce over the winter and mead making was no priority. Cormaic joined them, a burly eyebrow raised in question.

"No thanks to you," Winn muttered. He glanced at Maggie's cousin. "And no thanks to you, as well."

"What harm is it, if it gives her peace?" Cormaic said. Winn winced at the whiff of Cormaic's ale-tinged breath.

"It will give her no peace when she is dead. If there is a fight, she must take our children to safety. That is all I wish of her."

Cormaic and Eric erupted into laughter, with Cormaic staggering into Winn with the force of his guffaws. Winn scowled.

"Do ye not *see* the Norse in yer woman yet, ye bloody fool?" Erich asked, taking a gulp of his ale. "Our women fight, they doona hide. 'Tis not in 'er nature to do anything else."

"Ah!" Winn growled, shaking his head. There were differences between how women behaved in Norse society and Powhatan, but Winn refused to consider that his wife might fight at his side.

"Go easy on my niece," Erich said as his laughter dimmed. He placed a hand on Winn's shoulder.

"I will not, and neither will you," Winn replied. "There is more to this. I spoke with Pepamhu. Some of the Nansemond will join with the people at Basse's Choice."

Erich and Cormaic both quieted, the mood turning decidedly somber.

"So ye think we should as well, is that yer plan?" Erich asked.

Winn nodded.

"We know what the future brings if we stay here. We cannot stop it. Maggie says some of the Nansemond survive to her time, and they come from those who live at Basse's Choice." Winn turned to Cormaic. "And what do you want? What say you?"

Cormaic downed his ale and wiped the back of his hand over his mouth.

"To lay down my head at night without fear of being killed in my sleep? To have a woman and some weans, like ye? Aye, it's nothing much, really. I just want to live. Just *live*," Cormaic answered. He muttered something under his breath and walked away, shaking his head. As Erich shrugged and took the opportunity to refill his tankard, Winn followed Cormaic out of the Northern Hall.

Cormaic staggered into the courtyard, taking a seat on the edge of the well. At first Winn thought he engaged in drunken nonsense, but he quickly realized Cormaic's mood was much more dangerous. The copper haired Norseman shouted a slew of oaths in his ancient tongue seeming directed at the sky, then idly sliced his own palm with his knife. As he reached for something inside his shirt and Winn came closer, he could see it was Cormaic's Bloodstone pendant.

Winn watched, frozen, as Cormaic closed his bloody hand around the pendant.

"No!" Winn shouted.

Cormaic grinned. His eyes met Winn's and he started to speak, but Winn could not hear what he meant to say before he faded away.

"So it was tonight. I thought ye had more time here, son."

Winn turned to Erich, who had come up beside him.

"What do you mean?" Winn demanded, his head spinning at the realization that Cormaic had just disappeared in front of him. Eric seemed exceedingly calm for a man who had just watched his drunken son fade into time.

"He's not meant fer this time. He ne'er was," Erich replied. Winn was shocked to see him take a long swig of his drink, as if neither of them should be concerned with Cormaic's leaving.

"Where will he go?"

"Oh, to the past," Erich replied. "How do ye think I knew what to name him?"

Erich muttered something about speaking to Gwen and made his way across the courtyard, leaving Winn standing alone. Winn stared for a long time at the well where Cormaic last sat, until finally he thought he might have the words to explain it to his wife.

13

Makedewa

It was dusk when Makedewa reached the village. He hunted alone, unwilling to walk among the Powhatan men who hunted in groups. Although he took shelter at night with his uncle's family, he rarely remained near them, choosing instead to spend his time away from the others. He could see they feared him from the way the children stared, and the way the women stepped back when he passed.

It mattered not. He had never been well liked, in the Norse village or with the Powhatan.

Through the cover of swamp Cyprus he sat for a moment to watch, crouched amongst trailing Spanish moss with his feet burrowed in the mud. His toes ached with the numbness of the cold, and in another time he might have asked his wife to bring him a dry set of moccasins. Ever attentive, always his partner, Rebecca had known his needs before he even knew them himself.

Yet his wife was cold in the ground. *Gone.*

That tightness in his chest returned, sending his heart racing into a frantic tempo until the pain exploded between his ears. It tore through him, a scream of all his tears unshed, until he gasped for a breath and gripped his head in his hands.

Cool mud smeared over his face from his fingers, the heady scent of earth a temporary distraction from everything that was her. It did not soothe him, but it reminded him of when he was a boy and played in the woods with Winn and Chetan.

Winn, the brother who controlled the power of time travel. The brother who could wield that power to save Rebecca.

Winn – the brother who would do no such thing.

A rumble of laughter surfaced, followed by gleeful shouts. The hum of a rhythmic beat called to him. So it was a celebration in the village, he thought as he rose to his feet. The Powhatan village was well-attended, especially around the *yehakin* where his uncle slept. Makedewa recognized the men standing guard and was relieved; he knew them well, and he was sure they would permit him access.

He stepped away from the wood line and made his way to the yehakin. Weapons were drawn as he approached, and he was not surprised to hear the rustle of footsteps following him from behind. It eased him to know his uncle had so many warriors guard his people, unlike other tribes who had abandoned the old ways and opened their homes to the English.

"*Tawnor nehiegh Opechancanough?*" Makedewa asked, keeping his tone respectful as he spoke with the guard to inquire of the Weroance. Although he knew his uncle must be inside, he dared not assume, especially when he had been gone from his Powhatan kin for so long. He must be forthright with his requests, leaving no cause for distrust.

If they suspected he was an assassin, he would be dead before he passed through the door.

The warrior smiled when Makedewa lifted up two hares tied together by the feet. With a nod, the guard let him pass, and Makedewa entered the *yehakin*.

Opechancanough sat by the fire, tended by only one of his wives. When Makedewa approached, the old Weroance waved the woman away.

"Son of my sister," Opechancanough said.

Makedewa obeyed the flick of his uncle's hand and sat down before him. Although it was well known the Weroance preferred his solitude in the evening, Makedewa wondered if he was suffering from some malady. The Great Creator had favored Opechancanough for many years, but even the grace of the Gods was not enough to hide the evidence of his decline. Opechancanough was not well. His eyes were mere slits hidden beneath drooping lids, his skin a yellow pallor despite his brown color. When the Weroance raised a shaking hand to reach for a cup, Makedewa quickly fetched it for him.

Opechancanough sighed but did not thank him.

"You hunt alone again." The words from his uncle held the tone of accusation, and Makedewa responded by placing the dead hares in front of him.

"I need only my two hands, uncle," Makedewa replied.

"So I see. And when I have need of your two hands, what kind of man will serve me?"

Makedewa frowned.

"One who is loyal. One who honors you with the death of many Englishmen."

The Weroance uttered a snort.

"My warriors say your brother will not send men. They say he is a woman who will not fight."

At the mention of Winn, Makedewa felt his throat go dry. Although he was aware Opechancanough sent men to Winn's village, it had not occurred to him that Winn might refuse a request for aid. Surely, Winn had lost all sense. Was his blind devotion to his Norse kin worth more than the Powhatan people who raised him? Was his vow to protect the magic bloodlines the only vow he would honor?

"His Blooded One tells him what must be done. She claims the Powhatans will not win this battle. She says our end is near, and it cannot be changed," Makedewa said, the words tasting bitter on his tongue. He refused to speak her name, refused to feel any remorse for his words. Maggie had deserted him, just as Winn had.

Yet the image of Rebecca burst through his hatred and he could almost smell the scent of her hair as it lay across his skin. The memory of that morning burned bright.

"It is her birthday today," Rebecca said as she snuggled closer against his chest. He absently twisted one of her golden curls between his fingers, enjoying the feel of her palm placed flat over his heart.

"So? Why must I care?" he muttered. She immediately pinched her fingers together and squeezed his chest.

"Because she is my sister, and we shall give her a marvelous gift!" she shot back. With a grin, her deflected her outraged blows and tossed her onto her back, dropping kisses along her neck and breasts until she screamed with laughter.

"Fine," he growled through his smile. "A gift for your sister then."

Rebecca loved Maggie. Yet Maggie stood by and let his wife die. Had Rebecca meant nothing to Maggie?

"Tell me more of what the Red Woman speaks. Tell me about the end," Opechancanough demanded.

Makedewa raised his eyes, staring at his uncle yet not truly seeing him. Instead he saw his despair, swirling as a haze in front of his eyes as the thud of his heart slammed against his ribs.

Rebecca was gone. *Why should he hide their secrets any longer?*

It was a tale that would take some time to tell, but his uncle was a patient man. Makedewa started the only way he knew how.

"She says that *Tsenacommacah* will be no more..."

PART TWO

14

Norse Village 1638

Maggie

THE DAY WINN made his decision was fresh in her thoughts. Four years prior, her husband sealed a pact with John Basse. Since that time, those in the Norse village blended with the Christian people at Basse's Choice, visiting freely and sharing resources as they gradually found trust in each other. She understood why Winn wished to form an alliance, especially knowing what she did of the future. Yet using their daughter to seal that alliance by marriage was not something she agreed with at all.

"Ouch, Mama!" Kyra cried as Maggie tried to mend her torn sleeve and pricked her with a needle. Kyra seemed a bundle of nerves, either unwilling or unable to stay still for the few moments it would take to fix her dress.

"Be still," Maggie replied. "It's not easy to do."

"I can mend it myself," Kyra said.

Maggie sighed. "No, I'm almost done. See? All fixed."

She watched her daughter glance down at the sleeve and raise an eyebrow, but the girl shrugged and made no comment. Maggie knew it was not the most impressive line of stitches.

"Perhaps we should find you something more fitting for hunting," she commented. Maggie knew Kyra hunted most days, despite Winn forbidding her from doing so alone. Maggie recognized the flame of independence in her child, one she readily identified with, her heart sinking at the knowledge of what was to come. *How would her brave daughter react to the news of her betrothal?*

Kyra stared warily back at her.

"What I have will suffice," Kyra said quietly.

"I suppose it will," Maggie said. "Do you at least take one of the boys with you? It's the being alone that worries your father, especially when you're too far from the village."

"I do not go alone."

Kyra focused her attention on her loose shirt, fiddling with the tie as Maggie watched.

"Good," Maggie said. "You know there will be many people here during the gathering, and we'll all be very busy. I want you to stay in the village – no hunting."

"Will Morgan White join us? Da said there shall be Englishmen 'ere, and Nansemonds, too. Surely Da willna mind it?"

Maggie smiled. Kyra kept her feelings about Morgan to herself, but Maggie had seen her watching the boy often enough to know her daughter's heart. It only made things more difficult, however, since it was Maggie's job to tell Kyra of her betrothal. Although Winn offered, Maggie felt it should be a conversation between mother and daughter.

"Yes, I'm sure all our friends will be here. John Basse will visit with his brother. Do you remember him?" Maggie prodded, trying to feel the situation out. She was not comforted to see Kyra's face scrunch up in a most displeasing manner.

"Of course. Ye always make me sit beside him. I shall not this time, Mama. I'm no longer a child, ye canna make me sit with an old man," she said. Kyra pushed her dark hair away from her face, tucking a wayward strand behind her ear. Her blue eyes, so much like her father's, darkened with her display of disobedience.

"Kyra, you will have to –"

"Good day, Mistress!" John Bass interrupted, leaning his head inside the door. "How fare thee?"

When Kyra uttered a heavy sigh Maggie shot her a glare, which immediately served to stifle her daughter's behavior. After speaking initial pleasantries with John, Kyra sat down on a bench and folded her arms while Maggie served their guest a spot of drink.

She supposed he was not an unattractive man for his time, with a swatch of muddy brown hair that seemed to be forever in disarray. He always wore a wide brimmed hat that hid his dark eyes, with a light homespun shirt buttoned neatly at his neck. Maggie glanced at Kyra, then back to John.

It could be a good match. Winn was right; they needed the alliance, and marriage was part of the bargain. Fathers had every right to arrange marriages for their daughters. It was the way of the time.

Once Kyra warmed up to John, they engaged in a lively discussion. Despite her opposition to sharing a meal with the older man, Kyra had been privy to many conversations involving religion. Although he had lived with Indians after his family perished in the Massacre of '22, John was a devout Christian who spent much of his time spreading the Good Word, which he explained was his duty as a servant of the Lord. Part of his arrangement with Winn was that those in the village would consider converting to Christianity. Unlike many of the English, John did not demand immediate conversion. He believed that by continued interaction and tolerance between men, those in the Norse village would eventually accept Christ.

As John preached to Kyra, Maggie questioned if Winn meant to consider Christianity. If ever there was a man who respected all beliefs, it was her husband. The product of a Paspahegh upbringing and adult blood ties to Old Norse religion, Winn somehow navigated the delicate task of leading a widely diverse group of people. He fought to maintain good relations with his Powhatan family, just as he did with the Norse. Now, as the Christian Englishman sat in front of them, Maggie wondered how it would all fit together.

"Did ye know, Mama, that they eat the body of the White Christ? So that He may live in ye forever?" Kyra asked.

"'Tis not his actual body, my dear," John chastised her, bringing a wry grin to Kyra's face.

"Of course not!" she laughed.

"I am glad to hear it," Maggie added with a smile.

Perhaps the path would make more sense as time wore on. As she watched her daughter debate religion with her future husband, she decided to let her news abide. She could discuss Kyra's betrothal another day, leaving the two of them to learn a little more about each other in the meantime.

15

Kyra

Kyra watched from behind the brush, laying on her belly on the flat rock. It jutted out over a waterfall, the perfect spot to jump from to make a splash in the pool below. There was a rope hanging from a tree limb just in reach swinging idly in the humid breeze, and she considered grabbing it. Instead, she dismissed the childish desire as a different sort of playful longing washed through her. Morgan stood waist deep in the water below, his back turned away from her. He shook the dampness from his blond hair and sank down to his shoulders so that only his head remained above.

She rose slowly to her feet, shedding her gunna dress but leaving on her thin cotton shift. Instead of using the rope, she drew back a few feet and then took a running leap from the ledge as she uttered a gleeful scream. She crashed into the water with a squeal next to Morgan, who jumped away in a fright in the wake of her splash. As she came to the surface, she felt two strong hands close over her shoulders and she was unceremoniously hauled upward.

"Jesus, Kyra! Yer too old to play these games!" he snapped. He pulled her onto a shallow shelf where they could both gain their footing, and although he looked fighting mad, she suspected it was more bluster than ire.

"We used to jump all the time, did ye forget that?" she shot back with a mischievous grin. He shook her gently as if to chastise her, and suddenly she was aware of the heat of his damp skin against hers. Her shift clung to her body, her cheeks flushed when she followed his gaze. His soft brown eyes were focused between them where she was pressed up against his chest.

"We're not children anymore," he said quietly.

"We're still friends," she whispered. His eyes met hers, and she had never seen him so affected. This thing between them caused an ache in her belly, her pulse throbbing madly as suddenly the distance of their years felt like nothingness. His eyes no longer held the curiosity of a boy, but the shadow of a twenty-year-old man, and she hoped with all her being that he no longer viewed her as a simple child.

"It's not a proper game for a lady to play, Kyra," he murmured.

"I'm no lady," she shot back.

"Oh, are ye not, now?" he said. She could feel her heart thudding through the wet cloth of her shift.

"No! Well, yes, I suppose I am, but – oh!" One of his hands twisted up into her hair, and he tilted her head back as he gazed into her eyes. Her lips parted with a tiny gasp as his mouth covered hers, seeking an answer she did not know how to give. Slow and sweet at first, then with budding urgency, she lost herself in his arms.

So kissing was a pleasant thing, she thought.

One of his hands slid downward and settled on her buttock, pulling her closer. She abruptly realized things were different from when they were children. This was no nervous boy who held her, nor was his body that of a youth. He was firm and broad, his muscles tensed, his fingers pressing firmly into her skin. A surge of ache assaulted her deep in her belly with his touch, her heart leaping at the thought that he finally saw her as a woman.

From a few sweet kisses their embrace turned heated, his mouth crashing down on hers with urgency. She sighed when he suddenly pulled back, his eyes glazed and his lips parted slightly open. It was as if he saw her for the first time, and then he clutched her close and buried his face into her hair.

"Morgan?" she whispered, confused at his abrupt change. He was shaking as he held her, but he would not let her draw away to see his face. His voice finally emerged, grated and hoarse against her ear.

"Go home, Kyra. Go now, before I canna let you leave," he said.

"I'm no child to be ordered about," she replied. Her body ached to finish what they had started.

He took her face into his hands, swallowing hard before he spoke.

"Aye, yer no child. And if ye dinna leave now, I'll forget we're supposed to be friends. Get ye gone, go home."

"Is that what I am to you? Only a friend?" she asked, feeling her heart shatter into pieces. All the years she had spent trying to grow up as fast as she could for him, so that they could be together again without judgment, and he looked upon her as only his...friend. She felt her cheeks redden and she squinted hard to block the rush of tears.

"It's not that–"

"Fine. Just forget this ever happened!" she shot back. She twisted away from him and climbed out of the pool as gracefully as she could muster. Her clothes were up above on the hillside, and it would be a climb to recover them.

"What are you doing here, cousin?"

When she raised her eyes it was to meet the dark stare of Ahi Kekeleksu, and by his stance she could see he was uncertain of what to do with her. She sloshed from the water and crossed her arms over her bodice, trying to avoid her older cousin's inquisitive gaze. Even worse, behind him were Iain and Tyr, both with an equally perplexed look upon their faces. The young men were bare-chested in their braies, only seconds away from shedding the last of their clothes before they spotted her.

"I was swimming. Now I'm leaving," she snapped, brushing past Keke. She felt some remorse over treating him so brusquely, but her cheeks were burning like cinders at the way Morgan refused her and it was all she could think of to get as far away from him as possible. All the years she had loved him, all the years he had waited. Finally, when she was old enough to matter to him, he cast her away without so much as an explanation.

Keke grabbed her upper arm. He was gentle, but his gaze darted from her to Morgan, who was still waist-deep in the water.

"Why are you upset?" Keke asked. He spoke close to her ear, low enough so that the conversation was between only the two of them. "Did Morgan ah, um, trouble you?"

"No. I am fine, and I thank ye for taking yer hand off me!" she hissed. "He'd rather swim alone, I'm just doing ye all a favor. Be off with ye, do what it is ye men do."

He dropped his hand away and his gaze shifted back to Morgan.

"Very well," he agreed. "Go home then, cousin." Keke tapped her on the chin with his fist, and with a grin and a shrug he left her side to leap into the creek.

As she left the sandy bank, the sounds of laughter and splashing chased her back to her senses.

It had been a mistake to show Morgan how she felt. An enormous, devastating mistake.

16

Winn

"HOW DO WE FARE?" Winn asked.

Erich glanced at the women before he answered, watching for a moment as they tended to their preparations for the gathering. The village was full with guests from multiple places, English and Nansemond alike. Winn intended to throw a productive celebration that would strengthen ties between them all. The future of his family depended on the alliances made, and he would not fail in his task.

"Good, my lord," Erich replied. "Enough to feed our guests and enough to keep our bellies full as well. Have ye heard if Pepamhu's tribe will stay?"

"Yes," Winn said. "There are not many, but they will join us."

Maggie smiled as they approached. She continued stirring the food she prepared, which was likely some sort of venison stew from the delicious scent filling the air. Gwen added a bowl of sliced carrots, which slid into the pot with a splash.

"Will ye send Kyra to Basse's Choice, or will ye wait until they wed?"

Winn shook his head. "She will stay here. John Basse will have a church wedding, so he says it must be. We will take Kyra there when they wed."

"Chetan says the Christians will Baptize ye in yer sleep if ye doona say ye love their White Christ – should I lay with my sword, then, just to be ready?" Erich demanded.

"Ah, Chetan tells tales. John Basse may push you in the river to make you Christian, but he willna bother your sleep," Winn laughed.

Maggie dropped her ladle. Instead of picking it up, she wiped a hand over her flushed face and left the Northern Hall. Gwen raised her brows but said nothing, and Erich shook his head with a sigh. Winn knew Maggie was opposed to Kyra's marriage, but the time had come to face it.

Kyra would marry John Basse and join their families. They would all leave the village and join with the Christians at Basse's Choice. Winn had arranged the match when Kyra was twelve, and now that she was nearly seventeen, he intended to honor it.

Winn found Maggie alone by the edge of the meadow sitting cross-legged on the ground. By the stiff outline of her back and the method with which she yanked random fistfuls of grass from the earth her mood was evident. As he stood behind her he let out a shallow sigh, giving her a moment to collect her thoughts before he pressed his intent. For all her strengths and faults there was one constant in his wife, and that certainty was that she hated being forced into anything. Most times they could come to an agreement, negotiate a truce. This time, however, was different.

There would be no other option. Kyra would do her duty. Maggie would abide. He could give his wife no choice this time.

"You didn't have to run after me," she said quietly without looking up. She resumed tearing at the grass, tossing each handful away as she liberated it from the ground.

"I walked. There was no running," he replied. He slowly sank down beside her. When she uttered a doubtful snort but gave no further resistance, he took that as a sign she would listen. "Does it make you feel better, doing that?" he asked.

"No," she murmured. He covered her hand with his when she reached for the grass again and she stilled, keeping her chin tucked down. Placing her hand carefully between his palms, he rubbed the dirt from her skin. She did not move away so he continued to hold her, pulling her gently toward him. When their shoulders touched, she let out a sigh and he felt her body relax against his. He smiled.

"Tell me a story about the future. There must be some things that stay the same," he said.

"Nothing is the same. It's completely different," she muttered. He grunted his disbelief, which brought a smile to her lips, so he took the opportunity to put his arm around her shoulder. Her head dipped down and she immediately snuggled into his chest.

"Ah, I do not believe that. What about the sky? Does the moon still shine at night, or does the future only have sunshine? Go on, tell me," he urged.

To his relief, he felt her shudder with a muffled giggle. He closed his fingers on her chin and tilted her head up as she laughed.

"What is so funny?" he demanded with a smirk. He loved to hear her laugh. There had been few reasons to smile of late and he would do anything to see the glow of her happiness once again.

"Oh, it's just an old saying. I couldn't possibly tell you there's no moon in the future. It's like blowing sunshine up your – up your *ass!*" she laughed. She shook so hard that tears spilled from her eyes and he could not help but laugh along with her once he gleaned her meaning.

"Blow sunshine up my ass? Is that the way women speak to their men in the future?"

She hiccupped as she struggled to control her giggles.

"It's just a funny saying, that's all." Her fingers twisted into his tunic and she sank back down into his arms. Her laughter faded. "Of course there's a moon at night. The sky is pretty much the same, I suppose."

He pressed his lips to her forehead, kissing her gently as her voice grew wistful. It would make her feel better to speak of the life she once lived, and he enjoyed hearing her tales of the future.

"The moon seems brighter in the sky here, I think because there's no light from the city. It's easy to see the constellations."

"What meaning is that?" he murmured.

"Constellations? It's the word for the stars. Well, it's more than that. The stars are in groups, and the groups are the constellations. See?"

she replied, pointing out over the treetops. "That one that looks like a cup? Like it has a long handle? That's the Big Dipper. One of the constellations."

He nodded. He knew other names for the spirits in the sky, but he wanted to hear what she called them.

"And the bright one, you see the one all alone? Across the Big Dipper? That's the Northern Star. It points the way."

"To where?"

"Home. Marcus said he could always find his way home by it. His father taught him to navigate when they sailed. I didn't know it back then, but he must have been talking about traveling on the long boats. It sounded amazing."

An ache surfaced in his chest at mention of his father. There was so much about Marcus that Winn would never know. He held no jealousy that Maggie had grown up in the care of his father, nor that he had lived his entire life bereft of the man. At least with Maggie's memories, Winn could know Marcus better in some small way, and it was that thought that gave him comfort.

"Those are things a man shares with his son. He gave you his trust."

"He was different then. I guess he was always a little old-fashioned, and he had weird ideas about everything. But he let me make decisions. He listened to me—and so did Grandpa. Whenever something important came up, we sat down and discussed it. As a family," she said.

"See? We talk, just the same as you did with Marcus," Winn offered.

He felt her stiffen in his arms then and her breathing slowed.

"Marcus changed when he came here. He turned into a stubborn bully, and suddenly everyone is running around doing his bidding!" she replied. "Chief this, Chief that! It was like some stranger standing in his boots."

"He returned here as a Chief. It would change any man," Winn said quietly. "He sacrificed everything to see you safe in the future. He was what you needed, when you needed him."

She twisted around to face him. Her slim throat tightened and contracted and he could feel her fingers grip his tunic.

"And you? Has it changed you, being Chief? Do you expect me to obey your every command, to never question you?"

His hand slipped up and he cupped her face in his palm, rubbing his thumb lightly over her cheek. Her green eyes blazed on the flicker of moonlight between them, her soft lips parted slightly open as she waited for his answer.

"I will always hear you, *ntehem*," he whispered. "I made you that promise. I will keep it."

"But Kyra–"

"I *hear* you. I *know* this is not how you were raised. When you want to rage at me for making this choice, I only ask you think of who I am. How I have lived, here in this time." She tried to dip her head down, but he held her face firmly in his hands. "John Basse is a good man. He will be a good husband to our daughter. And by making this match, our people–our *family*–will be safe. It is my duty to see it done. I cannot yield on this."

She leaned her forehead against his, closing her eyes, and her body tensed in his embrace.

"So I have no say in this?" she replied.

"You have my ear. But the decision must be mine."

"I want our daughter to have a choice."

"She will do as I bid her."

Maggie jerked away from him, but he caught her shoulders before she could flee. The stubborn anger flared like beacons within her, the last remnants of her resolve fighting to be heard.

"As I will? So I must shut up and bear it?" she seethed.

"Yes! As I will bear it! See me, Maggie," he growled, his voice trailing off as he gripped her arms. "*See* me. I do what I must. There is no one for me to argue with, no man to tell me yea or nay. It is on my head that this rests, this decision. Perhaps I am failing my daughter– and my wife. Perhaps this will lead our people into danger."

She shook her head, but her eyes were riveted on his.

"Yet I think this is right. I believe this is the best path. I do not know what your future was like, that place you came from, but I know what our future will be. It will be here, with these people. I must do what is right for us all. We must join with the English if we wish to survive."

He would not be swayed. His kissed her softly on her forehead and stood up, intending to return to his duties.

"Winn?" she said quietly. He turned back to her. Arms wrapped around her knees, she looked up at him with her soft green eyes.

"Yes?"

"I told her this morning. She said she will do her duty. She will marry John Bass."

He nodded. He wanted to say he expected nothing less from his daughter, but he did not think his wife needed that truth to be said. He left to join his men, giving his wife time to accept what she must.

***

There had never been such a large gathering since Winn lived in the village, and he found it fitting that they would leave their home after the pleasure of a grand celebration. It was a diverse assortment of people, with Norse, the English, and the Nansemond sharing the space. Winn knew his efforts to live apart from the war cost him the loyalty of many of the Powhatan, but he was strong in his convictions. Change would come and his family would endure.

A few of the Nansemond already lived at Basse's Choice, more open to accepting the Christian ways than the Norse. John Basse was a devout man yet a patient one, and he believed that he was honoring his God by bringing more people into his fold. The Norse, however, were still suspicious, and it was not until after Kyra's marriage that they would be willing to go. Winn knew he asked a great deal of his people by joining with the Christians. If they needed the promise of his daughter's marriage to seal a commitment, then he was willing to give it to them.

Winn stood up from his chair, raising up his carved drinking horn. It had once belonged to his father, and his father before him, and each time Winn held it he was reminded of those who came before him.

"Hear me!" he shouted. The cries of celebration ebbed away with his declaration and head turned in attention.

"*Ja, Ja!*" was returned in agreement by the Norsemen, rising above the expectant murmurs of the crowd.

"Tonight we shall drink to the blessings bestowed upon us. This man, John Basse," Winn announced, pointing to the Englishman in the crowd, "will wed my only daughter, the lovely Kyra Alfrun Neilsson!"

His last words were muffled by the roar of the crowd, the sounds of Norsemen thumping the tables and smashing their tankards drowning him out. Winn did not mind. He grinned and finished his ale with one long swallow, sending the people into another chorus of joyous shouts.

Winn knew he made the right choice when he saw Maggie lead Kyra to John's side. There his wife placed Kyra's hand into John's, and Winn felt a surge of pride. He knew what it cost Maggie to concede her beliefs.

"*Winkeohkwet.*"

Winn glanced to his side at the sound of his name. Leaning heavily on his walking stick, Pepamhu joined him. Winn offered him his seat, which Pepamhu gratefully settled into, and Winn crouched down at his side as they watched the celebration.

"Did you enjoy the Norse meal, father?" Winn asked. Pepamhu smiled at the endearment and nodded.

"I did. Your Norse women may cook for me again."

Winn chuckled.

"Though I fear this will be the last time our families share food," Pepamhu said.

"Why is that?" Winn asked, taken aback. It had already been decided that Pepamhu's people would join the other Nansemond at Basse's Choice. Winn was eager for the day his family would all be safe in one place.

"Some Nansemond will stay here. But I will go north. We have friends with the Lenape who will welcome us."

"I thought you meant to stay," Winn said, trying to keep his voice level. It was Pepamhu's choice to make, but his decision still fell heavy on Winn's ears.

"At one time, I did. Now...now I see this is no longer our home. I wish you peace on your journey as it parts from mine, son."

Winn swallowed. His dry throat tightened.

"I wish you peace, as well, father," he said, his voice hoarse.

Pepamhu placed a hand on his shoulder. They watched their people dance and eat, enjoying what was left of their time together.

17

Maggie

The edges of the shells felt like smooth rocks beneath her probing toes. She thrust her feet beneath the sand, delving deep into the shallow seawater pool. It was a spot she often found a nest of clams, and the thought of having a basket full of fresh seafood made her mouth moisten in anticipation. She dug one out with her big toe until it released from the sand with a faint sucking sound, popping up where she could snatch it with her fingers. She swished it around until the grey shell was clean, then tossed it in her basket which sat a few feet away on a flat rock. They would eat well tonight.

The gathering took a toll on her. Winn stayed up with the men until the sun graced the sky, and she spent a sleepless night in their bed alone. With her worry over Kyra's arranged marriage, it was probably best she had some time alone with her thoughts.

She pushed her skirts up between her knees with one hand, holding the layers in one fist as she bent to snatch another clam from the pool. Too engrossed in digging out her dinner, she did not hear Winn until he was well up upon her. She let out a squeal as he swept her up off her feet and deposited her firmly on her backside on the rock beside her basket.

"You scoundrel!" she laughed, shoving him back with one hand as he tried to plant a kiss along her low-cut neckline. She had shed her dress on the beach and wore only her old threadbare shift, unwilling to risk salt-stains on any of her better dresses. She had not expected any company when she set out to gather clams.

"I've been looking for you," he chastised her. She leaned back as he bent over her, his eyes darting playfully from her face to her bosom. When he hooked a finger in her loose bodice and plucked it downward, she swatted his hand and squirmed back away from him.

"What has got into you?" she asked, unable to resist his attentions when his warm mouth descended over hers.

"I missed my wife. Is that not enough?" he murmured. She relented a bit, relaxing as he gently lowered her flat against the rock. She closed her eyes and moaned when his lips settled on one nipple, teasing it to a tight peak through the thin cotton fabric of her shift. Her head fell limp to the side, and she felt him gathering her skirts.

"Here, hold this, so I can bury my face in your–"

Her eyes fluttered open, and she let out an indignant squeal.

"Winn! The boys are with you!" she hissed. Dagr and Malcolm were indeed running down the beach toward them, with a full view of their mother sprawled like a harlot beneath their unrepentant father. Winn let out a low snort and shook his head, distracted for only a moment before he bent his head back down.

"They will see we are busy and go away," he reasoned, his voice edged with boyish petulance as he stared down hungrily at her. "Now, put your heels on my shoulders, woman, and let me service you," he grinned. She bit back her own laughter as she squeezed her knees together, eliciting a frustrated groan from him. He rested his head against her belly for a moment, then uttered a sigh.

"Boys!" he shouted. His words were somewhat muffled, being his mouth was still half-buried in her skirts, but they heard him and came to attention at the sound of their father's voice. Twelve-year-old Dagr was the image of Winn, his expression shielded with both respect and curiosity as he faced his father. Malcolm stared openly at them, his blue eyes wide across his round little face.

"Yes, Da?" both boys echoed in unison. Winn sat up slightly and cast a stern glare at them.

"I have an important duty for you," Winn said. The boys nodded eagerly, their attention seeming entirely on their father rather than the spectacle of their disheveled mother, for which she was grateful. "In the woods where the trail splits there is a nest. I think I saw a few goose eggs. Gather them for our dinner," he ordered.

"Yes, Da!" the boys answered, taking off in a sprint back toward the wood line. As Maggie watched them race away, Winn resumed his attempt to emancipate her from her dress. She swallowed hard as his hand ran up her bare thigh, squeezing and molding until his fingers splayed beneath her buttocks. Clearly pleased with himself for the clever distraction, he grinned up at her.

"I think I lost my way," he murmured. His lips found the correct spot, however, and he sucked gently in an experimental manner as she let loose a moan.

"You've found it," she answered. She felt his lips turn into a smile against her flesh as he attended to his task, and soon she was sent into a shuddering oblivion under his touch. Weak and wordless, he took everything from her, every bit of pride and shame that threatened to darken the bond between them. In the end she felt nothing but need, but wanting, the grasp of fulfillment as it swallowed them whole.

Afterward he shed his braies and carried her into the water, beyond the shallow pool to a deeper spot next to the tall rocks. There he made no apology when he held her and joined their bodies, seeking his own primal release as he buried his longing in her flesh. When he had need for her, he made it known, and she felt the meaning in his touch that he would not convey in words. She often felt lost in his world, but this joining, this bridging, this was the thing she could give him. She could help him breech that pass, reach that moment, where only their flesh needed to speak as they sought completion in each other.

Remnants of afternoon skittered away, leaving a glimmer of amber-kissed echoes across the water. She pressed her lips to his chest, over the shallow scar that marked him, and he clutched her so close it took effort to draw in a breath. One of his hands held her bottom, her legs still wrapped around his hips beneath the water, and he whispered sweet words in his native tongue against her ear.

"Da! We found the eggs! Shall we cook 'em?"

She nestled her head into his shoulder as Winn muttered an oath. Dagr and Malcolm stood a few feet away on the beach, their arms filled with large pale eggs.

"Put them in the basket, we will tend to them. Go find wood for the fire," Winn answered. She felt him sigh.

"They did what you told them," she smiled.

"Yes, they did," he replied. He slowly parted their bodies, and her shift swirled like white ink in the water around them. "But I saw no eggs, I know not where they found them."

Maggie giggled, smacking him lightly on the arm.

"So you sent our sons on a wild goose chase?" she asked. He shrugged.

"I thought it would occupy them longer." He caught her hand and raised it to his lips, kissing it solidly. "I would do much more than lie to have you to myself, *ntehem*," he whispered. His eyes still shimmered with boyish charm, but she glimpsed a shadow of darkness in his gaze before he dropped her hand and pulled his damp braies back on. He left her to chase the boys down the beach, making terrible whooping sounds to urge them on.

She twisted as much water as she could from her sodden shift, and then pulled her brown gunna dress over it. She was not a fan of such brazen displays in front of her children, despite Winn insisting that children saw no shame in nakedness. Living with the Norse, however, lent to a blending of cultures, so it was only in the privacy of their own home that the topic arose. Despite her attempts to meld into her life, she had an inkling that some issues would always be a struggle.

Malcolm made it back to the fire before the others. He plopped down into her lap without invitation, his narrow little chest rising and falling as rapid as a bird as he recovered from the run. He was a wiry sandpiper in her arms, covered in grit and damp with seawater. Even his hair was saturated, and when she kissed the top of his head she could taste the salt in his locks.

"You need a bath when we return," she murmured. She stoked the fire with a long stick and gripped him with the other hand as he squirmed.

"Aww, no Mama, not today!" he whined.

"Yes, today, if your mother says so," Winn interrupted. He deflected a blow from Dagr and grabbed his elder son around the waist, throwing him up over one shoulder as the boy screeched. "And you, too, mud-face. You stink like sons of a bull, not the sons of a Chief."

Malcolm scrambled from Maggie's lap and joined his brother. The boys took turns poking the eggs with a stick as they cooked over the fire next to the clams. Dagr crouched down, his long black hair falling tangled around his face, his lean arms extended out as he wrangled the crackling fire. Malcolm stood next to him, watching, always the shadow to his older brother's sun. Both boys resembled Winn, and in Dagr the resemblance was most stunning, but Malcolm held a bit of what Maggie recalled of her grandfather. Even with his sun-kissed skin tone and dark hair, young Malcolm had the squared jaw and straight nose that marked him as Norse, different from that of his father and brother. His hair tended to curly rather than straight, and when damp it wrapped around his ears in ringlets. Despite their looks, in essence the boys belonged solely to Winn; whether from sheer admiration of their father or the image of their shared mannerisms, they clearly came from his blood. Norse or Indian, it did not matter, only that it was the same blood he passed from his ancestors onto them.

Winn settled down next to Maggie, sprawling out beside her on the sand as he perched on one elbow. She felt the warmth of his skin as his hand slid over her thigh, resting there as if she needed any other reminder that he was with her. Her lips formed a smile as she felt him gently squeeze her leg.

They took the meal amidst gleeful conversation, the boys filled with stories from the gathering of the night prior. Dagr was most impressed with the weapons the English men had, the strength of their firepower seeming to have left a lasting impact on the boy. He chattered on about it, his admiration flowing over in an excitable jumble. Malcolm, however, was not so impressed, pointing out that Winn's *bryntroll* could fell a man as easily as a musket, and with no need for the fire-powder that the English required to make the guns work. As their bellies filled, the boys soon fell silent, resting on their backs as they stared up at the stars.

"Our daughter seems pleased with John Basse," Winn said. Maggie shrugged, unwilling to agree entirely.

"She didn't say much," she replied.

"She did not object," Winn persisted.

Maggie sighed.

"No, she did not. She won't disobey you." It was the most Maggie was willing to concede. Yes, Kyra agreed to the match and had spent much of the evening on the arm of her betrothed, but Maggie worried with the way Kyra acted so subdued. She knew she had difficulty accepting an arranged marriage simply because of the way she had been brought up in the future. It was all she could do to keep her opinions to herself, especially when she knew it was what was best for their future. After all, arranged marriage was the norm in the seventeenth century. Having a say in those matters as a woman was not.

"We should go back," Winn commented. Maggie could hear an easy snore from Malcolm, curled up beside his brother.

"All right," Maggie replied. Although she had enjoyed the quiet afternoon away from the village, it was late, and the others might worry if they did not return soon. A war party searching for the Chief's family was the last thing they needed.

They left Malcolm sleeping while they gathered their few supplies. Winn surveyed the site with a nod, and then bent and gathered his youngest son in his arms. Maggie reached for Dagr's hand but the boy slipped away, as he often did, his lips graced with an apologetic, but stern smile. Dagr had told her earlier in the week that he was too old to hold her hand any longer, and she grimaced at the memory but let him go without a fight.

"Da?" Dagr asked. The boy trailed behind, dragging a long stick with the empty clamshells tied to it.

"Hmm?"

"Do ye think ye ought to stop trying to make more weans with Mama? We have enough to bide," Dagr said. If Maggie had not heard it with her own ears, she would not have believed the words from his mouth, but at the sight of her eldest son's serious face she clamped her mouth tightly closed. Winn raised an eyebrow, slowing to meet Dagr's pace.

Dagr planted his heels shoulder width apart in the sand as Winn placed a hand on his shoulder.

"Is that so, Dagr?" Winn replied evenly. Dagr glared past Winn, refusing to meet his gaze, his chest heaving with short bursts as he seemed to fight some demon unknown. She had never seen her son so agitated, but Winn seemed to know what ailed him. Winn gently set the sleeping Malcolm in her arms and whispered softly against her ear.

"Go on ahead, *ntehem*. We will not be long."

He kissed her cheek, a grin on his lips, and patted her bottom as she walked away. She tried to give Dagr a smile, but the boy refused to acknowledge her gesture. Maggie heard Dagr utter one of the half-snort, half-grunts that the Indian men were known to make and she knew Winn had his work cut out for him. She left them on the path and made her way back to their Longhouse.

Malcolm was snoring soundly in his cot when Winn finally slipped beneath the furs beside her. She nestled back against her husband, her hips fitting into him as he molded his warm body to hers.

"Dagr?" she inquired. She did not know what to ask, or if she even wanted to know what sort of conversation they had, but her curiosity won the better of her as Winn kissed the nape of her neck.

"He had many questions. I think I answered them all," Winn replied with a chuckle.

"About what?"

"Oh, it seems he saw Ahi Kekeleksu with an Indian girl. They wandered away from the gathering, and the boys watched them. Dagr had...questions."

"Was Mal with him?" Maggie hissed. She groaned when her husband nodded.

"He and a few others. It seems I should speak to my nephew as well," Winn muttered.

"Mal is too young to–to know about that yet! And so is Dagr, for that matter!"

"Shh," Winn admonished her, covering her lips with his mouth. "Dagr is still awake, and he will hear you. Do not shame him, he is old enough to speak of it."

"So what did you tell him?" she asked, trying to control her tone enough so that only Winn could hear her. He kissed the tip of her nose.

"I told him when he is a man, he will want to lay with a woman as well," he replied. "And that he will find great pleasure in that task."

"You make it sound like a game," she replied. He took his head in his hands and stared down into her face, shaking his head.

"No, I did not. I told him someday he will want only one maid, and until then," he whispered, "I told him to keep his little prick in his braies and forget about pleasuring woman. And that if I wish to make children with his mother, I will do so, and it is none of his concern."

He stifled her laughter with his mouth.

"I think we need more practice," he grinned.

18

Kyra

SHE AVOIDED MORGAN for the remainder of the week, her heart broken and battered after the gathering. It was easy to adjust her hunting times rather than risk running into him again. After all, how could they go back to their normal routine when he had rejected her so horribly? Although she missed his company, she was sure it was better for them both. Even if Morgan suddenly declared his love for her, she was betrothed and there was nothing she could do to change it.

So when he sank down beside her in the tall grass one day as if nothing had happened between them she was near startled into silence. Nearly, but not quite.

"What are ye doing here?" she demanded.

He grimaced, avoiding meeting her stare as he adjusted his bow.

"Hunting. What are ye doing?"

"Hunting," she whispered with a scowl.

After that they resumed their afternoon outings, neither speaking of the day at the waterfall nor making any acknowledgement that anything might be different between them. Things gradually resembled the easy way they had with each other, talking about everything... and nothing at all. It was not perfect, but they continued to spend each afternoon together.

It was a day like any other when they sat crouched over in the tall grass, the soft cattails brushing her skin with the rhythm of the afternoon breeze. The meadow was a clever spot for tracking prey in the early spring as the reeds were still short yet tinted to a yellowed hue, hiding them well as they lay in wait. As she shared a sip from his flask, she wondered if she had the courage to follow through with her marriage and berated herself for the doubt. Of course she would do it. She must obey her father.

Yet as Morgan glanced over at her with his soft brown eyes, gleaming with a gentle curiosity, she felt the heat rise unbidden to her face. They had not spoken of that day at the waterfall. They continued on with their afternoon hunting escapades as if it had been only a dream.

Across the meadow, a spotted doe looked up. Her wide eyes turned in their direction and her tiny snout lifted, as if she caught their scent as they stalked her. Kyra adjusted her bow before she moved from her crouch, notching the arrow and drawing back the string. With a practiced motion she rose up on one knee and let go, the arrow spearing the air ahead of the soft twang sound.

She lowered her eyes as the doe skittered away, unharmed.

"That was terrible. Have ye webbed fingers today?" Morgan laughed.

"Not likely, ye bloody lout."

"Then what are ye afraid of?" he asked, his hand settling next to her as he tilted his head in wait. It was her chest that felt like a bowstring then, plucked tight and tensed to burst. His face was entirely too close to hers, his breath teasing her skin with a presence that was not entirely unpleasant.

"Fear? I think not," she scoffed. She spoke the words bravely to hide her discomfort, but he knew her better than that and she watched his mouth twist into a grin. She drew back away from him but did not go far, unwilling to diminish his amusement. It made her happy to see him smile.

"No?" he murmured, his fingers brushing her cheek. His touch sent a flurry of tingles through her skin, down through her chest where it settled as an ache deep in her belly. Yet it did not seem like her belly that ached. It was another spot, an entirely foreign sensation she had only glimpsed once before in his arms.

"Yer barmy, if ye think I fear anything," she whispered, her voice trailing off. His lips curled into a grin. "If I recall correctly, ye were the one who was afraid to kiss me." She instantly regretted her words, her heart thudding so hard against her chest she thought surely he could hear it.

"'Twas not fear," he muttered.

"Then what?" she whispered. Before she belonged to another, she needed to know *why*. After all the years she had loved him, why could he not love her in return? Yet still he hunted at her side each day, meeting her in secret despite what her father would do to them if they were discovered.

"There are things ye dinna understand," he said.

"Because I have no sense?" she asked, defensive when she thought he meant to insult her.

"No!" he sighed, rolling onto his back. He ran his hands over his face and through his thick blonde hair. "Ye are clever and pleasing in every way."

Utterly confused, she leaned over him, placing one palm flat on his chest. Her fingers rested between his opened shirt buttons, and he sucked in a breath at the shock of the connection. *Yes, she would be married, and yes, she would do her duty, but she would ask one last thing of her oldest friend before that happened.*

"Morgan?" she said softly. "Would you kiss me again?"

His breathing slowed and he stilled. Her eyes moved slowly from his chest to his face, which seemed scrunched as if he were in pain.

"Please?" she murmured, intent on wiping the pained look off his face.

"Kyra," he whispered, his voice strained.

She parted her lips and pressed her mouth to his, letting out a sigh as she quickly pulled away. *There.* It did not seem nearly as intense as their last encounter but it was not so bad.

"Was that proper?" she asked. His pained look remained, yet intensified, his cheeks flushed as he looked at her.

"No," he murmured. "I fear I must show you the proper way."

With a swift motion he placed her gently on her back and his mouth descended upon hers. This time it was his fingers tangled in her hair, and his hand cupping her jaw very carefully. His opened lips were soft, yet she yielded to the pressure, his tongue meeting hers in a delicious torture. His thumb caressed her throat, and he pulled her closer so that her body fit snugly within his embrace.

"Oh," she sighed, her head tipping back as she lost herself in the delicious sensation. *So that was it.* That was what she had been missing since their time at the waterfall!

His lips trailed over her cheek, to her jaw, and then down her neck, closing over the spot where her pulse throbbed just below her ear. She felt his fingers brush her throat and she let out a sigh, unsure of how he made her feel but eager for more. Suddenly, he broke their connection and pulled away with a low uttered curse.

"Did I do it wrong?" she asked, breathless. He shook his head, but the pained look on his face was worse than before.

"No, you did it quite well," he said, his voice hoarse. "We canna do this. I shall go."

She felt her stomach drop. Had she been truly awful?

"But why? I–"

"Because kissing ye like this makes me want ye more."

"Then kiss me again," she insisted. Her heart raced and her pulse pounded in her ears when he looked at her, filled to bursting with knowing he wanted her. It seemed she had waited her entire life and it could only be him. She resolved to see it through. *Let me be with the man I love,* she thought, *before I must wed a stranger.*

"No. Ye know not what game you play, nor how it will end. Yer too young to..."

His voice trailed off as she plucked at the binding of her kirtle, and heard him gasp as it fell open. She shrugged off one shoulder, then the other, and inched closer to him so that their skin collided.

"I'm not too young. You know I'm not.""

"Kyra, please…this is madness."

"But you've done this before, haven't you?"

He closed his eyes and his words were shallow through tight lips.

"Yes, I have."

"Then you will show me," she whispered.

"Do you truly know what this means?" he answered. She nodded. She knew what she was doing, she was certain. If she were meant to be a wife to an Englishman, then she would do her duty, but she would at least have a notion of what it meant to be with one she loved. She did love him, after all, the flustered man who held her. It was him she thought of when her father proclaimed her betrothal, and when the Chief announced it was John Basse she would wed she thought her heart would be torn from her chest.

They lay together afterward side by side, hands entwined, staring up at the willow leaves above them. She worried he was angry, but she did not regret it. She would never regret a moment of their stolen time, even when she became a wife to another.

"They're making me wed John Basse."

"What?"

"I have no choice. My father arranged it."

He rolled over and covered her body with his, leaning on his upper arms as he looked down at her.

"I will speak to yer Da. Do ye think I would let ye marry another, after this?"

"After this? But you would let me marry him if ye hadn't swived me, wouldn't ye? So what is the matter of it?"

"You think that's all ye are to me?"

"You didn't want to do this. I made you."

His eyes narrowed.

"Ye *made* me? I think not," he said.

"You didn't want to."

"I have always wanted ye, ye wee besom! Have I not met ye here, every day I could steal away, even knowing yer father would kill me if he found out?"

"We've been friends forever," she whispered.

"Aye, friends. And now ye'll be my wife."

"But what about John Basse?"

"I'll not let ye marry another. Ye could be with child—my child—did ye ever think of that?"

She paled. *No, she had not considered that notion.*

"My father will kill you," she whispered.

"Aye," he agreed with a sigh. "He will."

***

When the village was in view she made to run toward it, frustrated tears blurring her vision, but he pulled her back into the sanctuary of trees. He kissed her hard as if he meant to possess her, then softer as he brushed away her tears. She twisted her fingers in his hair, holding him close when he tried to draw back. Panting, he rested his forehead to hers.

"Go inside. I will follow to speak with yer father," he murmured.

"Today? Ye mean today?" she whispered, glancing off toward the Northern Hall.

"It must be today," he insisted.

"I will wait for ye."

"No, go to yer mother. I must speak to yer Da alone."

She stepped back away from him, and although their hands were still entwined she avoided his gaze. The depth of what they had done felt like a weight across her chest, and she prayed her father would not hurt him when he found out. Chief Winn was not known for being a subdued man, and in fact, when it came to his family he behaved like a rogue. One simply did not argue with her father; once his will was declared, it was done.

"Ye do not need to do this," she said softly. His round brown eyes narrowed into slits as he squinted down at her.

"I canna let ye wed another when I've taken yer maidenhead."

She felt the confusion rise again, that sliver of doubt.

"So it is only because of that ye'd ask for my hand? If that is yer only concern, then consider yerself free. I willna speak of it. I'll marry John

Basse and pretend it never happened," she whispered, turning her back to him. She heard him chuckle softly and she was not at all pleased. His hands fell onto her shoulders, gripping her gently as he spoke close to her ear.

"D'ye think a man would not know, lass? For a woman who knows it all, ye know too little," he teased. She swung around.

"I know ye wouldna stopped my marriage if not for today," she snapped. He frowned.

"I would have if I had known! Ye should have told me!"

"Ye dinna seem interested!"

"I was! I am! For the love of Jesus, woman, why do ye think I return here to meet ye, when I know yer father would see me dead? It's not to shoot rabbits, that's fer sure!" he shot back, letting out an exasperated sigh.

"So ye pretended to be my friend?" she hissed. He threw his hands up in the air.

"If I came to ye as a man wishing to bed ye, I'm damned. If I came to ye as a friend, I'm surely damned. What answer would ye have of me, ye thorny hellcat? What, then?" he bellowed.

"Ugh!" she screamed, her voice echoing shrill through the woods. He lurched forward and clamped a hand over her mouth.

"Are ye daft? We'll be seen, and then yer father will never give me his ear!"

"Well, what would you have my ear for, Englishman?"

Kyra felt her blood drain to her toes as her father and uncle stepped into view. Uncle Chetan wore a smirk, but her father was not amused in the least. He looked quite murderous, in fact, and by the way Morgan swallowed hard she could see he noted it as well.

"My daughter. Unhand her," Winn ordered in a clipped tone. Morgan dropped his hand.

"Da," she said. He scowled at her and uttered a half-hiss, half-grunt condemnation, so she clamped her mouth shut. She was sure her cheeks must have been scarlet.

"I thought I told you to stay away from my village, boy," her father said.

Morgan ignored the question and stepped forward, pushing Kyra slightly behind him. Uncle Chetan tried to hide his amusement as he placed a hand on Winn's shoulder.

"Do not kill him now. Wait until after the meal, brother," Chetan advised. Kyra shot him a seething glare over Morgan's shoulder.

"I-I would ask for yer daughter's hand. I wish to wed her, without delay," Morgan said bravely. She felt her heart soften a bit with his words. Perhaps he did care for her, after all.

"Oh? Why so quickly?" Winn asked through gritted teeth. Kyra closed her eyes. Surely he would not tell her father. He would not...would he?

"Because she is no longer a maid, and I would not forsake her."

She was suddenly shoved out of the way when her father reached for Morgan's throat. Uncle Chetan tried to pull him off, but it was no use. Winn pinned him up against a tree and lifted him onto his toes as he gasped for air.

"Da!" she screamed, scrambling to grab his arm.

"I'll kill you!" Winn shouted. "She's betrothed, you bloody fool! And you!" he hollered, turning on her. "Have you no sense?"

"Oh, great Odin!" she snapped, rolling her eyes as the men struggled. She was thoroughly tired of men questioning her intelligence.

"Odin will not help you, Kyra! Go to your mother, I'll speak to you later," he ordered.

Morgan shoved Winn, surprising them all as Winn took a step backward. Although his face paled, Morgan grabbed Winn's collar and shoved his face close to her father's.

"Ye'll keep yer hands to yerself, ye hotheaded fool!" Morgan shouted. Winn's eyes flared wide. She felt her heart skip as her father drew his knife and put the blade to Morgan's neck.

"Please," she pleaded, grabbing Chetan by his tunic when Winn ignored her. "Stop them!"

Winn let go of Morgan before Chetan could intervene. Morgan staggered backward against the tree but recovered quickly, standing up straight to face her father. Winn's chest heaved, his eyes narrowed on Morgan.

"Leave. Never return here."

Winn turned to Kyra, grabbing her by the upper arm. She bit back the hot tears as he hauled her back toward the village.

"I love her. I will marry her."

Abruptly her father stopped, shaking his head. She tried to twist her arm away but he was not yet ready to let her go. Morgan stood defiantly in Winn's path, refusing to retreat when Winn approached.

"Ye do?" she asked.

"I do. I've always loved ye," Morgan replied. She ignored the chuckle from her uncle.

"I didn't know –" she said.

"How could ye not? Dinna I tell ye as much when we –"

"Enough!" Winn roared. "Must I kill you to stop hearing this?"

"You cannot kill him, brother," Chetan interrupted. Kyra thought he winked at her, but she was not certain. "He once saved your life, do you not recall?"

Kyra winced when Winn released her. He placed his hands on his hips, pacing away a few feet before he glared at the three of them. Chetan motioned at Morgan to follow.

"Come with us. My brother may want to kill you later," her uncle quipped.

19

Winn

WHEN JOHN BASSE ARRIVED unannounced, Chetan offered to help Winn look for the wayward Kyra. At the time, he believed his brother only meant to help, yet as Winn sat staring at Morgan White, he suspected Chetan knew what they would find all along.

He glared at Young Morgan across the expanse of the long table. Yes, as a child Morgan had delivered a message to save Winn's life, but Chetan was surely mistaken if he believed that fact might keep Winn from gutting the man. With every moment that passed, his desire to throttle Morgan grew, and it took all his willpower to stay in his seat.

Kyra sat next to her mother, her gaze focused on the far end of the table where Morgan sat with Keke. He noticed Maggie elbow their daughter, and the way their heads tilted together as they shared whispers between them. His fury only flared more knowing his wife had no issue with what Kyra had done.

Seated to his left was John Basse, who did not seem at all displeased with the lack of attention Kyra graced him with. If Winn had not been so blinded by anger he would have questioned both the unannounced visit and John Basse's disinterest in his daughter. Chetan, however, was the most jovial of the group, chuckling with Eric and making sure to include John Basse in their discussion as Winn sulked at the head of the table.

"I thank ye fer this meal, friend. I regret the short visit, but there is much I need to discuss with ye," John commented as he shoved a piece of meat in his mouth.

"My home is yours, as you know," Winn replied. "The husband of my daughter is always welcome at my table."

Chetan snorted and took a gulp of ale as he smiled.

"Ah, well, yes, of course. The reason I trouble ye today is –"

Winn dropped his tankard and jumped to his feet, his chair slamming over onto the floor as he rose. In the few moments his attention turned to John, Kyra had left the table.

His vision blurred crimson as he went after her. *He should have killed Morgan on sight.* And his daughter? She needed to be inside, at least making the pretense that she liked the company of her suitor. How could she behave in such a manner, when there was so much at stake? It cut him to know his daughter had so little care for her people. They *needed* the alliance with the English to survive.

"Get back inside. You'll take my seat next to your betrothed," Winn barked as he approached his daughter. She stood with her arms crossed over her chest, her dark hair trailing back off her face in the evening breeze. He did not care for the way she glared at him, unaccustomed to defiant behavior from her. Yes, she had always been strong willed, owed entirely to her obstinate mother, but this was much worse.

"I will not. And I shall not marry him. Ye canna make me!" she shot back. Her lip quivered but she held her ground, even when Winn came closer.

"Yes, I can," he growled. "*I will.*"

She shook her head.

"I love Morgan!"

"It matters not! You will do your duty!" he bellowed. He heard Maggie approach but he shrugged her hand away, too focused on the defiant young woman in front of him.

"Winn –"

"Leave us, wife," he snapped.

"Ah, a word, if ye please, Winn."

He turned at the sound of John's voice. His daughter's betrothed stood nervously next to Maggie, and Winn immediately regretted his rash display of anger. Kyra's cheeks blared bright pink, her blue eyes so like his own reflecting every bit of her fury. John cleared his throat, scraping a finger around the collar of his shirt as if he could not find words for what he meant to convey.

"Well, have at it," Winn replied. He knew his voice was curt, but considering the circumstance, he thought John might forgive him.

"I beg yer leave; I must confess why I called upon ye. I ask release from thy marriage contract. I know we signed on this matter some years ago and I do not intend to change our terms, but if ye would grant me this consideration..."

Winn did not hear most of what was said after he realized John was breaking his vow. He watched Maggie go to Kyra, and the way Kyra smiled in relief. Chetan negotiated with John, and in the end their alliance survived and John was free to marry another. They would move to Basse's Choice as planned, regardless of the lack of marriage bond.

After John gave his regrets and left, Winn looked for Kyra. She stood with Maggie, arms entwined, silent as she waited for him to act.

"Chetan," Winn said, his voice low. "Show Morgan back to town. If he tries to return here, kill him."

Winn ignored the gasp from his women. He turned away from them and went back into the Northern Hall.

***

Winn did not return to his longhouse until morning. When he looked in on Kyra, he was not shocked to find her pallet empty and her horse missing. Considering the events of the previous day, he decided to set out alone to retrieve her, unwilling to ask for help when he knew it was his anger that drove his daughter away.

If there was remorse in his heart, he did not know. Yet despite his sheer frustration at the woman his daughter had become, he would not allow her to wander into trouble.

For her flight, he blamed himself.

For keeping the truth from her so that she did not truly understand the dangers in town? That was his burden to bear as well.

Winn did not know where to find Morgan White, and he did not wish to waste time. When he arrived in town he went directly to the tavern, confident that Benjamin would know where to find the young Englishman. Although Elizabeth City had expanded since his last visit, the tavern was easy to find. All he had to do was follow the trail of soused men to the door.

The stares were easy to ignore. With a purposeful gait he made his way to the back, his eyes scanning the establishment for a glimpse of his brother. To his dismay, there was no sign of Benjamin, nor of anyone else he recognized. The only attendant was a comely serving wench, tending the place alone. Disgusted with his poor fortune, he left to resume his search.

As he entered the alley behind the tavern, he felt a presence behind him. The footsteps were hesitant, likely a slight man, and whoever followed him made no attempt to tread quietly. Without turning, he drew his knife.

"I have no quarrel with you, stranger," Winn said slowly. "And I have no time for trouble. Be on your way and I shall be on mine."

"Yer searching for the girl, are ye not?"

His swift movement startled the woman, for in the span of a moment he swung around and snatched her by the arm. It was the wench from the tavern. She cried out when he slammed her up against the wall, her head hitting the wood with an audible thump. Her eyes glistened but she did not cry, her mass of dark hair shielding most of her face as she glared at him.

"Unhand me!" she hissed.

"Where is she?" he demanded, ignoring her request. He squeezed her arm and shook her, thrusting his face close to hers. "Tell me!"

"I will! Why de think I followed ye, if not to help? She was asking questions inside and he saw her. Agnarr knows what she is – they're riding to Wakehill now. Ye can catch them if ye ride hard."

Winn loosened his grip but did not allow her to flee.

"And you? You know what she is as well?" he asked. Although he did not relish the thought of harming her, he would not let her live if she was in league with Agnarr Sturlsson. He did not understand her duplicity, but it was even more of a reason to cut her throat with little remorse.

"I – I...yes. I do know what she is," she said softly, her face losing color as he raised his knife.

"Your loyalty leaves room for question, my lady," he murmured. "Why should I not kill you now, since you betray your own kind?"

He saw her throat constrict as she swallowed.

"Agnarr's not my kind, and I am loyal to my husband. It was he who asked me to watch fer ye, ye ungrateful cur!" she shot back. She lowered her tone a notch when he pressed his knife into her neck. "Benjamin said he will not let him harm her. My husband will keep his word."

Winn released her, his breathing slowed. So his brother had taken a wife amongst his enemies? There seemed no bounds to his treachery.

"Benjamin may be your husband, but that will not save you if we meet again. Pray no harm comes to the girl. Yours will be the first heart I cut out if she is damaged."

She slumped back against the wall as he left her. He would spare no accomplice of Agnarr's should harm come to his daughter. Not Benjamin, nor his wife.

20

Benjamin

WHEN HE NOTICED HER enter the tavern, the breath left his chest in a rush. It had been years since he saw her, a headstrong girl with her mother's temper and her father's dark hair. Yet there was no doubt that the young woman before him was his niece, grown into a stunning beauty who captured the attention of every man in the room. In another time and place, Benjamin might have been proud to call her kin, but at that moment, he had a dangerous problem.

Not only did she have the notice of every eye in the tavern, but that of his benefactor as well. Agnarr studied her, surveying her from head to toe, until suddenly a glimpse of recognition surged across his face.

"She reminds me of a lady I once knew," he murmured.

"Oh?" Benjamin replied. The glass he held in his hand cracked in his fist and he dropped it discreetly into the barrel of rubbish behind the bar. He wiped the blood away with a flannel cloth.

He was helpless to warn Kyra. Unless he was prepared to kill Agnarr in front of a tavern full of Englishmen, which he was not, there was little he could do. He watched, his chest tight, as Agnarr spoke with Kyra and invited her to sit. Too far away to hear their conversation, he decided offering her a drink would not arouse suspicion.

"Who is she?" Jora asked. Benjamin glanced at his wife. Her mood was difficult to discern, be it jealousy or curiosity he did not know.

"I know not."

Jora looked at Kyra, then back at Benjamin. "Ye lie," she said simply. She grabbed two cups of ale and stalked toward the table where Agnarr sat with Kyra, destroying his means to hear what was said. He felt his face flush with anger, yet he could not fault her. There were too many secrets and lies between them for anything less than mistrust.

As Jora bent and placed the cup in front of Kyra, she made a purposeful movement to touch the girl's hand. Agnarr's eyes narrowed and he made a sharp retort to Jora, and Jora quickly finished serving them.

When she returned to his side, he could see she was shaking. As Agnarr left the table and made his way toward them Benjamin realized there was no time for deceit.

"She is a Blooded *MacMhaolian*. If a savage comes looking for her, ye must help him," he whispered briskly.

"But where did she come from?" Jora demanded.

"I will tell ye when there is time. For now, ye must promise ye will do as I ask."

"Benjamin, ye must meet my young friend," Agnarr declared, approaching the bar with Kyra's hand tucked under his arm. Benjamin saw Jora silently nod and he released his breath in a sigh. *At least he could count on her.*

Agnarr looked like a smug cat, proud of the mouse within his paws, and Kyra appeared anything but reserved. Her eyes widened in recognition when she met Benjamin's gaze.

"Oh, I know –"

Benjamin quickly cut her off.

"Pleased to make yer acquaintance, mistress," he said with a nod. "What brings ye here on this fine day? Surely I've ne'er seen ye in town before?"

His warning seemed to resonate with Kyra. Her smile faded.

"Why, no, of course not. I only traveled here in search of a friend, and then I shall be on my way."

"I promise we shall locate yer friend, my dear. There is no person I lose sight of in this town, man or woman alike, I assure ye," Agnarr offered. "Will ye ride with us, Benjamin? I am sure it willna take long to locate her friend."

"A ride?" Benjamin asked, bile rising in his throat.

"Yes. What, my dear, did ye say was yer family name?" Agnarr hummed, his surly voice little more than a contented purr.

"Oh, it is –"

"Of course," Benjamin interrupted. "A ride. Right away. Shall we?" He took a chance by offering his arm, but he was relieved when Kyra took it and Agnarr did not seem to object.

One of the King's men engaged Agnarr as they left the tavern, and it was all the opportunity Benjamin needed. He hurried Kyra out the door.

"Doona tell him yer name, nor where ye live. Say ye are from Jamestown, or anything ye like," he ordered. "Ye do not know me, and ye know nothing Norse. If ye were not grown, I'd tan yer hide fer coming here!" he added, frustrated with the girl for her foolishness. "Dinna I tell ye never to return here? Let me guess, yer searching for Morgan White? I'll kill him myself if this ends badly!"

"Why must all ye men wish to kill each other? First my father, now ye! I'm going to marry Morgan, and all of ye can stop yer yammering!" she hissed in reply.

"If yer dead, ye'll marry no man, will ye? Now quiet yerself and do as I say until I figure out how to get ye gone!"

Benjamin lifted Kyra onto her mount as Agnarr joined them with a handful of his men trailing behind.

Dusk settled over the horizon as they set off toward Wakehill. Agnarr continued to make casual conversation with Kyra, but Benjamin was reassured to hear her divert his questions. It was not long before he was jarred from his thoughts by the sound of a rider approaching.

He heard the men whisper as Winn met their party.

"*A savage,*" they said.

Winn did not meet his gaze, his attention focused only on Kyra. When he seemed satisfied that she was well, he addressed Agnarr.

Although they had never met, it was clear who was in charge, and Winn was not the sort of man to waste time with anyone else.

"I thank you for your kind escort, but I shall ride with my daughter now," Winn said, his voice unwavering. It was impolite not to introduce oneself, and Benjamin could nearly see the questions spinning in Agnarr's mind.

The Norseman's eyes narrowed, his lips pursed as he considered the savage making demands at his side. Winn leveled his gaze in return, refusing to give Agnarr notice he might be swayed.

"May I ask yer name, friend, before I release the lady? Surely ye understand I must consider...her safety," Agnarr replied.

"*Winkeohkwet*, of the Paspahegh people."

Benjamin hid his grin. *Yes, Winn was a clever one.* It was a name without ties, one Sturlsson could not track. If he looked for those that remained of the Paspahegh people, he would surely be disappointed.

"He is my father, sir, and my only kin. I thank ye as well for yer kindness. 'Tis my luck to have met ye today," Kyra interjected. She moved her horse to her father's side.

"My pleasure, mistress," Agnarr murmured. "How fortunate yer kin has recovered ye. I shall pray we meet again. Forever your servant."

Winn did not wait as Agnarr gave a tight bow to Kyra. Instead, he urged his mount into a gallop and Kyra followed behind. Benjamin finally let go of his tension, assured that his niece would be safe.

With a flick of his wrist to one of his men, Agnarr pointed at the departing riders.

"Follow them," he said.

***

As Agnarr continued on his way to Wakehill, Benjamin left him with the claim of returning to the tavern. He immediately doubled back, and although it was dark and he was unskilled at tracking, it was not too difficult to find the way.

He needed to find the scout. If the man found the village, all would be lost.

Moonlight lit the sky, shimmering down upon the sandy path. Shadows plummeted around him as he rode, taunting him with memories of what once had been, and the promises he had made long ago.

He saw Marcus as he lay dying, demanding an oath from his sons. Despite the years, the sound of his voice was clear, ringing through Benjamin as if his father still stood before him.

"The power of time travel must remain our secret, and ye are sworn to protect it. Put aside yer quarrels, for the good of your people. I left my family, and all those I loved, to see it safe. Do not make it for nothing. Keep them close, see that they live on. I was born to protect them, and so are ye. I ask ye both, as my sons, to make it so."

The memory was fresh as he came upon his brother in the woods. Kyra, still astride her horse, was waiting by the edge of the tree line that opened to the meadow, silently watching her father. She was an eerie outline in the light of the moon, her dark hair streaming back off her face with the cool night breeze. In the middle of the path before her Winn crouched down, pulling his knife from the body of the tracker sent to find them.

As Benjamin stopped, Winn wiped his blade off on the dead man's jacket. The hilt of the knife flashed in the glare of the moon, and Benjamin could clearly see the rune engraved on the end.

It was the knife their father used to seal their bond. Brother to brother, blood to blood. They made a promise, and as Winn stood up and stared back at him, Benjamin knew it was only the beginning. They exchanged no words before Winn left.

He watched them ride away, safe for another day.

21

Maggie

THEY GATHERED THE SICK into the Northern Hall. When the fever affected only a few, they cared for them in their homes, but when the number of those sick became greater than those who were healthy, the only way to care for them was by having them all in one place.

Maggie did not know what ailed them. At first she suspected it was a simple flu, with the fever and body aches that accompanied a virus. Yet soon she realized it was a more serious illness. It spread rapidly, claiming the life of an elderly woman as the first victim. Several children deteriorated, and she feared there was nothing they could do to stop it. They received word the Nansemond people suffered as well, pointing to some contagion likely spread during the gathering.

"How does he fare?" Winn asked. She wiped the sweat from Dagr's brow. Her son smiled in thanks but did not open his eyes.

"The same," she said quietly. "Have you seen Kyra?"

Winn shook his head and his jaw tightened. She sighed. Kyra and Winn had not spoken since they returned from town. Kyra avoided her father at every turn, taking her meals alone in the longhouse and settling down to sleep before Winn finished his duties with the men. Winn did not seem eager to fix the situation, making no effort to mend things with his daughter as the days wore on. With so many sick in the village, Maggie knew it was not a priority, but she could not help but wish her husband and daughter would resolve things.

"I sent a rider to Basse's Choice. We cannot go until all of our people are well again."

"I know. We'd just make more people sick," she murmured. She placed a hand on Winn's lower back and was surprised to feel him tense. When Morgan entered the Northern Hall, she understood why. Morgan searched the hall, obviously looking for someone, and Maggie bit her lip when his gaze settled on Winn. With the tension still fresh between them, she hoped Morgan had more sense than to confront Winn.

"Come quick, it's Kyra. I canna rouse her," Morgan stammered.

She lay quiet on her pallet when they arrived, her skin dappled with sweat and colored a sickly shade of grey. Her breathing was shallow, her pulse rapid. Maggie clutched her daughter's hand, as helpless to do anything as she had been long ago when Kyra was stung by a bee. All of her future knowledge meant nothing, all of her magic blood meant nothing. Those she loved were suffering, and there was not a blessed thing she could do to stop it.

Winn sat down beside her. He brushed the damp hair from Kyra's face and kissed her softly on her forehead. The regret was etched into his eyes, his anguish reflected back at her.

"What is this? What can we do?" he said, his voice hoarse.

"I think it's an infection. I don't know for sure," she replied.

She stood up abruptly as the solution occurred to her. No, she could not go back to change the past, but was there any reason she could not go to the future to save them all?

At home on the farm in the future she came from, she had a cabinet of medicine. It was full of bulk bottles, with several different types of antibiotics one might use for sick animals. As far as she knew, the medicine would work the same for people. Bactrim was Bactrim, wasn't it?

"Winn," she said. "I have an idea."

***

Maggie intended to go, but Winn would not allow it. As she watched Erich paint the runes on Winn's arms, Gwen reminded her she could not go to a time she once lived. It was impossible for Maggie to use the Bloodstone; it must be Winn. Reality did not ease her mind, nor did it sway her husband's resolve. Presented with a way to save his children, Winn could not turn away.

Erich explained to Winn how to return, and how the order of the runes on his skin would take him to the place he meant to go. The only belonging she still possessed from the future was her wristwatch, and she gladly surrendered it to her husband to guide his way.

"But how can we be sure he'll return to us?" Maggie asked her uncle. Erich's face clouded at the question.

"The runes will help point the way, and yer bracelet will steer him there. But to return here, to this time, he needs one of these," he said, taking one of the figurines from the mantle. It was a turtle, with a rune engraved on the shell.

"Can't we give him this one to take?"

"No. It will keep him tied here, or confuse the magic. He must find one in the future. It is the only way."

"What if it's not there waiting for him?" she demanded.

"I buried a few in a place only Marcus knows. Marcus must have looked fer them, there's no o'er way he could have 'em in yer future time. If he gave ye the raven, and gave Benjamin the eagle, then I suspect he must have looked for the others I buried as well."

It made her head ache to think of it. She knew in the future she had her raven, and she suspected Marcus had other figurines as well, yet she could not be sure. If Winn did not have a figurine to return, he might not come back to them – or worse yet, he might go somewhere else.

Yet he made his decision and there was nothing Maggie could say to sway him. With the strength of his purpose bending her into submission, she tended the task of preparing him for the future. She thought it was best that he make an attempt to blend in, and it was only with Erich's persuasion that Winn allowed her to shear his hair. If Winn should find himself lost in the future or worse yet, go too far ahead, she feared he might run into trouble if he appeared too out of place.

She did not expect the simple preparations to bother her. Yet standing over her husband with his fresh shorn hair in her fist was the strike that sent reality crashing home.

Although she bit down on her lip, he still heard her sigh. He turned his chin slightly as he placed his hand over hers where she braced it on his shoulder.

"Do you know," he said softly, "that our history was written even before you were born?"

She swallowed back the rush of despair that gripped her as she shook her head. Not trusting herself to speak, she clenched her fingers into the thick of his shoulder.

"Before you took your first breath, I had already loved you for all my life." He turned on the stool to face her, his hands slipping around her waist as he gazed up at her.

They kneeled down together on the fur by the hearth, neither speaking lest the words make it all too real. They had only a few stolen moments before he must go. Maggie knew he might not return to her, but she pushed that painful truth to that dark place deep inside where it could not hurt them yet. As she peeled the clothes from his body, she took him in with hungry eyes. Each inch of his skin, every crease. Every sculpted muscle covered by taut flesh. She knew his body as she knew her own, but she felt the need to score each part of him into her memory to ensure he would always be hers.

He removed her dress, and she suspected he was thinking the same as she, except that Winn needed the touch, the feel of her. It was one way he communicated when he could not speak the words of his heart. Ever the warrior, he fought against despair, but when he traced his fingertips over her face, she knew what he could not say.

As his hands trailed down her neck and then her shoulder, she shivered and moved closer to him. If she touched him now, she feared she would lose her last grip on reality, but at the same time she could not stop from reaching for him. She placed her palm flat over his heart, over the puckered scar where he had once been shot. The wound was shallow and long healed, the skin smooth yet tough. She could feel his hand twist into the hair at the base of her neck as she dipped her lips to his warm skin. The salty tang of his sweat seared her tongue as she licked him, and she heard him moan when she bit gently on his nipple. *This was her husband, her man.* He uttered a guttural cry when she bent down and closed her mouth over him, wanting every bit of him to keep selfishly to herself. She wrapped her hands around his buttocks and surrendered to him, loving the way he cradled her head as she brought him to the edge.

"Stop," he whispered, his voice hoarse. She obeyed him, panting as she rested her head against his belly. He pulled her down onto the furs beside the fire. The flames danced across his skin as he rose above her, giving him an amber shimmer in the flickering glow.

"Please," she said. It was all the invitation he needed. With one swift thrust he joined them, pinning her down beneath his body. He pushed her hands above her head and held them there, their fists clasped together so that their flesh melded that much closer. She felt his lips on her shoulder where he would often curl into her, but this time his teeth bit down as he plunged. The pain was brief, but it was possession he meant to convey and she yielded to it. If ever in their lives they fought, it was this that made them whole again, the act that bound their lifeblood as one.

"Mine," he growled. *"You are mine!"*

Frantic and needful, they clung together through the shuddering release, their breaths coming in near unison as they collapsed. She slowly lowered her arms around her neck, feeling bruised from the restraint, yet cherished. He tried to lift his weight away, but she held him tighter.

"Stay here. Please. Don't go," she whispered. He sighed with a shake of his head. She felt him shudder as he wrapped his arms tighter around her. Her words were a simple request, yet they both knew beneath simmered so much more.

"You must listen to me," he said quietly. Every muscle in her body tensed. She knew what he was about to say and she did not want to acknowledge it. If they spoke of it, then it meant it could happen.

She could not make that recognition; she felt like she was giving up if she did.

"Please, Winn. I'll be waiting for you. That's all we need to say."

"No. You will listen!" he said, his voice rising an octave and his blue eyes gleaming. She swallowed, and he closed his eyes. "I ask you to listen."

"All right," she whispered.

"Erich will protect you and the children. Chetan will watch over you as well. You will move into town and join with the Nansemond and English at Basse's Choice."

"But Winn–"

"It is the only way to keep you all safe. I cannot take on this task without knowing you, and our children are safe. Promise me you will abide. Give me your word."

"You must come back to me," she whispered.

"Time is nothing to us," he said, kissing her tear-stained cheeks. "For all that I am, I am nothing but yours. Every moment of every day. In this life and all others. I will not let you walk alone, *ntehem*. I will find you again."

She took his hand and placed it over her heart. As their breathing moved in unison, he laid his cheek against her, his arms surrounding her in an unbreakable hold. When he clutched her close, she bit back her denial, knowing it was time to let him go.

Maggie helped him dress, knowing it might be the last time she ever completed that task. He handed her his knife and her hand shook as she slit his palm, but the blood flowed quick in response.

With his eyes fastened on hers, he closed his hand around his Bloodstone and faded into nothingness.

22

Winn

He closed his eyes for a moment to steady himself before he entered the house. With the knowledge that Maggie would soon be taken by the Bloodstone, he knew he had precious little time to speak to Marcus. If Winn did not get what he needed before that happened, he doubted Marcus would be willing to listen to anything he had to say.

His father sat at a small table, his head bent down over a book. He seemed to be scribbling in it with some sort of quill, one without a feather or ink. A heaviness surged through him, squeezing his chest as he watched his father.

As Winn pushed open the door, Marcus did not glance up.

"Change yer mind? Good. We can worry over the barn another day," Marcus said.

Winn cleared his throat.

"Marcus," Winn said, not entirely sure how to start the conversation. Marcus lifted his eyes and dropped his pen. He surveyed Winn, much as Maggie had done. Winn could see some sort of denial, and then recognition change his features, and Marcus stood slowly up from his chair.

Winn had never seen him without a full beard. His father seemed younger, and if Winn was correct on the date, Marcus was a few years younger than they day they met. He wore a snug black shirt with short, tight sleeves, similar to what Maggie wore, and a pair of blue trousers that looked terribly uncomfortable. Marcus backed up against the cabinet before he spoke.

"Who are ye?" Marcus asked, his voice betraying no hint of welcome.

"Sent by Erich," Winn replied evenly.

"Oh, aye? I know no Erich. Perhaps ye are mistaken, lad. I think ye found the wrong house."

Winn saw Marcus move his arm, but he could not see what his father was doing. Winn suspected Marcus was grabbing a weapon. Winn knew he had to diffuse the situation before it escalated into a brawl.

Without hesitation, Winn dropped to one knee in front of Marcus, holding both his hands out in front of him. He thrust his palms upward and bowed his head to his father, knowing his father could see the fresh Bloodstone scar branded into his hand.

"Chief Dagr, your First Man Erich sent me here. I give you my word, as your servant, that I bear you no ill-will. I have come for your help in a grave matter."

"Why should I believe ye, Time Walker? I know ye not. What tribe do ye hail from?" Marcus growled. Winn kept his head bowed, praying that Marcus would not lop it off before he could explain.

"From your own tribe. The Clan of the Neilsson Chief Protector of the blooded *MacMhaolian*."

Marcus grabbed Winn by his neck and jerked him to his feet. Winn winced when his father threw him up against the cabinet and thrust a knife to his throat.

"Now I know ye lie, as all my kin are long dead! And ye, an Indian? Yet a Time Walker? What game do ye play, and what do ye know of my Clan?"

"I know if you kill me, Maggie's daughter will die," Winn ground out through his narrowed airway.

Marcus loosened his grip, only slightly, but enough for Winn to speak without his throat being compressed. His father's suspicious gaze wavered and his slate-colored eyes widened.

"Speak," Marcus ordered.

"Maggie's daughter is sick. She needs medicine, Maggie says it is called *antibiotic*. She says it is the only way to cure her fever. If you don't believe me, take me to your storage closet, I will prove it to you. She told me you keep it there."

Marcus remained silent, but lowered the knife and stepped back. He pointed to a door next to a series of waist-high cabinets. Winn walked slowly past him, keeping eye contact lest his father try to kill him.

Winn opened the door and struggled to recall Maggie's description of the jars. She called them bottles but explained they looked like white jars, and that there would be six of them stacked next to each other on the third shelf from the top. He scanned the contents of the closet, his eyes nearly blurred with the assortment of brightly colored boxes inside, and when he spotted the white bottles he let out a sigh of relief.

"Here," Winn said, picking up one white bottle. "She said you had these for the horses, but that they would work for people. Are these the ones for fever?"

His father's face had paled considerably. Marcus dropped the knife onto the table and put a hand on the edge as if to steady himself.

"Take them all. Whatever ye need, take it," Marcus whispered. Winn dropped all of the white bottles into his satchel. He had satisfied two of the tasks he set out to do, and with that knowledge the panic ebbed slowly away. His last task was to return safely to his family, and for that he needed one more thing from his father.

"I need something to return. Erich said you had something of his that you would give me," Winn said quietly, keeping his eyes averted. It was too difficult to look at his father, standing before him. Although Marcus was confused and worried, he was still blessedly strong and alive. Winn ached with the memory of the short time they had to know each other, wishing with the longing of a youthful heart that he had known his father as Maggie had.

"Ye say yer from my Clan, that I am yer Chief. Then I must have returned to the past. What is it that will make me risk taking Maggie back there? I can think of nothing that would make me risk her life that way," Marcus asked.

Winn was aware that his actions in this time would not change the past he meant to return to, but the loop of time travel magic was an uncertain thing. He did not know if it was wise to share many details of the truth with Marcus, or what impact it might have to do so.

"You did not bring her back. It was an accident, and you returned for her," Winn said.

"We must be friends, then, if I sent ye on such a journey."

"You did not send me. I made the decision, and Maggie and Erich aided me."

Marcus crossed his arms over his chest, his brown furrowed sharply downward.

"But ye said...oh, aye. I see. So I will die in the past, as I always thought I would," Marcus murmured. "Tell me one more thing, then I'll ask ye no more. Is Maggie happy...and safe?"

Winn nodded. "I would give my life for her. And for our children."

Marcus startled at that, his eyes widening as his mouth fell open. Winn thought he had said too much, and he regretted to cause his father any distress. Perhaps the knowledge would help his father, in the future time he was in, somehow.

"She is my wife, and our children are sick. Many of our people are dying," Winn said.

Marcus took in that information, his mouth closing in a tight line. He ran his hand through his hair as Winn had often seen him do, and then leaned over onto the table with both hands sprawled out. Winn was shocked to watch him sit down hard in a chair with a long sigh.

"Then by my blood vow, I should stop her from leaving. When does it happen, and how can I stop it?" Marcus asked, running his hands over his tired face.

Winn froze. If Maggie did not return, she would never belong to him. They would never have their children and never share a life together. So many things would be changed. Opechancanough would be dead from poison. Winn would have remained in the Paspahegh village, never knowing what he missed. And Winn would have never met his father. Yes, there were things any man looks back upon with a wish for another outcome, yet despite the ache in his heart for those he had lost, still, Winn knew the power of time travel was not meant to change the story history had already written.

No, Marcus could not change what was done. Winn did not know how this future would affect anything, but he felt strongly it was not up to him to alter it. As he stood before his father, Winn's head ached with the implications of his actions, and he knew with every ounce of his being that this was the reason the blooded *MacMhaolian* must be protected. It was too dangerous a magic for any man to wield.

"No," Winn choked. "You must change nothing. You, of all men, should know that. I made you a vow that I would protect her, that I would protect all the Blooded Ones with my last breath. She will return to my time, and I will serve her with my life. You will follow her. It is what is meant to be."

"Who are you?" Marcus whispered. Winn stared into his father's face.

"I am Chief Winn Neilsson, Chief Protector of the blooded *MacMhaolian*. Husband to Maggie and father to our children. Brother to Benjamin," Winn replied. "And first born son to Pale Feather of the Paspahegh people, our Great Chief Dagr."

Marcus turned grey as Winn spoke, and although his father braced his hands on the table, Winn could see him shaking.

"I made a blood vow to you, and now I honor that pledge. We swore an oath to protect this magic so that it would not be used by selfish men. Help me return to my time now. Erich told me to ask you–he said you would give me a token so that I may return," Winn said. He tried to keep his voice from wavering. It was difficult to see his father so distressed, especially since there had been such little time they spent together.

"All right. Wait here," Marcus said, his voice strained. He left the room but returned quickly, his fist closed around something small and a book tucked under his arm. Winn wondered what object Erich had in mind, and when Marcus held it out to him he nearly gasped.

The crafted grey metal was worn smooth in places, but Winn could easily see the detail of the bear figurine in his father's hand. It stood upright, arms extended, as if it were the same bear he had fought for Maggie so long ago.

"I have few things left to tie me to them. Take it. And this, as well," Marcus said, holding out a dagger. It was the Chieftain's dagger with the Bloodstone mark on the hilt. Marcus had used it on his deathbed to draw blood from his two sons and seal their vows. It was the same dagger Winn now had strapped to his waist.

Winn drew his own blade, and both men looked down upon them.

"No, father. Keep your knife. You will have use for it yet," Winn answered.

Marcus did not seem startled at that confession, merely setting his knife down flat on the table. He then turned and lifted something from the surface of the tall cabinet, holding it out to Winn. It was a tiny painting, yet, it was *not* a painting. Young Maggie was in the middle of the portrait, flanked on one side by a much younger Marcus, and on the other, a man Winn did not recognize. He clutched the image in his hand and it flexed, then bounced back into place.

"It's in a plastic sleeve. Keeps it protected," Marcus said.

The second man in the miniature had bright green eyes, like Maggie, and his face was round with a pleasant grin. Between his brows were two furrows from age or laughter, and creasing his chin was a deep dimple splitting it in two. With that consideration, Winn suspected the identity of the second man.

"Erich looks much like old Malcolm," Winn murmured.

"Aye," Marcus said softly. "He was a good man. Maggie misses him something fierce. Take it, put it in yer sack. This book, as well. But hold the bear in yer hand when ye go, it will help point ye back. It helps, I think, to send ye where ye belong. My mother once said so, but I don't know for sure."

"Thank you," Winn said.

They clasped forearms for a long moment. Winn did not want to let him go, but thoughts of his duty reminded him of his task.

Winn let him go, and left the house. As he stepped into the yard and looked toward the barn he could see Maggie holding something heavy in the bottom half of her cloak, which she had pulled up like a make-shift sack. He felt that pulling sensation his chest, that ache to return to his family, and with a smile he drew his knife. Bright red blood welled up immediately when he sliced his palm, but before he grasped his Bloodstone, he turned to Marcus.

"When we meet again, tell me time is short. Tell me there is no time to waste in anger over old wounds. Tell me that until I listen to you, father."

23

Maggie

DAGR RECOVERED, as most of the stronger young men seemed to do. Some, however, still lingered between light and dark, wavering in the decision to live or die. Maggie thanked all the Gods she knew for the blessing of her son's health, yet at the same time she wanted to curse them for Kyra's decline. As the days went by and she watched her daughter succumb, the ache in her heart was replaced by despair.

She promised Winn she would go on. She would not fail him.

She needed to think of it in a sensible manner, as Winn might do. It was one of the things she admired in him, his way of deciding on a course of action and then his determination to see it through. In previous times she lost her composure when faced with adversity, and she was the first one to admit it. Her future life had not prepared her for the challenges she faced in the seventeenth century, but as time wore on, she realized she could change, too.

The fact remained that Winn had not returned.

He might never return.

Yet she needed to help Kyra, so it was with that pledge she granted Finola leave to perform the ancient ritual.

"Bring her into the woods," Finola demanded.

Morgan carried Kyra, cradling her limp body against his chest. He followed the old woman, and Maggie could see he still did not trust their Norse magic. Although Morgan knew what Kyra was and why she was special to them all, he told her he agreed to the ceremony for one reason, and that was because he loved her daughter, nothing more.

It was enough, and Maggie was grateful for his help. Finola insisted only those closest to Kyra could attend her during the ritual. When she saw the long sickle-shaped knife Finola brandished, Maggie thought she would agree to anything the old woman asked.

A waxing crescent moon graced the sky above, casting a mystic glow upon the grove of trees. Covered in a white robe that dragged behind her on the ground, Finola appeared somehow younger, her face softer in the glow of moonlight. The old magic woman pointed above to the boughs of a great oak, where the tendrils of a mistletoe twined through the tree. She handed Malcolm the sickle, which he fastened to his belt. Malcolm shed his grey cloak, and after he placed it gently on his sister, he began his climb up the tree.

"Careful," she whispered, watching him climb. He was strong for a youth of seven, agile enough to scale the golden oak yet still skilled enough to grab the mistletoe with one hand. Maggie gasped when he wrapped his legs around a branch and used them to steady himself.

As Malcolm cut the mistletoe away, he let it fall from his hands. It caught the breeze as it descended, gently drifting down until Finola could catch it with her white cloak.

"Will she wake after this?" Morgan asked.

"Yes," she replied, at loss to believe in any other certainty.

Maggie placed a hand on her hip as she took a moment to gather her thoughts. Morgan leaned over and ran his hands through his thick blond hair, watching Kyra's shallow breaths. The strain was clear on his angled jaw and creased brow. Seeing the way his eyes glazed hollow at Kyra, Maggie was struck by the change in him. He had always been a quiet, pleasant young man. Even as a boy he had been polite and respectful, never one to show too much or too little emotion. He was merely level-headed and true, even the day he rode into the Norse village as a young boy and confronted Marcus. Morgan had saved Winn's life with his errand; it was something Maggie would never forget.

"She'll get better. She will," Maggie said softly. Morgan raised his eyes, and his throat contracted as he swallowed.

"She will. She must," he replied.

Maggie reached for his hand. Unabashed pain was clear in his face as he gripped her hand. One might think it was a weak gesture for a man to make. She thought it only a measure of his love for her daughter, and she was glad for it. Morgan was steady and thoughtful. He was brave when needed, but otherwise he tempered his actions with quiet strength and resolve. Perhaps he was exactly what Kyra needed.

His face shadowed in grief, he looked warily at Finola as she approached. With her clouded eyes suddenly clear, Finola smiled, a rare moment of normalcy from a woman they feared was not sane.

"Of course," Finola replied. She pressed a vine of mistletoe into Maggie's hand and whispered in her ear. "Make a tea with this and have 'er drink. In the morning she will wake, I promise ye."

As the mist settled among the trees, they brought Kyra back to her bed. Maggie had a feeling there was some task left unfinished, as if they had missed something in their quest to tamper with ancient magic. When a figure appeared before her through the fog it became clear, and she flew into Winn's waiting arms.

Was it the ritual that would help Kyra, or the magic of future medicine? Neither Maggie nor Winn was willing to choose. Maggie ground up the antibiotics and placed them in the mistletoe tea, which Winn helped their daughter to drink.

Finola spoke true. When the morning sun split the sky, Kyra finally opened her eyes. Yet Finola's eyes closed forever.

24

Makedewa

HE WATCHED FROM above as they buried the old woman. He did not like that they gave her a Christian burial, or that they planted her body near that of his wife.

Rebecca should be free to soar, without the ghost of a Norse witch woman haunting her resting place.

Makedewa drew back on his bow. In his sight was a head full of red hair, a banner streaming down her back as she bowed her head in mourning. When he moved slightly, the dark head of the Chief came into his range, one he could easily pick off by letting go of his arrow.

Why had Winn cut off his hair? No warrior would ever do such a thing.

With a shake of his head, he stood up. *Winn was no warrior.*

He surveyed them for a moment longer, taking in the group of Norsemen he once called kin.

No more. Let them rot.

If they were not Powhatan, then they were nothing. Let them meet the same fate as the English.

PART THREE

25

Kyra

SHE FELT SOMETHING in the bed beside her as she stirred. Opening her eyes took some effort since she been ill for so long, but she was curious to see what shared the space with her.

On top of her quilt was a thick book. It was unlike any book she had ever seen, and granted, there had only been a few. She did not have much use for reading, but she did still keep the fairy tale story her father gave her as a child. It was tucked under her feather pallet, safely away from her brothers who would tease her for girlish foolishness.

She picked it up as she sat up in bed. The motion made her head swim, but she was too curious to lay back down. Running her fingers over the smooth brown cover, she wondered what it was made of. It was not hide or polished wood, nor could it be metal for being so light. The pages were the thinnest of parchment, the lettering crisp upon the page without hint of smudge marks.

When Winn sat down beside her she did not look up, too engrossed in examining the book to give him any mind.

"My father gave this book to me," he said quietly.

"Oh?" she replied. She knew he visited the future. Mama told her as much. She peered curiously at him, wondering if he still was angry. She deserved his anger, for surely she had behaved insolently. If John Basse had not wished to marry the Nansemond maiden, her actions could have put her family in great peril. She realized her selfishness now, her shame rushing to her cheeks at the thought of it.

"Your mother showed me this passage. Here, read this," he said, turning to a page marked with an unusually flat piece of what she assumed was wood. She squinted her eyes and tried to recall her teachings as she read the English words.

"John Basse married ye dafter of ye King of ye Nansemond Nation by name Elizabeth in Holy Baptizm and in Holy Matrimonie ye 14th day of August in ye yeare of Our Blessed Lord 1638 Dyed 1699 A.D."

She raised her brows as she finished the sentence.

"Da, what is this?"

Winn closed the book.

"There is more, for another time," he said softly. She felt tears spring to her eyes as her father took her face in her hands, his gaze cutting through straight to her heart. "I am sorry, daughter. I know not what saved you, be it magic or some God, but I thank them all the same."

"Da," she whispered. She buried her head in his strong shoulder, relief strumming through her like a melody. "I'm so sorry. I though ye hated me, I failed ye so miserably –"

"No," he said, shaking his head. He smiled as he stood up, taking the book from her. "I love ye, daughter of mine."

He turned back to her before he left the room, a sad smile upon his face.

"Your history is in this book. You will marry Morgan White, and I was a fool to try to stop that."

She pulled the quilt to her chin, staring at the door long after he left.

26

Winn

"SOMEDAY," MARCUS SAID, *"ye will leave this place. Ye will know when it is time."*

"Why must I leave, father?" Winn asked. There was scarce respect between them then. Winn did not yet trust his father, nor did he wish to hear his advice. "I was born of this earth, raised in this place. No man can make me leave it."

Marcus shook his head, his blue eyes cast sadly downward.

"No man can make ye leave it. Yet ye will know when it is time to let go."

Winn thought of Marcus often since his journey to the future. Although the memories were few, he cherished them, wishing to hold onto that tiny piece of connection he kept with his father. The sadness of loss held constant in their lives, but the recollections of those they loved could never be erased.

Marcus was right. *It was time to let go.*

He found Maggie in their longhouse. Finola's white cloak lay over a chair by the hearth, the bright white fur a stark reminder of her death. Maggie wanted to bury Finola with it, but Gwen insisted a Norse woman's cloak was meant to be passed on. She claimed it was magical, and after seeing Kyra pulled back from the hands of death, Winn had no doubt. Be it the magic in the medicine he brought from the future, or the hum of an ancient Norse ritual, to Winn it was all the same. The force that saved his daughter was sacred, no matter which God sent that blessing.

"Hey," she said softly. Red hair shrouded her face, her head dipped down over a shirt she was attempting to mend. Winn smiled, taking it gently from her hands despite her objections.

"Did my wife do this? These stitches are fine, indeed," he declared. She snorted, snatching the linen from his hands as she rolled her eyes.

"Hardly. I know it's terrible," she muttered.

"No, it is the truth. I have many shirts for you to fix," he insisted, raising his brow to peer into her lap. She scrunched the shirt into a ball as he traced his finger over the crooked stitches. "Well, I can do it myself I suppose."

"That's not funny, Winn," she shot back. She smiled, however, so Winn knew she was not too angry at him. His laughter dimmed as he shed his tunic, the reminder of his purpose resounding through him.

"What you told me of the future...the *reservations*...," he said, losing his thought for an instant. No matter how many times they discussed it, it was still difficult for him to accept. "You said the Powhatan will be no more, but you know the Nansemond survive. That in your time, Chief Basse leads them."

She nodded. "It is true."

"I know it cannot be changed. It is too late for that. We will leave this village. Our time here will end," he said. "You will travel with the others to Basse's Choice. I shall meet you there when I return."

She immediately objected.

"You can't *leave* – not now, Winn! We need you here –"

"If what you say is true, then no more warriors should die for this war. He never believed it from your lips – but I can tell him what I have seen with my own eyes in the future."

Maggie quieted. She bit down on her lip as she returned his stare.

"It won't matter to him. He won't listen to you. He won't listen to anyone," she said quietly.

"I went to your time, *ntehem*. I walked on Tsenacommacah land. There was no sign of my people – nothing to say we once lived here, that we once were part of this place. All of this that I know," he said, spreading his arms wide, "all of this is gone. As if it never was. No, my uncle may not listen to me. Still, I must try."

His hands fell to his sides. He did not like to speak the truth aloud, as if saying the words somehow made it an unchangeable truth. Maggie did not argue. As much as he often wished she would follow his commands without question, when his wife simply lowered her eyes and nodded it gave him pause.

"I will leave today," he said.

"Go quickly, then, so you will return to me sooner," she whispered.

Who was the woman before him? Downcast gaze, her mouth tightly closed, it was some stranger that handed him his traveling satchel. *Fight*, screamed the voice inside him. *Show me the one I love, the one who will stand down to no man!*

She gave no answer. Her red hair fell across her face, hiding her eyes as she murmured farewell. He should feel triumphant that his wife supported him, proud of her silent acquiescence.

Yet as he rode away his limbs were numb and it seemed there was a hollow thing where his heart should be.

27

Makedewa

PÌMISKODJÌSÌ JABBED a bony elbow into Makedewa's flank. He glared at the warrior. Although Pìmiskodjìsì was a favorite of Opechancanough, Makedewa would tolerate no aggression from the man. Since his arrival in the village, there were frequent attempts to challenge his loyalty; Makedewa met each action with swift response, and this insult would be no different.

"Your traitor brother joins us," Pìmiskodjìsì said, his words coarse in their native tongue. Makedewa followed the direction the warrior noted and was stunned to see Winn surrounded by a crowd of villagers. Soft light from the stars seemed to illuminate him, his blue eyes shining despite the cover of nightfall as he smiled at the women. It was a much better reception than Makedewa had endured on his own return to their uncle's village.

It was always that way. *Beloved Winn. Honorable Winn.*

Makedewa grunted an oath and turned away.

"I have no brother," he snapped. The words were sour on his lips, but he said them anyway.

"Hmpf," Pìmiskodjìsì replied. "We shall see."

The others did not know what wall stood between Makedewa and Winn, but Makedewa felt the distance once more when he met Winn's gaze. He returned his attention to the warmth of the fire, focusing on the flickering flames to dampen the surge of anger in his blood.

"So you guard our uncle now. This is where you lay your head."

Makedewa did not look up at Winn's voice. He noticed the warriors stepped away. Not far, because they tended the fire in front of the Weroance's *yehakin*, but it was enough to give them some semblance of privacy.

"Scurry away, Norseman. They do not care for traitors here," Makedewa muttered. Before Winn could reply, Makedewa left the fire. He stalked off into the woods, unwilling to abide the ache in his heart when he said words to his brother in hatred.

When they were children, Makedewa stole a spear from one of the warriors and hid it in his mother's yehakin. It was not long after Makedewa returned from Henricus, angry at the world and longing to make the pain go away. As a youth of twelve, he had no words to explain what had been done to him there, nor a way to calm the despair of helplessness in his soul. He stole the spear and hid it, intending to leave the village and return to Henricus. Killing the Englishman was the only way.

A furor soon arose over the missing weapon, quickly found in their *yehakin.* Although Makedewa did not speak of it, Winn somehow knew what his young brother endured, and when Winn saw the panic in Makedewa's eyes, he spoke softly to his brother. Winn stood up and claimed the spear, and then his older brother took the punishment in Makedewa's place.

"Worry not," Winn whispered. "I will see no harm come to you. You are my brother. As you will always be."

Now, as a man, seeing his brother stalk toward him with rage in his eyes sent him deep into despair. How had they fallen so far?

"Traitor? Is that what you think of me?" Winn demanded.

Makedewa glared back at him.

"Would a traitor care for your son, take him into his home – protect him as if he were his own?" Winn shouted.

He gritted his jaw, lowering his gaze from Winn's. He did not wish to consider his son. Only in the dark of night did he think on him, when Makedewa watched the Norse village from afar. Then he could think of him, as he caught a glimpse of the boy in Maggie's arms. He could bear no more than that, and the words from Winn's mouth stung him.

"Enough," he whispered, his voice hoarse.

"Would a traitor bury your wife? Would he wrap her in her marriage blanket, would he place her in the ground?"

"Stop it," Makedewa growled.

"You were not there. It should have been you. Instead it was a traitor that buried your wife. And a traitor that cares for your son, even now."

He could take no more. Makedewa lunged at Winn, shoving him back into a tree with the force of his assault. With a roar he pummeled his brother with closed fists, striking the man before him as if his pain might be swallowed whole. It did not help, the truth too much to bear, and slaking his rage on his brother only served to worsen it. He felt the blow to his chest as Winn drove him down and he knew that if Winn truly meant to hurt him, he would be dead.

His chest shuddered as he struggled for air. Winn's hands gripped his face, and Makedewa let his weary forehead rest upon his brother's. Brow to brow they sat there, until their breaths slowed and their tempers faded.

"Your son needs you," Winn said. "Come home."

Makedewa closed his eyes, his answer pained. "My brother will kill me. I would do the same to one who harmed my wife."

"You are my brother," Winn said quietly. "As you will always be. I will see no harm come to you. And I know you will do no harm to my wife."

The pain faded, washing over Makedewa as he nodded to his brother. It was still there, as he knew it always would be. Yet somehow, he thought, he might find the strength to go on, if not in the love of his brother, then the heart of his son.

***

Although Winn slept peacefully that night, Makedewa was restless. His dreams were usually of her, visions of the woman he loved so much. Yet under the glow of the moonlight, Makedewa saw a different vision, once where he held his son in his arms and promised the boy he would never abandon him again.

He heard them before he saw them. A rustle of footsteps beside his head, and then suddenly his vision exploded as he was struck in the temple. As he rolled away he landed on all fours, shaking his head to regain his senses as screams pierced the air around him.

The scent of dirt filled his nostrils, his fingers digging into the damp earth. He scrambled through the ground cover, sliding on wet leaves as he struggled to his feet. Women ran through the village, chased by English soldiers.

They were everywhere.

There were too many of them.

Dozens swarmed the village, firing shots seeming at random into the *yehakins* where villagers lay sleeping. His heart plummeted when he saw them carry Opechancanough from the Great Yehakin, the Weroance guarded by a bevy of Englishmen as they took him away on a litter.

Makedewa turned toward the shouts and froze. A soldier stood a few paces away, musket leveled in aim.

Winn grabbed the man from behind, buried his knife in the back of the Englishman's neck, and then dropped the body to the ground.

"Go!" Winn shouted. Makedewa obeyed his brother, taking off in a run toward the woods.

As he ran he heard a shot and then his legs felt heavy. Suddenly he could no longer direct them. He stumbled to the ground, first to one knee, then to the earth. With his face buried in wet leaves he tried to rise, attempting to make his useless limbs do something other than falter. Perplexed at why his numb body would not obey, he ran his hand over his chest and he knew why.

"No!" Winn shouted. His brother's voice echoed, as if it came from another time. As Winn rolled him over, Makedewa smiled. He took his bloody hand and placed it on his brother's shoulder.

"She calls to me," he whispered.

Makedewa saw her there, in the shimmer of moonlight above the trees. Just as she was on their wedding day, sent from the Great Creator to smile upon him.

"Come to me, husband," she said.

He ran.

28

Maggie

"WILL WE BE THERE for the wedding, Mama?" Kyra asked.

Morgan was out of earshot, busy securing supplies on the cart. A new horse stood harnessed to the contraption, both gifts from John Basse. There had been several offerings from the Englishman after the broken betrothal, and in Winn's absence Maggie tried to decline, but John was insistent. Despite John's distress over the matter, Maggie could not fault him. John was in love with a Nansemond maiden, the beautiful young daughter of a Weroance. She went by the Christian name Elizabeth, one of the first from the Nansemond to convert. Maggie was more than happy to support John, especially when their alliance remained intact and Kyra could have a chance at happiness.

"Yes, we will," Maggie replied. "How does Morgan feel about going?"

"Oh, he has no worry. He knows where my heart rests," she said.

Morgan glanced their way and grinned.

"Have ye two done any work yet? Truly, I will let ye help," he called out.

"Nay. My father says this is man's work. I willna not disobey him," Kyra announced.

"Oh, of course not. You're all about listening to your father," Maggie laughed. She wrapped her arms over her belly and enjoyed the good humor, but it was tapered by the reminder that Winn was still gone.

Intent on doing her duty, Maggie tried to carry on without her husband. It was what he asked of her. If she was useless for all things women should do in that time, at least she could follow her husband's orders.

Seeing everyone safely to Basse's Choice was a task she was going to fulfill, and when Winn returned, he would be pleased to see he could depend on her for *something*. It was a coordinated effort. Erich and Gwen left with a small caravan of villagers two days prior, taking Dagr, who had recovered sufficiently with them, and Malcolm, who had never been ill. Maggie stayed behind with those still recovering from the sickness, only a handful of Norse who were near ready to travel. She was not thrilled with the prospect of staying in a near-empty village, but she knew Chetan and Keke would return soon from helping the Nansemond move.

When Winn returned, they would be settled in their new home near Basse's Choice. Kyra was eager to plan her wedding day celebration, and Maggie was just as anxious for some sort of normalcy. Finally, she believed their struggles neared a conclusion.

"Keke?" Kyra called out. Keke thundered into the yard, jumping off his horse before the beast stopped. He left the animal ground tied as he ran to them, his chest heaving as he tried to speak. Sweat streaked his dark skin, his long hair twisted in a careless knot at his nape.

"They captured him," he panted, leaning over and placing his hands on his knees. He spit into the dusty earth and struggled to recover his breath. "Opechancanough. They took him to Jamestown."

"The others?" Maggie asked, not truly wishing to know the answer.

"Captured. All of them. If *Winkeohkwet* lives, he is with them."

✳✳✳

They argued on what plan to take, with both young men insisting they should go straight to Basse's Choice. Morgan agreed to see her daughter safely there as they had already planned, and since Kyra was not well enough to travel alone it was easy to convince Morgan he must go. There he could alert Erich and the others to what had happened, saving them precious time.

Keke was another matter entirely.

"If he is there, my father will find him," Keke argued.

"How will he do that? Chetan won't get anywhere near Jamestown without being captured himself," Maggie replied. Her nephew was insistent, shaking his head vehemently at her plan, but she knew what was going to happen to the prisoners and she would not be swayed.

"Winn will kill me if I let you go alone," Keke said.

"You can't go near the English, either. We have no choice."

Keke knew few details. Opechcanough led another massive attack on the English, a virtual re-enactment of the 1622 Great Assault where over three hundred English were killed. The shrewd leader coordinated a repeat battle, this time killing more than five hundred English, yet the results were less than desirable. In 1622, a few hundred deaths nearly ended the English colony; years later, the English population had grown to such proportions that the deaths of five hundred made little impact.

Opechcanough risked everything to drive the English away, yet his reign had come to an end. Captured at a village upriver in Pamunkey, the Weroance was transported to Jamestown for trial. It was difficult for Keke to relay the story to her, so she gently reminded him that he need not give her all the details. As his dark eyes softened and he insisted on telling her, it was clear by his adamant tone he needed to speak of it. He knew as well as she did what Opechancanough's capture meant. Perhaps by speaking it aloud, it provided the young warrior some solace.

Keke traveled with her most of the way, however as they drew near to the English settlement, she reminded him he could not go any closer to town. The risk of taking the young brave into Jamestown was too great, even though he was a free man that she would vouch for. She left him in the woods, and as she glanced back, she saw he paced like a trapped wolf.

She sympathized. *It was a feeling she knew well.*

Maggie was allowed through the palisade gates without issue. It had been many years since she visited Jamestown, but still she was struck by the change. Most mud and stud building were replaced with framed dwellings, and there were rows of houses lining a grid work of cobblestone roads. The old church had a new brick tower, standing tall and straight over the English city.

It was the tower she visited as a child, a standard school trip that all third grade Virginians made. Gazing up at it in wonderment then, how could she ever have truly understood what happened? A history lesson was one thing; living it was another matter entirely.

She made her way through the mass of people, patting the outside of her skirt pocket where her knife resided to steady herself. With the uproar over the captured Weroance keeping the English occupied, she had no reason to fear any trouble. Her moment of introspection was fleeting, however, for in the next moment she was shoved into an exceedingly tall Englishman and he grabbed her arm.

"I beg your pardon, sir," she said, slightly out of breath. Her eyes only met the embroidered shoulder of his waistcoat so she glanced upward at him. Her shock was immediate. "What are you doing here? And how did you find me?" she demanded.

"I ask ye the same thing! Yer a flaming banshee with yer hair like that, I saw ye as soon as ye reached the yard!" Benjamin shot back. He shook her by the upper arm and yanked her away from the crowd. "Do ye women have rocks in yer head? How many times must I tell ye to stay away from the towns?"

"I had to come," she tried to explain. He gritted his teeth, shaking his head at her in his distress.

"Every person in the colony is here, Maggie! None will miss the chance to see the Weroance. Find Winn and get ye gone!"

"Winn was with his uncle. I don't know if he's been captured or if he's – if he's dead," Maggie admitted, her words faltering.

"Oh, Jesus!" Benjamin swore. He stalked away a few paces then swung back to her, one hand gripping the butt of a knife at his belt. "There are *hundreds* dead, Maggie. Those who survived are prisoners. All these people are here to see the Great Weroance. I canna get Winn released if he is here."

She swallowed hard, turning her chin up to look him in the eye.

"Then I'll do it myself!" she insisted. "If he's alive, I'll do whatever I have to do!"

"No, ye will *not!*" he bellowed. "I know my brother told ye to stay safe. He would not want ye here. Why do ye MacMillan women ne'er abide?"

"The children are safe at Basse's Choice. I did my duty. I *know* they are safe. That doesn't mean I will abandon Winn."

His jaw was set and it was clear he would not be swayed. She would waste no more time discussing it with him. As she turned to leave, he snatched her hand.

"If yer bound to do this, I'll take ye to the magistrate. If Winn is there, perhaps we can buy his release. Pull up yer cloak o'er yer hair. It shines like a beacon fer all to see, and I am not alone here in town today. "

It was enough of a victory. Benjamin had standing with the English, so it would be foolish to decline his offer of assistance. She followed him through the courtyard, tugging her hood up as she tucked her hair back.

A convenient person to follow in a crowd, Benjamin stood a head taller than most men stand and he was able to navigate easily between the English. Although she was shouldered several times by those seeking a glimpse of the captured Weroance, she found herself mesmerized by the sight before them. It was too warm beneath her cloak, her skin sticky with sweat before they had traveled very far, her scent nothing compared to the stench of hundreds of Englishmen in the town common. Men and women huddled in every spot imaginable, each one endeavoring to see the display.

Even the English children were there to share in the joy. The chants of gleeful rhymes sent shivers through her bones.

"Three blind mice, three blind mice

See how they run, see how they run

They all ran after the farmer's wife,

Who cut off their tails with a carving knife

Did you ever see such a thing in your life

As three blind mice"

A boy with a sash covering his eyes stumbled into her, his outstretched arms hitting her at the waist as she walked through a game of blind man's bluff. The child lifted the edge of the sash and peered up at her with a grin, his missing front teeth reminding her of a malevolent jack-o-lantern. Maggie pushed past the little beast.

Opechcanough was held in a makeshift cell by the church. There was a prison nearby but it held only twelve spaces. From snippets of conversation around her, she realized the prison was full, so a temporary holding area had been constructed to house the captured braves. If Winn were inside, it would be dangerous to retrieve him. She prayed they would find him outside, where she could see a group of warriors held with the old Weroance.

"They treat him like an animal," she whispered to Benjamin.

"He's killed five hundred English this time, I'd expect no less."

"The English are not innocent in this," she snapped. *How dare he defend them!*

He pulled her to a stop, bending his head to her ear.

"I know that verra well. But this is something they never thought to see, and they shall make it a merry event. The Governor takes great pains to show us the threat is over."

He was correct. The English had Opechcanough positioned in a temporary cell, a long two-sided structure with a thatched roof. The weather was warm and his head was protected, so he would not suffer from cold or rain, but she could not help but think of how degrading it must be for the proud man. The construction was meant to put him on display to the English, not for privacy or protection from the elements.

Benjamin shouldered through the crowd until they found the soldiers guarding Opechcanough. Four English soldiers stood watch, with at least a dozen more scattered throughout the courtyard on patrol.

"I believe this lady's servant has been mistakenly detained. If ye please, we would like to look at the prisoners," Benjamin said.

"Oh? And who are ye?" the soldier replied. He was a tow-headed young man, barely out of puberty if she were to guess, his face dotted with the shadow of what might someday be a beard.

"Partner to Master Sturlsson, Inspector for Elizabeth City," Benjamin said.

The soldier's mouth dropped open and he nodded vigorously in a more congenial manner. "Ye can look just like the rest, but ye canna have any man released. Say farewell should ye see him, for he shall be dead soon enough."

Maggie felt the flush rise to her cheeks. Benjamin put a hand on her arm and held her lightly back.

"This lady is an apothecary, and I assure ye she has means to secure her servant's release."

An apothecary? *Fine, she would play along.*

"An apothecary…" the soldier mused. She could nearly see the smoke burning with the intensity of his thoughts. "I will release yer servant, if ye tend a sick man in return," the man said. Benjamin raised a brow in question.

"What sick man?" Benjamin asked.

"The old savage. Ye see, I think he's ailing, and I canna have him die before he stands trial. The Gov'ner willna be pleased, not at all. Mayhap ye have some cure for what ails him? So if yer wench – yer lady – will tend him, I shall let her servant go with ye."

"Fine. I agree," Maggie said quickly. "Take me to him."

Benjamin clamped his mouth shut from what he meant to say and mutely followed them. She was too focused on finding Winn to worry over anything else. As they passed by the barred side of the long holding cell to find the Weroance, her prayers were answered.

Winn sat against the wall in the back, but when he saw her he quickly stood up. She wanted him to come forward so she might touch him, and when he paused, she realized yet again that she let her emotions run rampant. She needed to convince the English that Winn was her servant, and it certainly would not help matters if she reached through the bars and kissed him.

"My servant is here. I have your word you will release him?" Maggie demanded, turning to the soldier. The young man scowled, but nodded curtly.

"Yes. Tell me what ails the old man and what ye may give 'im to fix it, and I shall release yer servant."

She hoped Winn did not hear the exchange, but he stood closer to the bars now and from the tight stare upon his face she determined he had. Pride be damned, he would just have to abide being referred to as her servant. She could explain later. All that mattered was getting him out alive.

Two guards accompanied her, standing with weapons drawn between her and the other captive men. Benjamin stood warily at the door with another guard, resting his hand on his weapon as he watched her.

Opechcanough lay on a pallet away from the others. He was not the man she recalled who had once threatened to shatter her skull with a bloody mallet, nor was he the strong warrior who commanded thousands of Powhatan braves. As he opened his heavy-lidded eyes, she kneeled down beside him and waited. It was all the respect she could give him in that moment.

"Sit, Red Woman," he said gruffly. The Weroance lifted his head, pushing himself up on unsteady arms. As unwell as he appeared, she wondered how he had led the warriors, until she recalled from her history lessons the details of his capture.

He was carried by litter to Jamestown, where he was treated with kindness by the Governor.

The skewed record of history was far from accurate.

"They asked me to see you. Are you wounded?" she replied.

He managed into a sitting position, his dark eyes mere slits across his weathered face under his drooping lids. His hands shook as he placed them in his lap.

"No, they came upon me whilst I slept. My guards cannot say the same, as they are all dead."

She bit down on her lower lip at his display of sadness, a rare emotion for the Weroance to show.

"Is there – is there something I can do to ease you? Some water, or food?" she asked. She was no healer, and for lack of an obvious malady she was uncertain how to help him. "They asked me to see to your comfort."

He uttered a coarse sigh.

"They ask ye to keep me alive, it is."

They both knew it to be true, so she did not attempt to deceive him.

"I can buy Winn's freedom. I will do what I can for the others –"

"Ah, ye know what is to come. Speak no untruth to me."

She glanced at Winn, who stood behind the guards. His eyes were fixed on her, his tension evident.

Opechcanough crooked his fingers and waved her to come closer, so she bent her head to his. The scent of the earth emanated from him, a wholeness that tied him to the place he so loved. It reminded her of the day she met Winn, when she rode with him and slept with her head on his chest.

Evergreens. Sunshine. Life. It belonged to those like him, and no matter what English did, they could never capture that spirit.

"Is it my time, Red Woman?" he asked.

She nodded, fighting the swell of tears.

"Yes. But it will not be by my hand," she said softly. He smiled and reached for her, taking her hand in his. He recalled the prediction made so long ago, just as she did.

"No. Not by this hand," he agreed. She feared to speak, unwilling to break down when she needed to be much stronger than that.

"Tell me, do they speak great stories of me, in your time?"

"Oh, yes," she whispered. "The greatest stories. Legends."

He seemed satisfied with that. Stunned when he straightened his legs and placed them on the floor, she heard the guards behind her react.

Opechcanough stood up, his dark eyes leveled on the one guard who stood between him and gate.

"I wish to speak to your Governor," he announced.

The young soldier shook his head furiously, pointing to the cot the Weroance vacated.

"Ye shall sit back down, savage, nothing more!"

Opechcanough did not falter. He stood up straight, extending his hands slowly from his sides, until he held them spread wide and palms up in apparent surrender.

"If it had been my fortune to take Sir William Berkeley prisoner, I would not have meanly exposed him as a show to my people," he said.

The soldier backed up a pace, then continued to retreat as the old Weroance approached. The cell was not wide and it was only a few steps before Opechcanough was out the door, still advancing on the soldier who screamed at him to stop.

Maggie cried out as she was shoved, bedlam exploding behind her. One of the two men tasked with guarding the warriors landed at her feet with a thud, his neck cocked at an unnatural angle. Another guard screamed from the middle of the cell floor, his shouts swallowed by the triumphant cries of the warriors who subdued him. With her head spinning in panic, she struck out when she felt a hand on her wrist.

It was Benjamin. She tried to pull her hand away as he dragged her from the cell but he would not relent. Screams littered the air, with English scattering in all directions as the soldier ordered Opechcanough to stop.

Unfolding as if she watched an old movie, her blood rushed cold as the soldier aimed his musket. Sounds ceased to be, the silence deafening to her ears while she struggled with Benjamin.

The Weroance shuffled his feet, a cloud of dust billowing up to frame him as if heavenly wings sprouted from his back. The shot struck him in the chest and she cried out as he fell.

"No!" she screamed.

Benjamin held her tight while the crowd surged. Women were trampled as they fell and children screamed in fear as the English ran from the shot. The imprisoned braves erupted in what seemed a single mass from the prison, and as Benjamin deflected panicking people around them, Maggie searched frantically for Winn.

A man struck her hard in the belly and her breath left her lungs in a single whoosh, sending her head to spinning at a time she needed her wits the most. Gasping for air, she clutched Benjamin as he swept her up into his arms. Through tear-filled eyes, she saw Winn, standing a few feet away.

Legs braced apart and bereft of a tunic, the dark skin of his chest was dappled with English blood. Men scurried between them, fighting and falling as screams echoed through the air. Another warrior called his name but he did not answer, his eyes fixed on hers.

"Keep her safe. I will come for her," he said.

Benjamin gripped her tighter, his voice hoarse as he answered his brother.

"I will," Benjamin replied.

Winn turned and left. In only a moment, she could no longer see him through the throng of bodies, his outline disappearing in the crowd.

Benjamin resumed pushing others out of the way until he found a spot they could recover. She wanted to tell him to put her down, to go after Winn. Too numb to speak, she heard Benjamin say something to her that she could not make out.

"Say nothing! I will tell ye who he is when we are alone!"

She shook her head, his words meaning nothing to her. It was then she saw the man who approached them, and she knew her dangerous situation was suddenly worse.

"I know who he is," she said. "He's my father."

29

Benjamin

WHILE HE TRIED to help Maggie secure Winn's release, he knew Agnarr was nearby. Every Englishman in the city wished to get a glimpse of the captured Weroance, and Agnarr was no exception. Although the thought of gawking at the prisoner was distasteful to Benjamin, he decided to accompany Agnarr on the trip that day, hoping he might hear word of what happened to the other tribes. No Englishman would know the name of a single savage, but if there were any news he could gather of Makedewa's whereabouts, he would consider it a trip not wasted.

When he spotted Maggie in the crowd he presumed he was not the only one who noticed her. The way she carried herself, the confidence in her gait – she was unlike any other. No good Englishwoman would push men aside and glare at them as if she meant to throttle them. Yes, the mane of bright red hair streaming down her back immediately captured the attention of others, but it was her manner that kept one captivated, and he was no exception. No, Agnarr would see her in the crowd, and since Maggie ended up squarely in the middle of chaos, it did not take him long to spot her.

He watched Agnarr stare at Maggie as if the man had suddenly noticed the sunshine above. Once before, Kyra stood in front of Agnarr, and Benjamin was sure the man recognized his own granddaughter. Yet Agnarr never made mention of the girl again after the scout was found dead, leaving Benjamin to believe Agnarr accepted the notion she was the simple half-English daughter of a Paspahegh man. Kyra favored Winn with her dark hair and tanned complexion. Maggie, however, was said to look just like her dead mother.

Benjamin recalled his father speaking of how striking Maggie's mother, Esa, had been, and how Maggie was her mirror image. The way Marcus spoke of Esa made Benjamin wonder of his father's true feelings for the woman. He could hardly blame Marcus if he harbored a love for Esa; wanting a woman he could not have was something Benjamin understood quite well.

They managed to weave through the crowd and make their way to the port, where a small dual masted schooner was docked waiting for them. It was the vessel they used for most of their business on the river, an efficient means of travel when they wished to avoid the deplorable roadway conditions.

Benjamin hesitated. He did not wish to bring Maggie aboard, but no polite Englishman would allow a woman to stay unaccompanied in Jamestown. At best, he would look like a cad if he sent her on her way; at worst, Agnarr would suspect Benjamin knew exactly who Maggie was.

"'Tis fortunate Benjamin secured your safety, my dear. Nasty business, with those savages escaping. Ye might have been injured."

"Yes, I know. He has been most helpful," Maggie agreed. She stared at Agnarr for a long moment. Benjamin feared her reaction if they did not speak privately soon. With Winn on the run and her being separated from her children, Benjamin doubted his brother's wife could maintain a calm façade for very long.

"Yer speech, it is quite odd. I mean no insult, be assured. May I ask where ye hail from?" Agnarr asked. "And how ye might know Master Dixon?"

"I – I was born here. In Jamestown," Maggie stammered. "I don't know Benjamin, he was only kind enough to assist me."

As the ship sailed smoothly toward Wakehill, Agnarr plucked his white gloves from his hands. Finger by finger, in the methodical manner he so enjoyed, he removed the gloves and set them aside. He pressed his hand lightly beneath his chin as he considered her, his green eyes narrowed.

"Reinn?" he called. Benjamin scowled as Reinn left the bow to join Agnarr. Reinn disliked his secondary status since Benjamin's arrival, so if ever Agnarr requested his presence the man was more than happy to oblige.

"So, my dear," Agnarr said slowly. "Tell me again, how ye know Master Dixon."

With that demand, Agnarr backhanded a crushing blow across Maggie's face, his assault sending her to the ground at his feet. As Benjamin leapt at Agnarr, Reinn and two others grabbed him from behind. Something solid struck him in the head, sending a blur of darkness through his vision, and he felt the sting of a heavy boot as he was kicked in the ribs.

He must stay awake. Agnarr knew her. He knew the truth.

He spit a stream of blood onto the deck as they held him down, his head hanging low as he tried to stand. Maggie writhed on the floor beside him, letting out a muffled cry as Reinn kicked her once more.

"Stop it," he demanded, as loudly as he could with a mouth full of blood. "Leave her."

Agnarr kneeled down on one knee in front of Benjamin. Benjamin had no strength to aid his partner when the man tucked his hand under Benjamin's chin. Agnarr lifted his head until he could look Benjamin straight in his swollen eyes.

"Tell me, then, friend," Agnarr said. "Who is she?"

Benjamin had no other hope. The words spilled out.

"She is my wife," he said.

Agnarr grinned. He nodded and the two men dropped Benjamin face down to the deck. As Agnarr walked away, Benjamin reached for Maggie.

He caught the tips of her fingertips in his hand. She did not stir. For that, he was most grateful.

***

Benjamin watched as Reinn carried Maggie up the wide staircase. A serving woman brought Benjamin a wet cloth, which he used to wipe the caked blood from his mouth and nose. Although he was not bound he had no illusions as to his status. With several armed men standing by, Benjamin knew he was just as much a prisoner as Maggie was.

"You said she was dead," Agnarr commented.

"I said my wife was lost in the massacre," Benjamin replied. Possibilities surged through his mind, any number of stories he might concoct to save them both. Without the guise of Agnarr's trust, Benjamin had no power – and no means to save the woman he vowed to protect so long ago.

Agnarr poured two glasses of dark malmsey wine, handing one to Benjamin.

"Where are her kin?"

Benjamin took a gulp of the wine, meeting Agnarr's gaze over the rim of the glass.

"Dead in the massacre of 'twenty-two. As I thought she was," he said quietly. *Give him his answers. Satisfy his curiosity*, Benjamin thought. *Gain his trust again if we ever are to escape.*

"You know what she is."

Benjamin nodded. "She is like us."

"No, not quite. She is much more than that," Agnarr said. "The blood in her veins is unlike yours or mine. Her mother was a *MacMhaolain*..."

Agnarr set his glass carefully on his desk.

"...and she is my daughter. I canna thank ye enough for bringing her to me."

Benjamin forced a grin to his lips. There was little else for him to do.

30

Maggie

ALTHOUGH HER HEAD THROBBED with each breath she took, she banged the window latch with the heel of her hand until the diamond-shaped quarrel sprung open. Once she stuck her head through the narrow opening, she could see the bedroom was on the second floor. There was no eve to crawl onto, and the fall was a steep one. Her only option was the door she arrived by.

As she sat down on the edge of the thick tufted bed to consider her options, the door opened and Benjamin stepped inside. With his dark hair curled wildly around his neck and his face littered with bruises, she had little faith he was any better off than she.

Maggie opened her mouth to question him when she thought better of it. His eyes held an unspoken warning, his stance tense as he held his hand out to her.

"Agnarr would like ye to join him downstairs, my lady," he said.

"I don't think I am up to that," she whispered, utterly confused. She noted the shadow by the door. *So Benjamin had company outside, someone he did not trust.*

"Here." He took a cloth from his waistcoat, and she eyed him warily as he wiped her face. "Are ye all right?" he said softly.

She nodded. "Yes."

"Better now," he murmured.

It felt strange to let him touch her in such an intimate manner. Yes, they had once been married, a time that was little more than a

213

sad memory to her. Nevertheless, there was something more to his actions, some reason for his behavior, and she suspected it had to do with her father.

Her father. Never had she called a man father. Even knowing he lived, the word was foreign to her. She had no father. There was only the man who sired her, who used her mother like cattle as a means to his own end.

She placed her hand in the crook of Benjamin's elbow and accompanied him downstairs. Despite the circumstance, she took in the extravagance around them. Leaded-glazed windows with wrought iron casements graced the walls, giving the plantation home a generous supply of natural light. Light-buff clay tiles surrounded the large fireplace, decorated with delicate blue motifs of varying design. The furniture was exotic for the colony, with a long carved mahogany table placed in the center of the room.

Agnarr sat at the head of the table, standing up when he noted her arrival. As he made a gracious effort to assist her with her chair, she shuddered. She could still feel the sting of his blow to her jaw.

They were right, she thought. *Winn, Erich, and Gwen. They knew what her father was all along.*

"I took the liberty of securing yer Bloodstone, my dear," Agnarr said. He leaned forward in his seat, her pendant dangling from his upheld hand. She shrugged. Didn't he know he could not use it? A Bloodstone could be used only by the one it bonded to. It was matched to the brand on her palm, and like it or not, it belonged to her alone.

"Keep it. It will do you no good," she replied. She took a swig of the red wine in her goblet, hoping it would calm her racing heart. Seeming to ignore her comment, she watched as he bent his head and used a quill to draw on a piece of thin parchment. Quite engrossed with his endeavor, he flicked a hand impatiently at the serving girl when she tried to refill his glass. Finally, he tucked a wayward piece of blond hair behind his ear and smiled triumphantly.

"This rune," he announced, handing her the parchment, "will take ye to my time. The time ye should have been born to."

She wanted to tear it to shreds.

"I won't help you. This is my time. This is where I'm meant to be," she said. Although her heart still pounded in her ears, her voice was steady.

"Ye will help me, I promise ye," he replied. "Jora, my dearest. Please, sit. It seems we have much to discuss."

Agnarr and Benjamin stood when a striking woman joined them. Her russet hair fell about her shoulders, her figure so petite that her silk gown brushed the floor when she swayed. Benjamin took care to help her sit, touching her shoulder gently before he resumed his seat.

"Jora, this is Maggie. My daughter," Agnarr said, his voice childishly musical. "And most unfortunately, she is also Benjamin's wife. His first wife."

The smile faded from Jora's face. She pushed her chair back and stood so quickly that her wine spilled across the table, her mouth agape as she rushed to the stairs. Benjamin cast a heated glare at Agnarr and then followed Jora. The sounds of their argument echoed from above even after Maggie heard a door slam.

"I'm not his wife!" Maggie hissed. "And who is she? Why did you try to hurt her so?"

"Benjamin says ye are his wife, so his marriage to Jora is not valid. One man cannot have two wives, my dear. Surely that has not changed in the time ye come from?"

She refused to be baited by games. She wanted to know what her father meant to do with her – and with Benjamin.

"What do you want with me?" she asked. She lowered her voice, trying to steady herself. Her ribs tightened, her breath shallow as she looked at him.

The man in front of her was her father by blood. *What should she call the father who meant to kill her? Daddy seemed horribly inadequate.*

"As if ye do not know," he replied. His meal remained untouched on the table before him, just as hers was cold on her plate. His eyes, lifeless under his narrowed brows, chilled her as he stared. *Did he see her mother, when he looked at her? Or was she merely a means to an end?*

"Perhaps I'd like to hear it from you," she said. "You are my father. Surely the things I was told of you are not true."

His lip twisted upward, a grin replacing his scowl. She bit down on her lower lip as he leaned back in his chair, crossing his arms over his chest. His face was softer, calmer; his voice steady and low.

"Did they tell ye how I loved yer mother?" he asked. "Or how they stole her away from me, because a lowly Sturlsson was not good enough for a *MacMhaolian*?"

He lowered his head, staring blankly at the table as he traced a finger across his napkin.

"I searched for ye both. Fer years, every waking moment I spent I searched for ye."

She swallowed hard when he rose from his chair and approached her. Standing behind her, he placed his hand on her shoulder, the tips of his fingers sending a shiver down her spine. The hollow of her heart tightened like a fist and her pulse raced beneath his touch. *Had she been wrong all along? Had she been cheated of the love of her father?*

"You did?" she whispered.

His fingers shifted, sliding up to cup her cheek. His breath was warm against her cheek, the illusion of fatherly love shattered.

"Yes," he said. "Because you will return me to my time, and then you will restore life to my father. *MacMhaolians* are not the only ones who keep their vows."

She tried to get up and he shoved her back down, her hope of seeing some goodness in him destroyed as he laughed.

"If you let me go now, I will tell my husband not to kill you," she said evenly.

Agnarr uttered a coarse snort, and too late she realized he thought she referred to Benjamin. His amusement however was short lived.

He reached for her, his reflex rapid, taking her hand in his. She cried out when he slammed it down on the table, palm up, twisting her arm so that any movement sent pain shooting up her shoulder. As she struggled he unsheathed the knife at his waist, a jewel-laden blade with a rune imprinted on the hilt.

She could not stop the angry tears that fell as he carved the rune into her palm, nor her cries. The wound was deep, the carving precise, and when he took all the time he needed to make it perfect he looked down upon it and grinned.

"No," she whispered. He sliced his own hand and placed her Bloodstone in his palm, then clasped it over her bleeding wound.

Darkness descended. It fell heavy upon her, blinding her eyes and searing her skin. She slid off her chair onto the floor, the force pulling her down until she thought she might meld to the earth below.

No, she screamed. Her voice never surfaced, her thoughts the only protest she could hear. *Please don't make me go.*

31

Benjamin

A CLAY PITCHER sailed past his head as he entered the room, shattering against the wall to his side. Benjamin ducked at the series of objects that followed – a chamber pot, a music box, and the brooch he had given her as a wedding gift – but he decided her tirade must end when she came at him with a fire poker.

"Jora!" he hollered. "Ye can gouge my eyes out later if ye wish, but please, now, let me explain!"

"Ye churlish, lying, hedge-pig!" she screamed. He plucked the iron poker from her hands and threw it across the room where it clattered on the brick hearth. When she moved to strike him he caught her fists, shoving her against the door where he could hold her steady.

"I dinna lie to ye!" he bellowed.

"Ye did! Ye said she was dead, that ye dinna love her, that she was not meant to be yer wife!"

Her breaths came uneven and he could see the flush across her skin from her anger. Even in the throes of fury, he could see the edge of softness in her eyes, that piece of her that trusted him despite the years of deceit between them.

"I said she was gone. I dinna say dead," he said, his voice low. "As the life left my father's body, I stood with my brother and we made an oath. I swore I would protect her kind."

Jora stared up at him, her struggles lessened for the moment.

"My father died because of my mistake. I betrayed my brother for my own selfish needs. This time, I shall not fail. If ever I held some honor in my heart, it is now I must claim it."

She stayed in place when he dropped his hands. The pulse throbbed below her throat, in that sweet place he often placed his lips. Her searching gaze demanded an answer he never intended to give, and as he turned his back to her, he struggled to form the words.

"Love is a weakness I meant not to dwell on again," he said quietly. "Yet my heart is bound to the woman before me, a woman who trusts naught which issues from my lips. Even so, I love my wife."

He sighed, letting his breath out slowly in the silence that followed. Perhaps his words meant nothing when so much mistrust lay between them. He closed his eyes, trying to steady the pound of his heart within his chest. As the quiet wore on and he thought all was lost, he felt her step up behind him.

Jora entwined her fingers in his. Her breath ran across his skin as she rested her lips on his shoulder.

"This woman trusts ye with her life," she whispered. "Tell me what we must do to stop this madness. Tell me how I will help ye."

He had never known what it meant to have her trust. The weight of it surrounded him, warmed him, as if it was an ember that raced through his veins. He welcomed it into his heart as he pulled her into his arms.

"We will end this. I promise ye," he whispered.

***

When he left Jora's side the house was dark, the lamps along the hallways dimmed as the stillness of evening fell upon them. Murmurs from the servants in their quarters assured him it was a night like all others, yet as he made his way through the narrow halls in search of Maggie, he was acutely aware it was not.

So familiar with Wakehill that he anticipated the squeak of the study door, Benjamin turned the knob carefully as he peered inside. He had searched the house and found no sign of Maggie, nor Agnarr. It was the only place he had failed to look.

Agnarr sat sprawled in his chair in the darkened room, holding a piece of parchment. His hair fell unencumbered about his drawn face, his jaw set tight above his loosened shirt. Blazing jade eyes flickered with the glow of the dying fire, focused on the woman who lay on the floor at his feet.

"We were in a place I did not know," Agnarr said, more to himself than to Benjamin. "I think it was that future time she was born to. I dinna care for it at all."

Benjamin winced when Agnarr reached over and kicked Maggie's foot with his booted toe. She did not stir.

"Ye canna control the Blooded Ones. Yer not meant to change the past. Do ye not see that, man?" Benjamin replied.

"Oh, yes. Yes I can," Agnarr answered. "I need another rune. Next time, we will go where I command. And this–" he snapped, throwing a tiny figurine onto the floor, "this *thing* – it will not return us here!"

Benjamin picked it up, kneeling down beside Maggie. It was her raven, the match to his eagle.

"Those bloody McMhaolians have their trinkets, their ways to control the magic. They forget my family once knew the same," Agnarr muttered.

As Benjamin lifted his brother's wife into his arms, Agnarr cleared his throat.

"See that Jora helps yer wife find a suitable dress. We shall have guests on the morrow and ye both will be at my side."

Maggie stirred, reaching blindly for him. A bloody trail streaked his shirt where her hand clutched his chest. Benjamin swallowed hard as he glimpsed her gouged palm.

He would find a way to escape – for all of them.

32

Winn

"A RED-HAIRED WOMAN was seen with Benjamin Dixon at the port. They traveled to Wakehill. That is all I have word of, I fear."

When John finally arrived at Basse's Choice with the news, Winn was not at all consoled. It had been three days since he escaped Jamestown and last saw his wife. He left her in the care of his brother, his only option at the time. As he turned away from John, Winn's hands clenched into fists.

Was she safe? Did she understand? Surely, she knew they could not escape Jamestown together, that he would come for her. No matter what stood between them, he would find her.

Standing in John Basse's home with the trappings of English luxury surrounding him, the very air in the room felt still. His leather-clad feet slid across polished wood floors as he paced away, the glow of an oil lamp guiding his way.

He could abide it for her – but not without her.

"Then I will go there," Winn said. "And I will let no man stand in my way."

John sighed, shaking his head.

"Ye canna go there with such malice in yer heart. A good Christian –"

Winn turned abruptly and stalked toward John, who backed up against the wall.

"I once was Paspahegh. I once was Norse. Will I be a Christian? I cannot say," Winn growled. "Yet no matter what God I speak to, I know this to be true: I will kill any man who harms my wife. I tell this to you so you have no doubt. That is the man I am. That is the truth I know."

The Englishman's neck contracted as he gulped.

"Then I imagine I must accompany ye," John stammered.

Winn scowled. He looked into John's eyes for a long moment before he gave the Englishman a curt nod.

"A good plan, Englishman," Winn replied.

***

It was years since Winn attended any sort of English gathering. When he was a young man, he lived with the Dixon family for a time, and with Benjamin, he learned how to behave in gentle company. The women valued their silk dresses and fancy petticoats. The men enjoyed the luxury of pipe tobacco and imported spirits. As Winn looked at the plantation house before him, he was reminded of yet another possession the English valued – their homes on the land they believed they owned.

The house was bright beneath the light of a crescent moon. Music and laughter hummed from inside the house, and Winn could see several couples touring the garden. He recalled how they destroyed the land and then planted beautiful flowers to look at in their leisure time.

Chetan nudged Winn with his elbow.

"She must be in the garden," Chetan said. Winn's eyes narrowed.

"I know this."

"You stare as if they may bite you. Go. I am at your side."

Winn grunted an oath at his brother. He tapped the knife on his belt, and then ran his fingers over his father's *bryntroll* harnessed to his back. Erich muttered something foul in Norse about Englishmen and swiving goats, and Winn shot him a glare.

"Carry on," Erich muttered.

"Weapons, gentlemen," John Basse called out. Standing at Winn's side, the Christian had a newly confident air about him. Wearing his good church clothes and a fine wool cloak, John lifted his chin and straightened his back as he spoke at the men. Perhaps the man would not be a liability after all.

They sheathed their weapons as they approached. Chetan and Keke said little, while the Norse filled the silence with playful banter. It was the first time Tyr joined them in battle and the Norse youth reveled in the camaraderie. Iain, the young half-English, half-Chesapeake man seemed thoughtful, his eyes searching the others as if he needed guidance. Winn felt Cormaic's absence, just as he was certain Erich did. Never had they engaged an enemy without the massive berserker.

Winn's fur mantle streamed behind him in the brisk night air, the sword at his side banging lightly on his leather-clad thigh. Under his grey vest his chest was bare, the winding tattoo upon his abdomen visible to all.

He was proud of who he was. All of it. Every moment, every death, every memory of happiness – it all belonged to him. He would wear it with honor as he led his men one last time.

There was an arch decorated with flowers stretching over the garden entrance. When Winn stepped through it with his men flanking his sides, he heard panicked whispers from the English guests as he passed. Men moved their wives from his path; others retreated into small groups to stare.

Erich liberated a piece of fresh venison from a woman's plate, bowing to her with a grin on his lips as he shoved the dripping morsel in his mouth. Chetan scanned the garden for threats, as was his usual task, and when he grunted Winn paused. At least a half dozen armed soldiers populated the spacious lawn, enjoying the celebration amidst the guests.

Ahead of them under a raised wood awning stood Benjamin and Agnarr. Winn noted the warning in Benjamin's stare and the way his brother's eyes flickered to the soldiers. Winn nodded his acknowledgement, hoping to ease his brother, but it did not matter. *The soldiers would not stop him.*

At Agnarr's side with her hand tucked in his arm was Winn's wife. Wearing a silk ruffled gown that dipped low over her full breasts, she seemed the perfect image of a pampered English lady. Yet the bruises on her face beneath the white powder told a different story.

"Master Basse," Sturlsson said. The crowd parted for Agnarr and the music faded, all eyes turned to the new arrivals. The trickle of a nearby fountain punctuated the silence, covering the gasps and whispers.

"Master Sturlsson," John replied, stepping forward.

Winn focused on Agnarr, knowing if he looked at his wife's face for one more moment he would explode.

Whatever the man had done to her, he thought, *I will repay him tenfold.*

"I was unaware ye keep the company of savages," Agnarr quipped. "And ye invite them here, to sit among English folk?"

"I fear 'tis a most serious matter. My friend –"

Winn interrupted him, his patience ended with the pleasantries.

"I am here for my wife," he said. His low voice rumbled in his chest, the threat beneath his statement evident to all those with ears. He noted the flick of Agnarr's wrist and the way the English soldiers moved slowly toward them, the crowd dispersing to safety.

The small band of Norseman was surrounded. It did not matter to Winn. Agnarr was within his reach, and if he only had time to kill Maggie's father before the soldiers descended, then he would consider that a victory.

"Your wife?" Agnarr asked. At first, the man appeared confused, but his disposition quickly turned incredulous. Agnarr glanced at Maggie, who was trying to yank her hand free, and then back to Winn, eyes wide. "I know ye, savage. I recall the day. So that girl indeed was yer blood – my own daughter's spawn."

"I told you my husband would kill you!" Maggie muttered.

Erich moved to Winn's side and Agnarr suddenly grabbed Maggie around the throat. As she tried to pry her father's hand away Winn noticed the bandage on her palm, which only served to enrage him further. Eyes darting wildly about, Agnarr pressed a blade beneath her chin.

"Do ye think ye can come to my home and take my daughter?" Agnarr hissed. "Ye filthy *MacMhaolians*, so haughty and proud! This is how ye raise yer precious Blooded Ones, Erich? Letting her breed with a savage?"

Winn surged forward when Maggie cried out, and Erich held him back. Agnarr shuddered as he shouted, his voice shrill as if he lost his wits. His green eyes bulged as he screamed at them, his coiffed hair falling around his face as he pulled Maggie away.

"Let 'er go, boy. Act like a man, fer once in yer miserable life," Erich demanded.

Agnarr pointed the knife at Erich, then quickly back at Maggie.

"Yer sister pleased me quite well, *MacMhaolian*," Agnarr taunted. "And it seems she was useful to me after all."

The soldiers moved in as Agnarr dragged Maggie away. The Norsemen roared an ancient battle cry as the two groups collided, the scream of swords piercing the air. Winn shouldered the burly soldier who charged him, running his blade through the man's belly as he dropped him to the earth. He stepped over the body, looking over the heads of fighting men for his wife.

Flailing and screaming, Maggie kicked at her father as he dragged her toward the riverbank. When they reached the top of the shallow hill and disappeared beyond, Winn shoved yet another Englishman from his path so that he could follow her.

"Not tonight, lad!" Erich bellowed. The old Norseman swung his sword, clipping the knees of a soldier who tried to flee. Blood and sweat splattered his face, mixing with the red-gold hair in his beard as he grinned. "Go on – we'll settle this here!"

One of Agnarr's less fortunate men slumped to the ground ahead, felled by Benjamin's sword. The blade flashed in the moonlight as Benjamin yanked it from the dead man's back, his eyes meeting Winn's across the yard.

"The river. He has a ship," Benjamin shouted.

Winn broke into a sprint. He could feel Benjamin keep pace with him, and for that he was grateful, but he would have raced to meet them without the assurance of his brother at his side. His lungs burned to bursting as he raced across the meadow, drawing his *bryntroll* from his back as he met the first Englishman. His gait did not falter as the man turned, and the man had no time to utter a sound before Winn slammed the axe across the man's chest. Winn flung all his weight into the blow, flinging the man onto his back with a thud before he reached the next man. They were stragglers of the bunch, only a few, and as the other soldiers turned to the sound of a man hitting earth Winn felt Benjamin reach his side. Winn and Benjamin stood still for a moment as a dozen more soldiers advanced on them.

Benjamin cut one man down with one blow of his sword, nearly severing the man's arm as he sliced through his sternum.

"Find her," Benjamin growled, and Winn nodded. Benjamin raised his blade, swinging it wildly above his head. The soldiers jumped back, giving Winn the chance to reach the hill.

He breached the hill with one shallow jump, and when he landed with two feet braced apart he slid all the way down the loose soil on the hillside toward the river. His hand trailed behind him, keeping him upright as he scaled the decline, and he could hear Benjamin shout behind him. Winn did not need the warning because he could see them as well. Englishmen swarmed over the hill and below them at the river, as Agnarr tried to drag Maggie onto a boat.

"Surrender, savage!"

Winn turned to the shout, weapon poised by his shoulder. His breathing was shallow, his hands slippery and warm.

Benjamin staggered to the top of the hill surrounded by soldiers. They slowly walked him down the hill, three guns aimed to ensure his cooperation. One man snatched Benjamin's sword; another hit him with the butt of a rifle and sent him to his knees.

Winn wiped the blood from his brow with the back of his forearm. A guard leveled his musket at Winn, aimed squarely at his chest.

Agnarr cocked his head slightly, his wild eyes fixed on Winn.

"Why do ye fight for this woman? She is not yer kind."

"She is mine," Winn replied.

With a lopsided grin, Agnarr motioned to the man at his side. "Kill him," he said simply.

"No!" Maggie shouted. "I'll do what you ask. I'll take you where you want. Just let him go – let them all go. I won't fight you."

Winn shook his head sadly. *It would hurt his wife to see him fall, but she would carry on. Two paces ahead to kill Agnarr. He could make it before they shot him.*

"No," Winn answered, his voice coarse. "You will *not*."

As Agnarr uttered a disjointed laugh, his gleeful face slowly turned into a frown.

"No. You will not," a voice echoed from behind him.

Winn followed Agnarr's gaze and turned back toward the hill. Surrounding the now outnumbered English, a line of Nansemond appeared. Draped in full war attire with bright colored grease streaking his face, Pepamhu descended the hill. The warrior pointed a spear at Agnarr as he came to Winn's side.

"This will be a fair fight. End it now. A life," Pepamhu announced, "for her life."

Agnarr glanced at the Nansemond who surrounded them. Standing straight as they waited for his answer, the decorated warriors looked down upon the scene, their readiness evident.

"So it is," Agnarr murmured.

Winn wiped his hand on his braies, which did not help much to get rid of the sticky blood. Agnarr thrust Maggie aside while drawing his sword, the motion sending her to the ground. Blood rushed to Winn's head as he raised his father's bryntroll and launched himself at Agnarr.

The blow radiated through his bones as his weapon met Agnarr's, his hands aching with the impact yet his aim was true. The older man was strong, but not enough.

Winn's gaze clouded into a haze of scarlet thunder. If it was the blood that he spilled or the rage in his heart, he had no answer. It seemed he watched from above as if he hovered in spirit, guiding the hand of his *bryntroll* with some unearthly presence. Perhaps it was his father's hand, or the aid of his ancestors, those valiant warriors both Norse and Powhatan. He found the mark. Bones shattered beneath his blows. His fingers were slippery with warmth as he gripped the long-handled axe, but his aim remained true.

Thank Odin. Thank the Creator. Guide my weapon. Let it be steady. A spreading stain erupted across Agnarr's chest. He lay before Winn on the ground, his shaking hand reaching for the wound. The old Norseman stared at the blood on his fingers for a moment, as if he had never seen such a sight before.

"Who are ye," he breathed.

Winn kneeled down beside the fallen Time Walker, bending his head to ensure Agnarr had his answer.

"I am only a man," Winn said, "And she is my wife."

Agnarr's lips parted with a sigh. It was his last breath.

Those who remained put down their weapons.

***

A crisp breeze graced the air as they placed Makedewa in the ground beside his wife. Winn wrapped his brother in linen, taken from a dress Rebecca once wore, and Chetan covered him with earth as Pepamhu looked on. There was no *kwiocosuk* to send Makedewa to the Creator, as all of the sacred shaman were long since scattered into hiding. It saddened him knowing what had become of those old rituals, and he wondered if the English would return Opechancanough's body to his people for proper ceremony. At least Winn was able to give that to Makedewa. He found Makedewa's body where he had fallen, undisturbed, as were many of the dead.

Winn closed his eyes. For a moment, as the air rushed over him, he could see the past. It was so clear he might touch it, lose himself in what once was, laughing with his brothers as they raced through the village to the beach.

One of the women said there was a canoe on the shore, filled with men of fair skin who spoke a strange tongue. She thought they might be Spaniards, but she said they did not speak Spaniard words. As the boys hid in the trees and watched the Paspahegh warriors greet the strangers, Makedewa looked up at Winn.

"Are they lost?" Makedewa asked, his dark eyes wide. Winn was only eleven, but he was the oldest of the three and usually knew the answers. This time, however, he did not. It had been a long time since Spaniards visited and these men were no Spaniards. They came to shore in a small boat, one that looked like the dugout canoes the Paspahegh used. Yet out on the water was a massive ship, and Winn felt with a certainty these men were anything but lost.

"I know not," Winn replied.

"Look at their weapons!" Makedewa exclaimed.

Chetan snorted and shoved their youngest brother.

"Ah, stay here and talk like women. That will make more food for me!"

Chetan took off back to the village, his laughter trailing behind him. As Makedewa uttered a slew of curses and followed, Winn glanced back at the beach.

Only a few men. What trouble could they bring?

He watched the English arrive as a boy with his brothers. Even if he had known, he could not have stopped it. Old magic and new magic, from the Great Creator or not, none of it could stop the story meant to be written. Winn knew that well, if he knew nothing else.

As they left Makedewa to rest and descended the hill, Winn could see the sadness in Maggie's face. Her throat was tight and her mouth tightly closed, a touch of dampness on her cheeks as they looked at the deserted village. He felt the ache as well, and he knew what thoughts played in her mind.

"Do you remember when Dagr was born?" she asked. He stood beside her as the other men prepared. She needed to speak, to somehow release those spirits, just as they had done for Makedewa upon the hill.

"His cry was so loud, I knew he was your son," Winn said. "Then little Malcolm came, and he was lucky to have a strong brother to watch over him."

Her mouth quivered as tears slipped over her cheeks, but she stared straight ahead. Erich lit a torch, the flames licking the air as he raised it, and Chetan peered into the Northern Hall one last time.

"I know this is what must be. But I don't want to leave them," she whispered.

Marcus. Finola. Makedewa. Rebecca.

"They will never leave us, *ntehem*," he replied.

Winn reached for the torch Erich held out to him.

The fire spread quickly, the thatched roofs of the longhouses perfect kindling. The smaller dwellings did not take long, nor did the bath house over the hot spring. Rune carvings in the trees smoldered into ash, and the well was dismantled and filled with rubbish. As the Northern Hall finally succumbed and the roof caved in, all evidence of their home was extinguished. Soon, the forest floor would rise up, new trees would grow, and the earth would take back the place the Norse had borrowed from it. Men could never truly own the land. It was no possession, it could not be bought. One might share it for a bit, but in the end, the earth would claim it once more.

The Norse would be erased from history, just as those at Roanoke. Just as the Spaniards who came before the English and the Dutchmen before them. God willing, the knowledge of Time Walkers would lay buried as well, only a legend that children might whisper of someday.

The Norse bid the Nansemond farewell. Winn and Pepamhu clasped hands but did not linger; they had already made their peace and Winn knew the Nansemond had stayed longer than was safe. Pepamhu's men claimed responsibility for the English deaths at Wakehill and it would not be long before the King's men attempted to bring them to justice. Pepamhu never meant to join the other Nansemond at Basse's Choice, and he considered it a final gift to Winn's family.

The Northern Hall finally collapsed, and Maggie twisted her hand into his.

"No one will ever know we were here," she said.

He nodded.

"As it should be," he replied.

33

Maggie

THE CRYING OF THE BANNS commenced on three Sundays, and a wedding occurred on the fourth. In the light from the tall glass window of the chapel, Kyra clasped hands with Morgan and said her vows. Her dark hair streamed down her back, decorated with delicate boughs of baby's breath Maggie twined carefully in her daughter's locks that morning. To Maggie's surprise, Kyra insisted on wearing a new gown for the occasion. Kyra sewed it herself, and Maggie could not be more proud of the lovely young woman she had become.

Maggie walked ahead of Winn outside after the ceremony. Their family and friends set off in groups, but she knew she would see them all soon at the celebration. She noted Benjamin and Jora talking with Erich and Chetan, and for once, she felt that all those she loved might remain in one place.

Intent on serious conversation with John Basse, Winn engaged in yet another religious quarrel. She smiled, swinging her arms a bit as they strolled through the town square. Their home was not far outside Basse's Choice, and it was a pleasant walk.

"Yer own daughter was just marrit' as a good Christian woman. Can ye not see 'tis the right path?" John argued.

"Does it make your God any less if I do not believe in him?" Winn replied. It was an answer that set John off, causing him to expel an abrupt sigh.

"Well, I suppose not. But I beg ye, consider more on this matter. Ye have my friendship even if ye keep yer ungodly ways," John muttered.

Winn laughed at the insult. It was rare for John to display such humor, but they all knew it was meant in jest. Winn moved his family onto English lands, banking on the pledge of friendship with John. There was little they agreed on regarding religion, but the strength of their friendship was unquestioned.

Beyond the town square she noticed a man approach. As Winn and John continued their banter, she stared at the figure. Tall and straight, with wide shoulders and a confident gait, the man strode toward them with a steady pace. In the distance she could make out a swatch of thick curling hair, his dark locks tied loosely back at his nape. She noted his clothes were odd, the snug fit of his trousers reminding her of a pair of blue jeans.

Oh, she thought as he came clear into view. *She was having a day-dream. It was Marcus.*

She stopped walking, content for the moment to simply stare at his ghost. God, she missed him! How he would have loved to see Kyra married, or to meet Dagr and Malcolm.

The ghost was young and strong, clearly a picture of health that she did not expect. She smiled, glad he did not return to her as some morbid version of himself with his death wounds on display.

He stopped a few feet away, so she closed the space between them, placing her hand on his cheek. The warmth surprised her, as did the pressure of his hand when he closed it over hers.

"I miss you so much!" she whispered.

"I dinna see why, as it's been naught but one day. Ye go on dates longer than that, ye silly chit," he replied. She shook her head, her senses obviously in failure.

"What did you say?" she demanded.

"Yer addled," he snorted. "And a bit older than I recall. D'ye have a husband yet?"

She heard Winn and John approach, their conversation suddenly ceased. "Of course I do!" she weakly replied. "And – and my daughter was just married!"

"Oh. I suppose I am late then," he grumbled. Marcus pushed past her and stuck out his hand. "*Winkeohkwet,*" he said with a nod.

"You are late," Winn grinned as he clasped arms with his father. Maggie was grateful when Winn placed his other hand on her waist, the way her head was spinning nearly too much to bear.

"I'll take some food, and I'll meet yer weans. I dinna make this trip for idle conversation," Marcus announced.

When the men resumed walking as if it were any other day, she jerked her hand from Winn's and ground to a halt.

"Wait a second!" she shouted.

All three men turned back to her. A boyish grin graced Winn's face, and John chuckled as she threw herself into Marcus's arms.

"You – you're breaking the rules! Is it really you? You're here!" she laughed. He was as young and strong as ever, swinging her easily in a circle while she hugged him.

"Ah, well, it's not a time I've once lived, if ye wish to be precise. So the time travel police can kiss my fine Norse arse!"

Tears streamed down her cheeks. Marcus smiled as he took her hand and placed it in Winn's.

"He said he'd have some good sweet mead fer me," Marcus said, nodding to Winn. "Let's get to it, I'd say."

"Of course," she laughed, wiping her tears. "Let's get to it."

***

In that magical time between dusk and dawn, Maggie found solace as she walked down the path. She left her boots at her bedside, needing to feel the cool sand beneath her feet and the sting of the air upon her cheeks. Winn slept soundly in their bed, and as she closed the door of the space they shared, she wondered how long it would be before Winn noticed her absence.

At Basse's Choice, the small chapel where Kyra was married sat in the center of town. Although Winn had yet to convert to Christianity, the Basse family welcomed the displaced Norse and accepted them as kin. Of the Nansemond that stayed, most had already converted, leaving only a few of Maggie's family for John Basse to worry over. She smiled. John was a good man and a good friend.

The elderly vicar grew accustomed to her early visits. Most mornings he simply sat beside her as she stared at the wooden cross above the altar. At times, he offered her consolation, placing his stubby hand over hers. Today, however, he shook his head sadly at her and did not sit. He clutched his linen robe, arms crossed over his chest.

"Yer dreams keep ye awake yet again, my dear?" the vicar asked.

Maggie nodded. He raised a brow at the position of her toes, which were propped gainfully on top of the pew in front of her. She dropped her feet and offered a wry smile in apology.

"It is in yer power to rest easy," he said.

"Oh, is it?" she replied, curious to know what answer he might give. She enjoyed hearing his pure thoughts, the strength of his conviction something she admired despite their differences.

"It is. Ye need to accept our Lord as yer savior. Pledge yer obedience and abandon yer heathen ways. Ye and yer husband are sinners, but God is great and he shall forgive even the likes of ye."

Uttering a sigh, she stared at the vicar. She was grateful when he patted her hand and shuffled off, since she was unable to form words to answer him. He could never accept the things she knew to be true, and as such, she could never truly believe his God was the only way. It was an impasse, one she lived with quite easily.

Soon she heard his footsteps pad across the plank floor and she closed her eyes. Winn worried, and for that she held regret. As much as he always protected her, she wished she could do the same for him. She did not wish to cause him distress over her scattered thoughts.

"What can I do," Winn asked, "to keep you in my arms until I wake?"

He took her hand and pulled her to the altar, where he looked at the tall wooden cross with curiosity.

"Does it ease you, *ntehem*? They say one must only accept this God, and then your burden will be lifted," Winn said softly.

"I have no burden," she replied.

He tilted his head toward her, his blue eyes slanted.

"I know your anger at me. I do not fault you for it. I killed your father. Someday...someday I hope you can forgive me."

With her fingers tight around his she let the tears fall. *Beautiful Winn, her faithful husband.* He blamed himself, and it only made her hate herself more.

"No," she whispered, her voice breaking. "Never. I don't think that at all. The only person I cannot forgive is myself."

He let her grip his hand, unmoving as she struggled to explain.

"I'm glad he's dead. What is wrong with me, Winn? Why am I glad my father is dead?"

"I think you are happy our children are safe. You are happy to live without fear. If that is wrong, so be it."

"I must be a monster to wish my own father dead. The vicar said –"

"Forget what he said."

As they kneeled together in the darkness of the church, he twisted his fingers into her hair at her nape. She bowed her head, resting her forehead gently against his.

"He said we were sinners. I couldn't tell him he was wrong," she whispered. Winn clutched her tighter, his breath warm against her cheek when he spoke.

"Should I ask forgiveness for what I have done? If it means I must take it all back, then I shall not ever ask it. If loving you makes me a sinner, I will gladly bear that title. And for every day that I breathe, I tell you this: there is no promise I would not break, no duty I would not abandon...no man I would not kill, if it meant you belonged to me. For today and all the days of time, you are mine. And I shall keep you," he said, "For I am not finished with you yet."

He kissed the tears from her cheeks as he swept her into his arms, cradling her against his chest as he took her to bed.

She slept in peace by his side, as she did for the rest of her days.

Epilogue

Chetan

LAST WILL AND TESTAMENT of Capt. Morgan White, of Isle of Wight County, in Virginia, and Born at James Town, near Savage Hill, in ye parish of James Citie in Virginia.

To my good Christian wife Kyra Neilsson one-fourth part of all my movable estate (that is to say) the same to be equally divided between my wife and three daughters Rebecca, Susannah Basse and Finola. To eldest dau. Rebecca my dwelling House near Basse's Choice, with ye land and houses from Pagan creek. To second dau. Susannah all the land that Daniel Neilsson now liveth on on the Easterly side of Bethlehem Creek, that land now named Bethsaida; To Finola another daughter, all lands and houses whlyeth on Red Pt. My brew house and land at James Town to be sold and monies to be divided between my said kinfolk Jonathan Dixon my wives cousin, to William Basse my nephew, to Peter Basse my son-in-law. My land in England by Berry and Alvenstoak in Hampshire, near Gosport and Portsmouth, to be redeemed if not to be sold outright and the proceeds divided between my three daus. To my relation by marriage and executor of this will Gabriel Basse, all lands on the hillside beyond James Citie, to include the site with the creek and a cave long since deserted. My will is that a new house and barn to be made as discussed with Gabriel Basse prior to my decline and that same place shall forever bequeathed to mine own children and mine childrens heirs. Also to honore my wives mother I give and bequeath four female cattle to remain for a Stock forever for poor Fatherless Children that hath nothing left them to bring them up, and for Old People past their labour or Lame People that are Destitute in this lower parish of the Isle of Wight county. My will is that the overseers of the Poor with consent of my children from time to time are to see this my will in this particular really performed as is in my will expressed and not otherways. Recorded 10 March, 1699.

Tall and fair skinned, Chetan's grandson Gabriel Basse could easily be mistaken for an Englishmen. Yet if one was looking and knew which features to consider, he clearly had a touch of the First People within him. As Gabriel worked with the other men to dig up the foundation, Chetan was struck with a pang of homesickness that would not ebb. With Gabe's head bent to his work and his raven-black hair falling over his shoulder, he reminded him of Ahi Kekeleksu, and an ache swelled in Chetan's chest. Yes, Ahi Kekeleksu had gone to the spirit world many years before, as had most of those Chetan held close to his heart. Yet watching the man before him, this blood of his blood, Chetan could not help but acknowledge that life continued on despite how men tried to change it.

His desire to see the stones won over. Although his bones ached with the strain of age and his fingers shook when he gripped the long handle of the shovel, he thrust it into the earth on that sacred spot. What he sought was not buried deep, and when the metal blade hit the ancient box, Gabriel heard the clatter and moved to assist him.

"What is it, Grandfather?" Gabe asked, squatting down beside Chetan. Chetan scraped the soil away with his fingers, clawing through it with increasing eagerness until he had a firm grip on two sides of the box. He could not lift it, however, nor could Gabe, so they split the lock with the shovel blade and opened it.

The breath left his lungs in a long exhale as the scent of old magic and memories assaulted him. Chetan took one of the stones in his hand. It was a deep green color, nearly black, with a vein of bright crimson running through the center as if it lived. Sitting in his palm, the Blood-stone felt heavy, more than a stone of such tiny size should feel.

"Ye had me there, I thought it might be treasure. 'Tis only a bunch of stones," Gabe laughed. Gabe picked one up, turning it over in his fingers, then tossed it back into the pile inside the old Viking chest.

Chetan made a low grunting acknowledgement. Only a stone, no less.

"'Tis a cave up near the waterfall, we nearly missed it, it was hidden so well. Looks like someone lived here once. D'ye know what tribes settled nearby, Grandfather?" Gabe asked. Chetan closed his fingers around the Bloodstone and nodded.

"Oh, there were many that lived here," Chetan answered. "This place holds their memories. Here, start the foundation on this spot. It is a good place for your new barn."

"Well, if ye think so. I suppose it's as good a spot as any," Gabe replied. The younger man wiped the back of his hand across his brow, then picked up his shovel. "I shall tell the others."

Chetan watched him join the others, the Bloodstone still clutched in his hand. Did he imagine that it felt warm, or that he could hear the murmurs of spirits passed whisper around him? The longer he held it, the stronger the voice surged, until like an avalanche of dust it filled him. He inhaled it, breathed in the heady scent of the past, letting it take him back to that time when it all started.

"What is so amusing, brother?" Winn asked as they rode back to the village together. Chetan continued to smirk, knowing Maggie was waiting for Winn and that the two had parted on bad terms. He also had the feeling Winn would only make things worse, and he wished to spare his older brother undue grief.

"Well, I look forward to returning home. The men speak of what women to take to furs," Chetan answered.

"So what?" Winn snapped.

"If you do not take your captive to furs, I will take her. I like her red hair and pretty pale skin." Chetan meant it in half-jest, but Winn needed prodding to see his way forward with the woman. He knew he made an impact when his brother's face exploded with rage.

"I am not ready to share my captive," Winn growled.

Chetan lifted one corner of his mouth in a wry smile. "Then claim her yourself."

"Why do you rile me, Chetan?" Winn demanded.

Chetan looked sideways at him, shaking his head with a sigh.

"If you do not claim her, another man will challenge you. Then I must challenge him, and I do not wish to fight. But if I must save my stupid brother from himself, I will."

Chetan smacked Winn's thigh with the long end of his reins, leaving a welt across his skin and a scowl on his brother's lips. Winn looked straight ahead, refusing to acknowledge the taunt.

"Any man who tries to take what is mine will die a quick death," Winn muttered.

"Then stop being a fool. Or I will take her from you and die smiling for it," Chetan replied.

He meant to urge his brother toward his path that day. Never in all the years they spent together would Chetan ever admit that it meant more to him, that a part of him wondered how things might have been different. If Winn had killed her when they met, instead of saving her. Or if Winn had simply not cared, and turned her over to his brother.

In the end, Chetan did not covet that which never belonged to him, but he thought of it now and then. Yet the memory of a lifelong friendship with the woman served him just as well, and he found solace in recollection of all the times they had shared. Quiet conversations, listening to her stories, sharing her delight in the life before them, those were the precious times. Her blood held a centuries-old magic, one more powerful than any should ever control, but it was not only that which made her special. Her smile, her fire, the heart of a warrior in her soul–those were the things that Chetan cherished.

Those were the things he recalled when the spirits visited him at night. They called to him more of late, asking why he did not join them. He did not understand such questions himself so he could give them no response, no reason why he should live to see ninety years when his brothers had not, when even Ahi Kekeleksu had not.

Makedewa, lost so young with his wife. Benjamin, who was buried with Jora. One of the young men helping Gabe was of Benjamin's blood.

And Winn. Well, Winn's ghost did not visit him often, but Chetan knew he was there. Maggie would be at his side, no matter what. They had lived as one and died with souls entwined, and no one expected anything less from them.

Chetan looked down at the stone in his hand as the voices whispered louder.

"Ride faster, brother, you're falling behind!" Makedewa shouted.

Chetan sighed.

"Are ye well, Grandfather? Ye look tired. Sit down, I'll move the rocks," Gabe said. Chetan felt the hand on his shoulder, guiding him to the ground, and he gladly sat down in the dirt.

"Yes, yes. This old man is tired," he whispered.

"Here, drink," Gabe insisted, pushing a flask of whiskey to his lips. Chetan gently pushed it away, shaking his head.

"Make me a promise, Gabe. Build this barn here, on this spot, over these stones."

"All right, just rest. I'll build it here, I promise ye," Gabe agreed, seeming eager to placate the old man. Chetan placed the stone back in the chest, carefully covering the tip of the pewter flask he noticed poking out. The old flask needed to stay where Maggie placed it, and so did the stones.

Finally, something he could do. A task he could finish, to see that they all lived on.

"Will you ride with me, brother?" Winn asked, his voice like an echo of a fading breeze.

Chetan closed his eyes. He could see them clearly now, those he loved. Winn on a sorrel horse, and Maggie galloping ahead on Blaze down the beach, her laughter trailing back to them.

"If you ask it of me, I will. You are my brother," Chetan replied.

The scent of salt and screams of seagulls took him down, down deep to that place where time stood still. So this was what it meant, to have a purpose greater than pure love.

Now he was ready. He closed his eyes.

This time he would join them.

THE END

PREVIEW: GHOST DANCE
The Battle of Bloody Run
James River Falls, 1656
Daniel

HAD HE KNOWN what was to come, would he still have traveled that same path? Not only for knowing that it *would* end, as all lives do, but for the when and how of it? For truth, it was a tricky question since he was privy to the history of time before it happened, yet despite that unfair advantage, Daniel knew the answer in his heart.

Yes.

Even as his face pressed into the sodden earth and he tasted the muddy grit on his tongue, his answer remained unchanged. The trickle of warm blood seeping into the corner of his eye would not sway him, nor the scent of his enemy's rancid breath upon his cheek.

Yes. I would do it again, he thought. *For what am I, if not a spawn of two worlds, a man beholden at once to all and to none?*

Blows from a club rained down on his back, taking the last of the breath from his lungs. Beneath his ribs, down deep in his belly, his muscles spasmed, and he could no longer draw air when he gasped. He could not see his enemy but he could still feel the presence of the man with the club, and although the attack had ceased, Daniel knew there was little time to catch his breath before it would resume.

Totopomoi – the Pamukey Chief – was dead. Their English allies deserted them like cowards, fleeing from the battlefield as the bodies of Pamukey warriors fell to the muddy earth. Had Colonel Hill ever meant to stand beside the Pamukey, or was it his plan all along to run, leaving the Pamukey to fight the Ricaheerians alone?

It no longer mattered. The Ricaheerian with the club standing above him would not spare him, and Daniel knew he would soon join his companions.

"Is he dead?" one of his enemies asked.

Daniel winced when the tip of a foot jabbed into his ribs.

"Not yet," another man answered. "Leave him. This is the one *Wicawa Ni Tu* wants. Let our Chief have the honor of ending his life."

The men laughed to each other as they walked away, their voices echoing through Daniel's skull and pounding in his ears. When he was certain they were gone, he buried his fingers in the damp ground and moved to raise his head. With all the damage done to his body it was no easy task, and it took a few moments before he could lift himself enough to look around.

By the tears of the Creator, he had never seen such a sight. Was this the *Hell* the Christian Englishmen spoke of? Only a few paces to his side lay dozens of fallen Pamukey braves. Limbs were twisted, heads bloodied. A man Daniel had stood with at Colonel Hill's side was propped up, run through with a spear that impaled him to the tree at his back. A lanyard of eagle feathers around his neck fluttered in the wisp of a breeze, tangled in long dark strands of the warrior's hair. Daniel did not want to look at him, yet he could not look away. The man's eyes stared straight ahead, an empty chasm, and for a moment Daniel swore his dead lips moved.

"*Run,*" the dead man whispered. "*Hurry.*"

So he did. Daniel forced the remnants of his strength into his limbs, clawing at the dirt until he started to move. He darted a glance over the bodies of the dead and saw no enemy near, yet he could hear them in the distance and he knew they would return for him. When he gathered enough purchase to rise, he crouched on one knee with his hand over his belly, the burning taste of bile searing his throat. The river was close; he could smell the dampness in the air and hear the rush of the water nearby.

It called to him, and he obeyed.

A Ricaheerian bellowed a joyful war cry, and it was then that Daniel knew he was the last one left alive. He scrambled down the steep sandy bank and slid into the cold water, stumbling through the shallow stream bed until he reached a deeper spot. He tried to steady himself but when he waded deeper the force of the current struck him like a barrel in the chest, and for a long moment he clutched the slippery root of a tree.

Death was assured if he stayed, yet fleeing could give him no certainty of survival. The sounds of war cries echoing through the trees drew closer and Daniel looked down at his fingers entwined in the tree root.

He let go.

The frigid water took what was left of him, welcoming him, and he did not object this time as the current pulled him away from shore.

It was not long before numbness settled deep into his bones. Even in his dreams, he had never felt so peaceful, so weightless. The gentle lapping of the current rocked him and washed over his wounds, licking them clean and taking away his pain.

If this is the afterlife, he thought, *then perhaps I have nothing to fear.*

Every few moments he reminded himself to raise his head and open his mouth, taking a breath of air into his bruised lungs as he was carried downstream. A part of him realized he could not stay submerged for too long and that he must make an effort to float, but another part of him wished to simply give in. *Let the water take me, wherever I am meant to be.*

Water flowed over his open mouth and filled his lungs. He choked it up by pure reflex, past caring to fight it any longer. In the murky depths of his scattered thoughts, visions of his fallen companions spoke to him, taunting him as he drifted farther away from the carnage. He could hear the voices of the dead call to him over the sound of his own ragged breaths.

"Go," the ghosts commanded. "*Live!*"

He listened to them as best he could until the current slowed and his legs found purchase in shallow water once more. Although he much preferred to remain floating, the Creator had a different plan for him. It was with that assurance that he left the water and made his way onto a quiet sandy bank where the only sign of life was a pair of spotted-back turtles resting on a patch of tuckahoe. Loose pebbles shifted beneath him when he crawled out of the creek and he felt the quick rush of a cold breeze take the air from his lungs as he gasped and coughed.

The panicked cries of sand gulls protested his intrusion and he could hear the flutter of their wings above him in the trees. His breath left him in a groan as he pushed himself up on one arm. He stilled for a moment, cocking his head slightly to the side. He was not yet too far gone to ignore the new sound coming towards him, the creeping echo of something walking through the brush that he was certain was no animal.

Yet when he raised his eyes and the last glimmers of amber rays from the fading sunset blinded him, the shadowed outline of a woman breached his weary sight. There, in front of him, she stood like a messenger from the Creator, her illuminated form taking the very breath from his tired chest.

Daniel squinted, raising his hand to shield his gaze. Was this the one meant to take him from this time, sent to guide him on his final path? She was not as he expected. Not with her honey-colored hair streaming free over her shoulders, nor with her pale face defined by the glow of the setting sun. She was dressed in a peculiar manner with her legs covered with some sort of tight trouser, and he could see heavy leather boots the color of doe skin on her feet. Perhaps the Christians were right about death, and this was one of their angels sent to gather his soul. He shook his head as if the motion might clear his vision, but when he opened his eyes again and she remained, he knew what to he must do.

He reached for her, his hand slipping down past her trousers to settle around one bared ankle.

"Take me home," he said, his voice hoarse. "I am ready now."

Instead of the comforting embrace he expected, she leaned forward and peered down at him. In her hands was an odd shaped flintlock pistol, smaller than those the English used, and as she raised it up in her fisted hand he wondered why a spirit guide might have need of such a weapon.

"Christ!" she hissed. "Not today. I am *not* doing this bullshit today!"

He had no time to wonder over her strange reply before she struck him with the weapon, smashing it into the side of his head. Darkness exploded around him. His hold on her ankle slipped away, and he sighed as the blessed sanctuary of the afterlife swallowed him whole.

~ end preview ~

PREVIEW: THE PRETENDERS
CHAPTER 1
Basse's Choice
Isle of Wight County, Virginia
1648.

"AH, ANOTHER GIRL! Can your sister make only female children?" Daniel asked.

Dagr kept his gaze focused on the ceremony at the front of the church and tilted his head slightly toward his younger cousin, keeping his voice low as he spoke.

"I do not care to think of my sister making any children," he replied. He winced and grunted a warning at Daniel as the youth elbowed him sharply in the ribs, but his reaction only served to encourage the rowdy behavior. It was difficult to be mad at Daniel for very long, especially when his cousin set his mind to getting a rise from him.

"Nor do I," Daniel agreed. "Did I miss the blessing?"

Dagr crossed his arms over his chest, his eyes focused on the ceremony taking place at the front of the church. Although he had converted to Christianity when his family moved to the Basse's Choice plantation, he did not routinely attend services or follow all the rules. Respect, however, was another matter entirely, and he knew it was considered ill-mannered to carry on conversations while a child was being blessed.

"Do you think the child is a Blooded One?"

Dagr shook his head.

"It does not matter," he replied. "Kyra will not allow the test."

Truth be told, Dagr knew the infant would be bled at some point before her first birthday despite his sister Kyra's objections – if not by his sister, then someone else in the family. When Kyra became Christian, she took it much more seriously than the rest of their kin. The Norse among them viewed the religious practices as something to be tolerated with good humor in order to live in peace; Kyra, however, was a different story. After her marriage to an Englishman, Dagr's sister became a strict believer in the church, denouncing her powerful bloodline and insisting her children would never know what it meant to be a Blooded One.

Dagr closed his fingers over the Bloodstone pendant he wore around his neck. The near black stone felt warm against his bare skin, which was a trait his elders told him was entirely normal. As much as he might like to join his sister and deny their power of their bloodline, it was simply not an option for him. He was the first-born son of the Chief Protector, and he could neither run from that fact nor pretend it did not exist. It was Dagr's duty to protect his sister no matter what God she chose to worship.

"Mal says he will bleed the child, even if Kyra will not permit it. He says we all have a right to know," Daniel commented.

Turning abruptly, Dagr stared down at the dark-haired youth beside him.

"Where is my brother?" he asked. With a twinge of shame, he realized he had not noticed the absence of his younger sibling. It was easier to leave Malcolm to his own devices rather than risk stirring his ire, but Dagr knew there would be much more trouble if Malcolm did not show up.

"Good question. Where is your brother?"

Dagr and Daniel turned to Chief Winn at the same time. At twenty-two years old, Dagr was the same height as his father, but Winn made him feel small when they stood beside each other. Winn was the kind of man others paid attention to, even if they were not aware of his identity. With long black hair and dark skin from his Paspahegh mother he was clearly native, yet the width of his shoulders and the mass of his muscular warrior's body was a gift from his Norse father. Some said Dagr was the image of his father, but he did not see it. He shared his father's light blue eyes and sun-kissed complexion yet Dagr felt they were nothing alike.

"I have not seen him, father," Dagr answered.

"Hmpf. And you, Daniel?"

Winn raised an eyebrow at fifteen- year old Daniel, who visibly paled beneath his dark skin, dipping his round brown eyes downward to avoid Winn's stare. As Dagr faced his father, he wondered what made the younger boy so nervous.

"I – I told him to come with me," Daniel stammered.

"Where is he?" Winn replied.

"On the hill beyond the woods."

Winn placed a hand on Dagr's shoulder. "Find your brother. Perhaps he is lost. I can think of no other reason he would disobey me."

Dagr nodded. As much as he was tired of covering for Malcolm and hunting his younger brother down when he took off, he knew Winn was equally as frustrated. It seemed as if Malcolm thrived on the constant discord, and over the last few weeks, there had been plenty to go around. Even a thorough thrashing had not tempered his careless behavior after Malcolm was caught with a Nansemond brave's sister the week prior. At the time of the incident, Dagr kept the warrior from hurting Malcolm too severely, but in hindsight perhaps he should have let the Indian pummel his brother more.

"I will find him, father. Worry not," Dagr said.

Winn smiled. "When I ask you to do something, I never worry if it is done," the Chief said. "Take Daniel with you and hurry back. Your mother will be unhappy if you miss the blessing."

"Yes, father," Dagr replied, dipping his head slightly to his father in a gesture of respect. Winn clamped his fingers tight on Dagr's shoulder and released him with a gentle shove.

As he motioned for Daniel to follow and they left the new brick church, Dagr pushed his hood off his head. The thick bear skinned-cloak was ceremonial garb he infrequently wore, given to him by his great-uncle Erich when he reached manhood. Lined with fur edging and embroidered with ancient symbols, it was a display of his position more than a useful garment. Since his village joined with the English at Basse's Choice, there were few times his position as Chief Winn's son had cause for acknowledgment. Yet even though his status was of little importance to the English, Dagr still felt the pull of responsibility toward his kin – and his wayward brother.

"What is he doing up there?" Dagr asked his cousin.

"I – I don't know. He has Old Dagr's *Leabhar Sinnsreadh*," Daniel replied.

Dagr glanced sideways at his cousin as a wave of unease settled in his chest. "What is he doing with my grandfather's book?"

"He wants to learn to use the runes. He says it is his right as a Blooded One."

"His *right*? Has he spoken to father about his rights?" Dagr demanded. "And why do you help him? You know we cannot use that magic. You know the risk."

"I know! I – I'm sorry, Dagr. I did not know what he meant to do."

"How did he get it?" he asked, suspecting the culprit before Daniel answered.

"It was me. I took it from Erich's longhouse. Malcolm stood watch while I looked for it," the young man admitted. Daniel was two years younger than Malcolm, but he was still old enough to know the consequence of what he had done. No one was permitted to use the ancient *Leabhar Sinnsreadh*, a book his grandfather Dagr Marcus had retrieved from the future. With the details of the original Five Bloodlines, the *Leabhar Sinnsreadh* was much more than just a book. It was a relic of days past and lifetimes that would never be lived. The Elders kept the book hidden to protect those it named – and Dagr was going to kill his brother for stealing it.

The last glimmers of an orange sunset cast a glow upon the hillside where Malcolm sat against a nook of stones. As Dagr inhaled the thick scent of Cyprus and Elm, he could see Malcolm sat cross-legged with the book in his lap, his head of dark curls bent down as he studied. *Why would he risk such a thing?* Dagr wondered. Even for Malcolm, stealing the *Leabhar Sinnsreadh* was beyond excusable.

Malcolm looked up as they approached. He placed the open book beside him on the ground and slowly rose up to his feet, meeting Dagr's hard gaze.

"I'm not going to the blessing, so your trip was for naught," Malcolm said, his voice wavering despite his apparent resolve. Dagr pointed a finger at his younger brother.

"Yes, you *will* go to the blessing," Dagr replied. "Even if I must drag you back there myself!"

"Of course. Do father's bidding, just as you always do," Malcolm muttered.

Dagr placed a hand on the knife at his waist, pushing his cloak aside. "This is about respect for your sister and your niece. Nothing more. Give me the book and I'll speak to father on your behalf."

With a low snort, Malcolm shook his head, darting a glance at Dagr's blade.

"Will you stab me with your blade, brother? Are you too cowardly to fight me with your fists?"

Turning his head slightly, Dagr motioned to Daniel, who was standing silently behind them.

"Return to the church. Tell father we will join him soon," he ordered. Daniel obeyed the command without question, which only served to remind Dagr that Malcolm never listened to anything he was asked to do. Despite the fact that all three men and Kyra had been raised in Chief Winn's household, somehow Malcolm had turned out quite different. Malcolm shunned every attempt to live in harmony with the English, instead focusing on what might have been if they stayed in the Norse village. Dagr knew it was that dream that drove his brother, the same notion that caused him to steal the book.

As soon as Daniel was out of earshot, Dagr stalked over to his brother and grabbed him by his collar. He was past patience with Malcolm. His father asked him to retrieve his brother, and by the Gods, he was going to do it.

"I am no coward, and you know that very well," he growled, his face next to his brother. As much as he wished to prove that fact to Malcolm, he held back as his father would have done. Chief Winn never let Malcolm get under his skin, even when Malcolm behaved like a child.

"Then listen to me. For once, listen!" Malcolm stammered, trying to pluck Dagr's fingers from his collar. "What good is it to have this sacred blood in our veins if we never use it? If there was a way to change the past – to make it better for us all – should we not do it?"

"You mean better for yourself," Dagr replied. He released his grip and Malcolm stumbled backward, going down on one knee.

"I am not meant for this time as you are," Malcolm said quietly. "Here, you are the Chief's son. Someday you will be the Chief Protector. "And I am only a second son, as I am when I stand here before you."

Dagr sighed, trying his best to keep his voice level. It took considerable effort, especially when his base instinct was to box his brother in the ears and drag him back to town. "Stop this foolishness now. Father sent me to bring you home –"

"The runes can take me where I belong. I know how to use them, Dagr, if you will only listen! You could go with me."

"You belong here. That is the truth I know," Dagr replied. "If you wish to leave, then you will face our father and mother and tell them yourself, and then you can leave on your own two feet. You need no magic for that."

Malcolm's green eyes blazed bright beneath his dark brows, his boyish face covered in dust as he frowned. "Someday you will envy me, brother. Remember this day. Remember that I asked you to stand by my side."

Before Dagr could move to stop him, Malcolm took a blade from his belt and sliced through his palm. When he took his Bloodstone pendant from his neck, Dagr lunged at him, sending them both sprawling.

"No!" Dagr shouted, slamming his brother's bloody fist to the ground. Malcolm crawled toward his Bloodstone and Dagr yanked him back, both trying to gain control of the pendant. Each of them knew what would happen if Malcolm touched the stone, yet Dagr was still stunned that his brother tried to do it. Malcolm had always complained about his role within their family, but the depth of his anger had never truly been so clear. As they fought beneath the dying embers of a golden sunset, Malcolm twisted in Dagr's grasp and grabbed the Bloodstone with a triumphant grin.

Dagr did not think of the consequence when he grabbed Malcolm's wrist and slammed it down. Instead of dislodging the Bloodstone, their entwined fingers fell upon the open *Leabhar Sinnsreadh*. As the earth beneath their tangled limbs began to shudder he closed his eyes, the sickening force pulling him down closer to the dirt.

Was that his handprint staining the pages of the Leabhar Sinnsreadh? Or did it belong to Malcolm?

He could see the outline of a rune on the ancient pages, obscured beneath a bloody handprint. His vision flickered like a fire bereft of timber, darkness engulfing him amidst the random surges of flame. Dagr never knew the power of his own blood until that moment, when he felt the air rush from his lungs and he thought he might die if he did not feel the cold earth upon his face. It engulfed him, embraced him, welcomed him, until finally, he heard a voice screaming and he realized the sound came from his own lips as he plummeted through time.

~end preview~

About the Author

E.B. Brown enjoys researching history and genealogy and uses her findings to cultivate new ideas for her writing. Her debut novel, *The Legend of the Bloodstone*, was a Quarter-finalist in the 2013 Amazon Breakthrough Novel Award contest. An excerpt from another Time Walkers novel, *A Tale of Oak and Mistletoe*, was a finalist in the 2013 RWA/NYC We Need a Hero Contest.

The author lives in New Jersey and is a graduate of Drexel University. She loves mudding in her Jeep Wrangler and enjoys causing all kinds of havoc the rest of the time.

CONNECT WITH ME ONLINE:
FACEBOOK www.facebook.com/ebbrownauthor
GOODREADS www.goodreads.com/EBBrown
OFFICIAL WEBSITE: www.ebbrown.net

BOOKS BY E.B. BROWN

Lightning Source UK Ltd.
Milton Keynes UK
UKHW022058250822
407860UK00003BA/172